SHADOW OF THE DRAGONS

THE PORTAL WARS SAGA
BOOK EIGHT

JAMES E. WISHER

SAND HILL PUBLISHING

CHAPTER ONE

Otto Shenk took slow, deep breaths as he centered himself both mentally and in the ether. The air held a faint mustiness. No matter what sort of cleaning he tried, either magical or mundane, nothing could fully remove it from the underground chamber. He stood in a very special room deep in the bowels of the imperial palace. Should a stranger visit it, an impossibility given the palace's security, they would no doubt be unimpressed.

Dimly lit by scattered Lux crystals, the stone walls were unadorned gray. In fact, there were no decorations of any sort. Or furnishings for that matter. Other than Otto, the only thing in the room was a tall glass cylinder topped with a deep-red crystal that a thief might mistake for a ruby but was in fact a great deal more valuable. The crystal, known as the Heart of Alchemy, was one of the most powerful artifacts in existence. Combined with the Chamber of Eternity on which it rested, it formed a device called the Immortality Engine.

For one that knew how to use it, the engine could transform a normal wizard into an immortal Arcane Lord. Unfortunately, or fortunately, depending on your point of view, the only person that knew how to perform the ritual was dead and his soul trapped in the netherworld.

And that was fine with Otto. Though he always sought ever greater knowledge and power, he'd also seen what became of a person when they were transformed into an Arcane Lord. The results, especially the mental changes, weren't pretty. There were many who would call Otto evil or a monster for some of the things he'd done. Not to his face, of course, but he knew the whispered rumors spoken when people believed his agents weren't around.

Those whisperers didn't have a clue about true evil. Otto had seen it for himself in a black pyramid in the Dead Lands. No sane being would do what Amet Sur had done. Better for the world if the Arcane Lords remained extinct. He would find his own path forward. A better path. Or at least a path that didn't turn him into a depraved monster.

His lips twisted into a thin, humorless smile. How many would claim it was far too late for him to avoid that fate?

He finally opened his eyes and smiled at the crackling power that surrounded the engine. It was primed and ready for today's session. Three strides brought him right beside the smooth glass cylinder. At his touch and mental command, a section of the glass vanished and he stepped inside.

When it sealed up again, he reached into his pocket and pulled out a piece of mithril the size of a marble. He'd invested a whole day in purifying it. There couldn't be even a hint of contamination if the infusion was to succeed. He checked it one last time just to be sure and found nothing save pure mithril. Nodding to himself, Otto switched the piece of metal to his left hand and sent his awareness into the Heart of Alchemy.

As always, he found the crystal's facets beautiful and dizzying in their complexity. It would be so easy to get lost in them.

And that was one of the Engine's many traps. Otto had enough experience not to fall for it and soon he was riding a wave of ether back out of the Heart and into the mithril piece. At his psychic command, the Heart's magic dissolved the metal and sent it into the flesh of his hand. He ignored the faint, burning pain and focused. This was where things got tricky.

Drawing the dissolved mithril into the bone of his index finger, he wove it into a fine lattice, merging metal and bone until they were indistinguishable and inseparable. He knew not how long the delicate process took, but at last he ran out of metal and had fully infused his entire finger.

An effort of will returned his awareness to his body. Otto flexed his finger and found his dexterity perfect and the pain gone. Good, another success. He'd already finished with his right hand and that was two fingers down on his left. Adding just that small amount of mithril to his body had already increased his maximum thread count to forty-one as well as increasing the threads' diameter by a tiny but noticeable amount.

He could hardly wait to see what he could accomplish once his entire body was done. Pity he figured it would take at least five years to fully complete the transformation.

Oh, well. It wasn't like he was short on time. He'd found that, in addition to infusing his bones with mithril, the process also repaired the effects of time on his flesh. Despite over a decade passing since his final battle with Valtan, Otto didn't look a day over twenty. He could've stopped the de-aging effect, but didn't care to expend the effort. His youthful appearance made people underestimate him and he found that useful and annoying in equal measure.

With a thought he made the entrance appear and stepped out of the chamber. Rather than feeling exhausted, the ritual left him invigorated. The Heart of Alchemy made it possible for him to channel ether without getting worn out, an effect he greatly appreciated.

He crossed the room and pulled the door open. Waiting a few strides away was Hans, the leader of his personal guard. The veteran soldier, unlike Otto, was showing his age. His short hair was fully gray and his leathery skin creased with wrinkles. His black-and-gold uniform was crisp and his back straight as he touched fist to heart. In his left hand Hans held Otto's baldric. From it hung his mithril sword and anti-mithril dagger, neither of which he could wear while using the Chamber. He hadn't had much use for the magic-negating dagger since he traded a young thief a mithril sword for it nine years ago, but better to have it and not need it than vice versa.

As he donned his weapons Otto said, "Have you thought any more about our discussion?"

"Yes, my lord. I've thought about little else."

"And?"

"And I haven't decided. I'm very grateful that you're willing to share the Chamber's magic with me, but extending my life that way..." Hans trailed off, clearly uncertain about what to say next.

"You think it's immoral to extend your life by taking the lives of others?" Otto asked.

"That's part of it. If I do this thing, how will Branik judge my soul when I die? Will I be cast into hell?"

Otto wanted to slap his forehead in frustration, but he respected Hans too much for such a display. After all, assuming he ever decided to die, Otto had a pretty good idea where his soul would end up and he preferred not to think about it.

"I can't answer that question," Otto said. "The lives we're going to use to power the ritual belong to criminals. They're going to die regardless. Using them this way at least lets their life force serve a useful function. I can't imagine executing prisoners would be regarded as an evil act. But as I said before, the choice is yours. That said, you're getting too old to lead the squad."

Hans winced. "Aye, I know it, my lord. It's a fact every soldier must face eventually. I've been a soldier all my life. I have no family and no hobbies. This *is* my life."

"There's a place for you as head of security at Franken Manor. Our guards could only be improved with you as their leader. Not to mention Abby keeps nagging me every time I show up in the main house about learning the sword. I keep telling her to ask her mother and Annamaria tells her to ask me. You can give her lessons. Maybe that will silence her."

"The sword isn't the best weapon for a woman, my lord. Could you not teach her magic?"

"She has no wizardly potential and even if she did, I have neither the time nor the inclination to teach her. As for the suitability of a sword for a woman, I couldn't care less. She lives at the mansion surrounded by guards. The odds of her having to actually fight someone are astronomical. Once she sees how much work the training is, she'll probably quit anyway."

"Can I have a little more time to decide, my lord?"

"I'm leaving for Shenk Barony in three days. I'll have your answer then."

"Yes, Lord Shenk."

"And Hans, the process is painless if that's part of what's worrying you."

"It wasn't, but thank you for the reassurance."

Otto nodded and strode up the empty hall. Hans fell in a step behind him as was proper. Otto hardly needed a guard at all, much less when they were in the heart of the imperial palace, however, having him along was all part of the noble image. As the second most powerful man in the empire, Otto had to keep up appearances.

Well, he didn't actually have to do anything, but keeping up appearances made things easier, so he did it to the extent he felt like. Mostly he figured it made Hans feel like he was doing something useful which made it worthwhile.

They soon left the less populated area of the palace behind and reached the main keep. Servants bustled about, clerks took their time, and the occasional noble ambled about. To a person they all made a path when Otto approached and bowed as he passed.

He nodded back but didn't slow. He had a meeting with Emperor Wolfric and it wouldn't do to be late. Not that keeping Wolfric waiting would be a big deal. He didn't have much in the way of duties despite being emperor.

When they made the final turn to the library, they found two imperial guards standing in front of the door. They wore mail covered in black-and-gold tabards and stood straight as statues. Both men looked as young as Otto. Hopefully they weren't new recruits. He hated dealing with new recruits. They always thought the rules applied to Otto.

Otto stopped a few strides from the door when the guards made no move to open it. He looked from them, to the door, and back, then raised an eyebrow.

"No one's allowed in the emperor's presence with weapons, my lord," the right-hand guard said.

Yes, definitely new recruits. "My name is Otto Shenk and…"

He trailed off as the guards hastened to open the doors.

"Apologies, Lord Shenk," the lead guard said. "I didn't recognize you at first. Please go right in."

"I shouldn't be long, Hans." Otto strode into the library and let the smell of leather and parchment wash over him. He loved it here.

He sensed only one person in the library, which made it easy to find Wolfric. His old friend lounged in a leather chair, one leg over the arm, and a thick tome in his hand. Otto recognized it as one of the ancient history books he'd brought from Lord Karonin's storehouse.

Wolfric must have heard him approaching as he lowered the book and looked up. He'd grown a beard and despite only being in his midthirties it had a few streaks of gray. The emperor smiled, stood, and the two men shook hands.

"My condolences on the loss of your father," Wolfric said.

Otto refrained from snorting a laugh. He'd hated his father and the feeling had been mutual. "Thank you. Are you enjoying the book?"

"Very much. Pre–Arcane Lord histories are difficult to come by. Have a seat."

Otto adjusted his sword and took the chair opposite Wolfric's and both men settled in.

"Have there been any issues I need to know about?" Otto asked.

7

"Nothing serious. Some minor bandit activity, some squabbles between barons, the usual. The provinces are reasonably calm as well. All in all, the empire is peaceful, secure, and rich. I almost hate to say it out loud lest we tempt fate."

"I don't believe in fate. We built this empire through hard work and blood and now we're reaping our just rewards. Should anyone try and ruin what we've built, they will be dealt with, harshly."

"I know I've said this before, but I'm glad we're not enemies."

"As am I. It's not like I have that many friends. Anyway, Father's funeral is in three days. I might hang around for a day, depending on how Mother is holding up."

"Take all the time you need. The capital will be fine."

Otto was less worried about the capital than he was about spending a day and a half with Stephan. Losing his patience and killing the new baron would cause all sorts of problems he didn't need to deal with.

CHAPTER TWO

As expected, Otto's chat with Wolfric hadn't lasted long. When all was calm and peaceful, there really wasn't much to discuss. Taking his leave, Otto joined Hans in the hall and the two men marched back the way they'd come. He preferred traveling the back halls. It wasn't strictly necessary for Otto to be out of sight when he became one with the ether, but he found the magic unnerved the servants. Since they already acted like they feared he'd blast them to ash for the smallest offense, Otto found it easier to just avoid using unnecessary magic around them.

He paused and turned to face Hans. "I'll be working at home for the next couple days, but I'll be by the warehouse before I leave. Think hard about what you want to do."

"I will, my lord. And thank you for your consideration."

Otto nodded. "You've been a loyal soldier and earned that consideration. Until later."

So saying, Otto became one with the ether.

A moment later he appeared in the closet of his suite in Franken Manor. He'd debated joining Illsa at Lord Colt's

Workshop, but didn't want to start a project only to have to stop in a couple of days. He smiled and stepped out of the closet. He'd never forget the day eight years ago when she emerged from the portal in Garen. A portal he'd believed it impossible to reactivate.

He'd returned to the workshop with her and together they studied under Lord Colt's simulacrum. His goal had been to create enough of the artifacts she'd used, ethereal capacitors Lord Colt called them, to reactivate all the empire's portals.

On the face of it, this didn't seem like such a big thing, but after nearly ten years they still had only one prototype built and it rattled apart every time they powered it up. Illsa was trying to work the bugs out now. Otto had worked on it off and on for a year and now when he looked at the boxy device all he wanted was to smash it into a thousand pieces. When such thoughts started filling his mind, he knew it was time to move on to a new project.

Happily, his mithril-infusion process was going splendidly which did wonders for his mood. And then he'd gotten word that his father had died which meant a trip back to the barony. That killed whatever good mood he'd been enjoying.

He shook his head and put the thought out of his mind. Lady White had requested a meeting and he was curious what the beautiful undead priestess wanted. She and Jet kept to their part of the mansion, seldom speaking to anyone outside of Jet's requests for meals. If nothing else they were excellent guests, though they did make the servants nervous.

In the hall outside he turned left and barely managed a stride before a high, clear voice called out, "Daddy!"

He stopped and snarled. Of all the people he didn't want to deal with, Abby was near the top of the list. Annamaria's little girl had grown into a precocious teenager who wasn't the least bit frightened of him despite his reputation. She still didn't know the truth about her father and Otto wasn't going to be the one to tell her. In a few years she'd be married off to someone and he wouldn't have to deal with her anymore.

He turned and found her standing a few feet away, a bright smile on her pretty face. Her long blond hair was unbound and she wore a simple white dress that reached her knees. When she was older, she'd be as beautiful as her mother, no doubt about that.

"Abby. Did you need something?"

"I need someone to teach me how to use a sword."

"How many times have I told you to ask your mother?"

"Mom says it's up to you."

Otto frowned. What was Annamaria playing at? She knew Otto cared nothing for the child. "Ask your grandfather."

"I did. Grandpa says girls shouldn't study sword fighting. He said I should learn to cook instead."

That certainly did sound like something Edwin would say. The rotund merchant thought food or gold could solve every problem. That he was still alive was something of a miracle given his eating habits.

"Well?" Abby asked again.

"I couldn't possibly care less. If you want to learn to swing a sword, be my guest. I have a meeting."

Otto spun on his heel.

"Can I come?" Abby asked, seeming in no way deterred by his cold attitude.

"It's with Lady White."

"Never mind. I'll go find Mom and tell her you said it was okay for me to learn sword fighting."

The thumps of Abby's feet soon vanished as she went to find her mother. For his part, Otto wasn't sure whether having to talk to her was better or worse than having to listen to her screaming. Both were miserable in their own way.

He shook his head and set out again. Why did he bother putting up with her delusions? He asked himself that question regularly and had yet to come up with an answer that suited him. Perhaps some remnant of his youthful weakness remained to curse him.

Whatever. She was such a minor annoyance on the grand scale of things it hardly bore thinking about. Putting Abby out of his mind, he strode through the empty halls to Lady White's suite. In truth it was more than a suite. He'd given her an entire wing of the mansion for her private use.

Edwin never complained about Otto giving away a third of his mansion and Otto wouldn't have cared if he did. Lady White was a powerful and loyal ally and he intended to keep her close.

Otto rounded a corner and the light seemed to dim. It was a minor magical effect that served no purpose beyond ambiance. A few strides further on and a deep growling filled the air. The door to Lady White's chamber was guarded by a pair of wolves that she'd transformed into warbeasts. Nowhere near as impressive as the giant cat he'd seen her make, the wolves stood about chest high and had stiff gray hair and glowing red eyes.

He stopped. Not out of fear. He could have easily killed the beasts with a thought. No, he stopped out of politeness. He understood that Lady White could see everything the warbeasts did. And sure enough the door opened and the woman in question appeared in the flesh.

Much like Otto himself, Lady White still looked exactly the same as she did on the day he first met her in the Land of the Demon Binders. Today she wore a black gown that revealed more of her bone-white skin than it hid. Her red eyes flashed when she saw Otto and her bloodred lips turned up in a smile.

"Thank you for coming, Otto." She turned to glower at the still-growling warbeasts. "Stop that! You know better than to growl at Otto."

The wolves fell silent and one let out a little whimper.

"I thought they were supposed to be smart," Otto said.

"They are, but they're also protective and sometimes the two clash. They wouldn't have attacked you without my direct order."

"Lucky for them," Otto said. "What did you want to discuss?"

"Won't you come in and sit down so we can have a proper chat? Jet can make tea."

"Do you drink tea?"

"Sometimes. While I don't require food, I do like the taste."

He shrugged and followed her inside. If Lady White wanted to play hostess, he'd go along with it. He had nothing else on his schedule for today after all, so there was no rush.

She led him to a sitting room decorated in black and red. There was a cherry table and black leather chairs. Jet stood behind one of the chairs, back straight, and far-too-human eyes looking straight ahead. Unlike Lady White, Jet had aged a great deal since Otto first met her. Her beautiful, pale skin had grown tight and wrinkles had formed around her eyes. She wore a dark-green dress in the style of her homeland.

Jet bowed to Otto. "Lord Shenk."

"Jet. I see Astaroth hasn't acknowledged your devotion yet."

"Unfortunately not yet, but soon my prayers will be answered."

If the Lord of the Undead hadn't answered her prayers in a decade, Otto had his doubts that he ever would, but then again, who could say? He would never claim to know the mind of a demon lord.

"Jet," Lady White said. "Brew us a pot of tea."

"Yes, my lady." Jet hurried out of the room and into the kitchen.

"Please, sit." Lady White gestured to the nearest chair.

Otto obliged her then asked, "So, what's on your mind?"

She sat across from him and said, "Something odd is happening in Astaroth's hell where it approaches our world. I don't know exactly what and that worries me."

Otto cocked his head and considered her words. The goings-on in the various hells had never interested him overmuch. There was enough to worry about with mortal politics. "Does this oddity pose a threat to the empire?"

"I don't believe so. The focus appears to be many thousands of miles from here. I can't get an exact fix on where."

"At the risk of stating the obvious," Otto said. "Is there some reason you don't just ask your master what's going on?"

"I have, but Astaroth refuses to answer me. He still grants me my magic, and my demonic servants continue to obey, so I'm confident that I remain in his good graces, but if that's true, I can't figure out why he won't speak to me."

"I wish I had some brilliant advice to offer you," Otto said. "Perhaps he's busy with other matters. The universe is a big place after all."

"I hope you're right. I may summon a demon tonight and question it. Would you like to sit in on the ritual?"

"Certainly. Is the process similar to what you did to create the warbeast?"

"Somewhat. Thank you for listening to my concerns."

Otto smiled and relaxed a fraction. "I visited with Wolfric this afternoon and it occurred to me that I don't have many friends. He is one of them. Over the past decade, you've become another. Anytime you wish to talk, I'm happy to listen."

"It's funny that you say that. If you have few friends, then I can say with complete honesty that I only have one. And you are my first."

"The first friend of a demon priestess? I'm honored."

Jet chose that moment to enter with the tea. Otto sighed in contentment. It would be nice to relax for a few hours in the one place he was certain no one in the mansion would bother him.

○

Annamaria slipped a stitch on her current embroidery project and scowled. She used to hate sewing, but after many visits from Otto's mother, she'd gotten to like the hobby. She still didn't come close to Katharina's skill, but she had improved. Today she was working on a cluster of bluebells that would decorate a pillowcase.

Why was she so distracted today? There wasn't anything unusual happening. Life in the city was quiet; Father said business was good and since she doubled-checked the books, she knew he wasn't exaggerating. They had nearly returned to their old profit levels. No doubt the fact that she was friends with the emperor and her husband was his chief advisor played a part in funneling a lot of business their way.

She worked on picking out the errant stitch and swallowed a sigh. Life was about as good as she had any hope of it being. That being the case, what was the problem?

"Mom!" Abby's shout from the hall startled her into pricking her finger.

The scowl turned to a snarl and she stuck her finger in her mouth. A moment later the door to her suite burst open and the bundle of energy that was her pride and joy came running in.

Abby smiled from ear to ear, her face glowing with joy. Father said she looked just like Annamaria when she was that age, but all she could see were hints of her long-departed Lothair. They were subtle; the curve of her nose and the shape of her eyes were the most noticeable.

"What's got you so excited, dear?"

"Dad said it was okay if I started studying the sword."

Annamaria tensed. She'd been encouraging Abby to try and get closer to Otto in the hope that he might eventually come to think of her as his own daughter. It was a dangerous game, but one that she hoped would ensure Abby's future. Of course, if she'd miscalculated, the results would be... unpleasant.

"You spoke to Otto? I didn't realize he was home."

"I was hiding around the corner from his room and caught him when he came out." She frowned a little. "We didn't talk for long. He was going to see Lady White."

Annamaria's face twisted in distaste. She'd had minimal interactions with the coldly beautiful woman. When Otto informed them that she'd be taking over the east wing of the mansion, Annamaria had been tempted to object. Then good sense got the best of her. Anything she said on the subject would've been ignored and Father hadn't complained in any case.

"Do you think Dad's cheating on you with her?" Abby asked.

Annamaria turned a laugh into a cough to cover her reaction. Though they were technically married, it was very much in name only. Otto did what he wanted, when he wanted and her opinion was of no concern to him.

"I don't think so, dear. They have a professional relationship, nothing more."

Abby had a thoughtful look, one that often led to questions she'd prefer not to answer.

"How come you two don't share a bedroom?"

Yes, that was just the sort of question she didn't want to answer. "Your father comes and goes at all hours. It would be difficult if he had to worry about waking me up."

Abby's face lit up in a smile. "I didn't think about that. Uncle Wolfric really keeps him busy."

Annamaria hated lying to her daughter, but the truth would serve no one. "He certainly does. Now, what exactly did Otto say when you asked him about the swordsmanship lessons?"

"Um, he said he couldn't care less if I wanted to learn how to swing a sword. That's the same as giving me permission, right?"

Annamaria winced. Clearly the plan to turn Otto into a doting father wasn't going as well as she'd hoped. At least he hadn't ignored her completely. That was progress, of sorts.

"It's close enough I suppose. We'll ask one of the older guards to start teaching you the basics when he has time."

Abby threw both hands in the air and whooped with joy.

Annamaria had no idea why her daughter had become so obsessed with swordsmanship, but seeing her happy warmed Annamaria's heart and that was enough.

"When can I get started?" Abby asked.

"We'll see. When I next speak to your father, we'll work out the details." She didn't add that given how seldom she spoke to Otto, that might be awhile.

CHAPTER THREE

"Why, exactly, does this sort of thing have to happen at night?" Otto asked as he followed Lady White down a long hall that led to a bedroom she'd converted into a casting chamber.

She'd changed from her black gown to an equally black robe that featured so many slits and cutouts that it exposed more skin than the skimpy gown. While she certainly looked fetching in it, the robe was yet another thing he didn't understand. If it served a purpose, he couldn't imagine what it might be.

Beside him, Jet was dressed in a matching outfit. She had the ecstatic expression of a true believer about to witness a miracle. While Otto might have questions about her sanity, he would never doubt her devotion to her beliefs. Ten years of being ignored and she still kept at it.

"We—and by we I mean followers of Astaroth—perform these sorts of summonings at night because that's what the demons prefer. If we show them respect, we're more apt to get the responses we want."

"I assumed that if you were sufficiently powerful, you could compel them to answer."

"That's also an option. But you have to remember that all demons I summon were created by Astaroth. Beating the information you need out of a being created by your master is a bad look. Coaxing is better when possible. At least that's my opinion. Astaroth has never given me any guidance one way or the other."

Demonic politics didn't interest Otto any more than human politics did, but for a priestess, these sorts of details were no doubt important. He certainly wasn't about to offer a critique of her methods. Lady White was the expert here, not him.

They reached the final door and she waved a hand. The ether shifted as, he assumed, some sort of ward was dispelled. The door opened of its own accord and the three of them strode through.

Any resemblance to a bedroom was long gone. There was no furniture, unless you counted the gold candleholders that surrounded a summoning circle drawn in red that covered half the floor. Another gesture saw the black candles spring to life, sending odd shadows dancing around the room.

"You two need to remain silent," Lady White said. "If you have questions, tell me now and I'll ask them."

"I simply wish to observe the magic," Otto said. "As long as whatever's happening is no threat to the empire, I couldn't care less."

Jet remained silent, hands clasped behind her back.

"Very well. I'm going to begin. No casting lest you disturb the ritual."

Otto almost took offense, but felt certain she was just being overly cautious. He was certainly wizard enough to know not to manipulate the ether this close to someone casting a powerful spell.

The light dimmed and corrupt ether gathered. Lady White directed the magic into the crimson circle and slowly the runes lit up. Normally this much corruption would leave him feeling ill, but tonight Otto felt nothing. No doubt the mithril he'd infused into his body played a large part in his comfort.

His focus remained on the spell, but Otto couldn't help wondering what would happen if he tried to use corrupt ether now. Would he even be able to touch it? His instincts said no and he was okay with that. Corruption might be beneficial for the undead, but as a living man, he doubted it would do him any good.

His idle thoughts quieted when a dark sphere appeared in the center of the circle. It grew until it was about the size of his head then popped like a soap bubble, leaving an incredibly ugly, two-foot-tall demon behind. The creature hung in the air, flapping rotten bat wings as bits of flesh dripped off its decaying body. And the less said about the smell the better. Hopefully the ward sealing the room would keep the stench out of the rest of the mansion.

"You summoned me, Priestess?" the demon asked.

"I did. Thank you for answering. I have noticed some odd changes in the master's hell in the vicinity of our world. Tell me what's happening."

"I can't."

Lady White frowned. "Does that mean you don't know?"

"No. All who serve in this part of Hell know. But by Astaroth's will we are forbidden to speak of it. It matters not how you seek to compel me, I can't defy the master's will."

"Can you at least tell me if whatever is happening will threaten this part of the world?"

The demon shook his head. "I can say nothing about it by Astaroth's will."

"That at least explains why my auguries revealed nothing. Very well, you—"

"Wait, please," Jet said. "I have to know. When will my devotion be rewarded? I've been praying to Astaroth for over a decade and he still doesn't acknowledge me. What more must I do?"

Lady White glared daggers at Jet. If she survived the night, Otto would be impressed.

"Human, what have you offered the master save empty words?" the demon asked. "Have you offered your true name?"

"I offered my soul and my loyalty. I thought that was enough!"

"It is if all you want is to be a cultist and lesser priestess. You've been praying for the same power as Lady White, yet you refuse to offer the same sacrifice. Either change your prayers to match what you can give or offer more." The demon turned to Lady White. "Have you not instructed her?"

"I thought I had, but it seems she needs a refresher. I release you."

The demon vanished, blessedly taking the stink with it when it left. Normal light returned to the room.

Before Otto could speak or move, Lady White lashed out, sending Jet crashing into the wall with bone-breaking force. Crackling bands of corruption held her in place.

"What part of 'stay silent and don't move' did you fail to understand? Your actions made me look weak in front of one of the master's servants. Like I can't control my own acolyte."

"Forgive me, Mistress," Jet said. "But I had to know. Will I truly never be like you?"

"Not without paying the same price I did. Too many people know your true name for it to have value. And you're certainly not strong enough to kill everyone that does. Set your sights lower, become a loyal cultist, and be reborn in Hell as a demon. It's the best you'll ever manage."

"But I want to be young and beautiful like you forever."

Lady White snapped her fingers and Jet fell to the floor, her body curled up in a ball of pain.

"We all have things we want. But that doesn't mean you can have them. Now get out of my sight before I decide to end you."

Jet groaned and crawled out of the casting chamber. Otto watched her as she passed but didn't speak. It wasn't his place and he had no words of advice in any case. Well, maybe "give up on becoming the slave of a demon lord," but he doubted that sort of advice would be welcome.

When she'd gone, Lady White said, "I apologize for that unseemly display. I can't imagine what got into her."

"Desperation makes people do crazy things. I can't blame you for Jet's behavior. In fact, I'm impressed that you decided to let her live."

"She's a useful servant. Hopefully she takes this correction to heart and adjusts her ambitions accordingly."

Otto had serious doubts that someone as obsessed as Jet would ever lower her ambitions. But it wasn't his problem and if it became his problem, he'd deal with her, permanently.

CHAPTER FOUR

Three days passed quickly for Otto and the time for his father's funeral had arrived. While he was far from eager to return to Shenk Barony, he wanted to be there for his mother. Heaven knew Stephan wasn't qualified to offer her any comfort and the less said about his wife, the better. Otto suppressed a shudder when an image of the hideous Griswalda popped into his head. He seldom pitied his eldest brother, but having to live with that woman was almost enough to do it.

But before he left, he needed to talk to Hans. His most loyal soldier had a decision to make. Otto hoped he made the right one, at least the right one from Otto's perspective. The other members of his personal guard were competent, but he didn't think any of them could take Hans's place and match his ability.

Otto rounded a bend into the industrial area. It was midmorning and the streets were empty. The late spring weather was beautiful, which was why he'd chosen to walk instead of travel through the ether. Though the clangs of hammers filling the air along with the sharp stink of smoke did spoil the trip a bit.

They'd never bothered moving the team to a new base. Instead they'd expanded the warehouse into a proper military facility. There were bays for the enchanted armor, now upgraded thanks to Illsa, and a large alchemy lab for Ulf. That lab was the main reason they didn't bother to relocate. The frequent stench that emerged from it blended right in with the foundries and forges. Had they moved closer to the palace, no one would've been happy, including Otto himself.

Four guards were on duty outside the gate that controlled access to the warehouse. They'd built a heavy, spike-topped iron fence to increase security. Not having to hide their work made it much easier.

As he got closer the guards straightened, touched fists to hearts, and opened the gate. Otto nodded in passing, but didn't speak. An open space separated the fence from the warehouse. Otto ignored the huge double doors that allowed the armor in and out and went to the smaller side door. It was locked of course, but a flick of ether popped it open.

He'd barely stepped into the main mustering area when a bright voice called out, "Master!"

Corina came running toward him. At twenty-six, she'd filled out into an, if not beautiful woman, at least one far more attractive than the skinny, half-starved girl he'd first taken under his wing. Her dark hair was tied back in a ponytail and she was dressed in her black war wizard robe. Once he was satisfied with her training, Corina had been reassigned to the team as their permanent wizard. She'd maxed out at seven threads, not amazing, but better than average.

Otto's lips quirked up in a faint smile. "Corina. Is Hans around?"

"The guys are playing cards. There's really not much else for us to do now."

"As a wizard, there's always plenty for you to do. Practicing and learning new ways to manipulate the ether is a lifetime's challenge."

Her face scrunched up. "I know, but it's hard to stay motivated when I've maxed out my power."

"Every wizard reaches that point eventually." Otto shrugged. Though he thought kindly of Corina, she wasn't his apprentice anymore. Should she choose to stop trying to improve, that was her decision.

"Are you really going to make Hans retire?" she asked.

"Perhaps you'd prefer if I let him keep going so he can get himself killed during the next emergency?" Otto shook his head. "He's getting old. If he follows me into danger, being half a second too slow might cost him his life. Or, worse from his perspective, he might get one of his men killed trying to cover for him. Do you imagine he could live with that?"

"No. That would gut him. I just can't imagine the team without Hans on it."

"I'm not thrilled about it either and he does have options. Whether he chooses to take them or not is out of our hands."

Otto gave Corina a pat on the shoulder and crossed the warehouse. The seven men that made up his personal guard along with their leader had abandoned their game and were standing at attention when they approached. They were all good soldiers, skilled and loyal.

Otto nodded and focused on Hans. "It's time."

"Aye, my lord. I've been thinking hard about what you said. If you're still willing to have me, I'll take that position at Franken Manor."

"An honorable choice, though I can't deny my disappointment. Sergeant, you are officially relieved of duty. Leave your uniform behind, but you can take the sword and armor. Everyone knows you at the mansion and I already told the guards you might be joining them. Present yourself at the gate by the end of the day."

Hans touched fist to heart. "Yes, Lord Shenk."

Otto turned a fraction to address the rest of the men. "I'll decide on the new unit commander when I return from Shenk Barony. Until then, Jax will serve as interim leader."

The men saluted and he turned back to Hans and held out his hand. "It's been an honor having you watch my back."

Hans stared for a moment before grasping his hand. "The honor was mine, Lord Shenk."

With a final nod, Otto turned back the way he'd come. It felt like the end of an era, but that was something he'd have to get used to. When you were immortal, change was constant. People got old and died all the time. The sooner he got used to that, the better.

CHAPTER FIVE

When Otto appeared in a shadowy corner of Castle Shenk's courtyard he found the rest of the space largely occupied by carriages and servants. It seemed many of the local nobles had turned out to pretend to mourn his father's passing. No doubt at the same time they'd be trying to chat with Stephan to find out just how insane he was. As someone that knew exactly how insane he was, Otto wished them all the best of luck with that.

He stepped out of the shadow and into the light, striding across the familiar ground toward the keep where soldiers in freshly polished armor stood at rigid attention. Otto didn't recognize either of them which was no surprise since he hadn't visited the barony in half a decade.

When he got closer the right-hand guard said, "Your name so we can announce you, sir."

"Otto Shenk."

Both guards' eyes about bugged out of their heads. Not an unusual reaction for Otto.

The speaker's throat worked as he tried to swallow. He finally coughed and said, "Lord Shenk. We didn't realize you'd arrived. One of the servants should have mentioned your carriage getting here."

"I didn't arrive by carriage."

"Right, magic." The guard coughed again. The way he was shaking, Otto expected him to piss himself at any moment. "What title should we use, my lord?"

Otto smiled faintly. "If you must announce my arrival home, chief advisor to the emperor will do."

The guard winced. "Baron Stephan's orders, my lord. We had to announce Captain Axel as well."

Otto's smile broadened. He was the one that made Axel a captain after all. "Well, mustn't keep the baron waiting. Go ahead."

"Yes, my lord." The guard took a deep breath and bellowed Otto's name and title into the great hall. "You can go on in."

He strode through the door and into the familiar great hall. It seemed strange not to see his father seated at the head of the table. And stranger still to see Stephan there. His eldest brother had lost the last few strands of his hair, but his massive build remained unchanged. He'd dressed like Father, in fine leather pants and shirt, both decorated with polished brass rivets. Griswalda sat beside him, looking even more porcine than ever in a poison-green robe.

Around the great hall, knots of the local who's who stared at him, their previous scheming forgotten. Of Mother, Axel, and the boys, there was no sign. Strange, but Otto would find them later. Much as he disliked it, he had to pay his respects, such as they were, to the new baron.

He walked through the silent hall to the table where

Stephan stood to greet him. "Little brother. I didn't think you'd join us."

"I came for Mother. We've known this day was coming since her last visit to the capital, but that doesn't mean it will be easy for her."

"No, but she's been remarkably strong when I've seen her. Will you be staying long?"

"One night perhaps. I'll decide after the funeral. Is Mother upstairs?"

Stephan nodded. "With Axel. We've got an hour before we head over to the Temple of Branik."

Otto held out his hand in a gesture of no doubt pointless goodwill. "I'm sure you'll keep matters in Shenk Barony running smoothly."

"Of course." Stephan gripped Otto's hand, and, being Stephan, tried his best to crush it.

Otto squeezed back, adding a little ethereal enhancement, until Stephan's face twisted and the bones were grinding together. "Don't try your pitiful power plays with me, Stephan, you're not remotely up to it. Run the barony, don't cause trouble, and hopefully we'll never have to see each other again. Understand?"

Stephan nodded, his jaw tight and his face red.

Otto finally let him go. "Good. I'll be upstairs with Mother until it's time. Griswalda, you're looking as lovely as ever."

Leaving the new baron behind, Otto made his way up the familiar steps to the second floor. He figured Mother would be in her bedroom and sure enough he found the door open when he arrived. She was sitting in her chair while Axel lounged on the bed. Both of them seemed to have aged since Otto last saw them, Mother especially. Her hair was now totally white and all the more shocking against her black dress. Axel had on his black-and-gold uniform. His hair had finally begun its inevitable receding. They made a glum, silent pair. Appropriate given the situation.

As if sensing him standing there watching, Mother looked up with red-rimmed eyes. She'd actually been crying for Father. That surprised Otto, though he knew it shouldn't have. Somehow the two of them had loved each other. It was one of the universe's great mysteries.

"Hello, Mother. Axel. How are you holding up?"

"I'm fine, dear. No need to fuss." Otto smiled faintly. He didn't need magic to see through that lie. "Come in and sit down. Did you speak to Stephan?"

"Briefly. He was almost cordial, for Stephan."

"He's on his best behavior with all the other barons and rich merchants around," Axel said. "He doesn't want them thinking he's a complete maniac."

"I'm curious to see how that works out for him. He does know that all these people have met him at least once before, right?"

Axel barked a laugh.

"He's trying," Mother said. "You should give Stephan some credit for that."

"He's not a child," Otto said. "And you don't give grown men credit for trying, only succeeding. But enough about Stephan. Have you thought any more about coming to stay at Franken Manor after the funeral?"

"I haven't decided. I'm sure Griswalda would like nothing better, which makes me want to stay. Though spite is a poor reason to do anything."

Otto's smile broadened and he sat beside Axel. "You might not be a Shenk by blood, but you've lived with us long enough to know that for a Shenk, spite is a perfectly reasonable motivation."

"You're too young to be so cynical," Mother said. "As far as I can tell, you haven't aged a day."

"That's a side effect of the experiments I've been running. A positive one. If you'd like to be twenty again, I can arrange it." Otto meant it too. If Mother wished it, he could keep her young and healthy forever.

"Thank you, dear, but no. I'll live out however many years I have left before my natural time comes."

"I keep offering people their youth back and no one wants it. I'm baffled by that."

"It's unnatural," Mother said. "A parent should die before their children. Why would I want to be younger than Stephan and possibly outlive the boys? Each generation has to accept when their time has come and make way for the next. That's how nature works."

"I'm a wizard. Nature works the way I want it to work. But if that's your decision, I'll respect it."

They moved on to lighter topics, mostly about Axel's work surveying roads and Abby's strange desire to become a sword fighter.

At last a voice from downstairs announced, "It's time for the procession to begin!"

Otto stood and helped his mother to her feet. Her hand trembled in his. When he tried to let go, she held on tight. If that was what she needed, so be it. They went downstairs with Axel a little bit behind. At the bottom, the gathered nobles were silently waiting.

Stephan approached and tried to take Otto's place. A single, hard look was sufficient to change his mind. The walk to the Temple of Branik didn't take long, thank goodness.

Though Mother still seemed healthy, her stamina wasn't what it used to be.

Outside the church, the priest waited by the door. He wore mail polished bright enough to gleam in the sun and carried an arming sword at his side. If he were any other man, Otto might have asked if he was expecting an attack. As it was, he offered a polite nod and led Mother to a pew at the front of the church. A little ways further in, a wooden coffin sat on a raised platform.

"Do you wish to take a look?" Otto asked.

"I've seen his body many times," Mother said. "And I have no desire to see it again in this state. Were it up to me, I'd skip this entire affair and consign his remains to the fire immediately. But Stephan needs to go through the motions and have the priest officially acknowledge him as baron."

Otto would've laughed, but this was far from the right time. Stephan needed Otto's acknowledgment far more than he needed some priest's. Luckily for his elder brother, he had it.

CHAPTER SIX

Hans sighed and picked at his plain tan tunic as he walked through the busy streets toward Franken Manor. It felt strange not wearing his uniform. He wasn't in disguise working on some secret mission this time. He was a civilian now, mostly by his own choice. Much as he hated it, he couldn't deny the truth of what Lord Shenk said. He was a step slower; a fraction weaker. It wasn't much, but in a fight, the sort of fights he might get into while watching Lord Shenk's back, it might be the difference between life and death.

If it was just Hans's life, he wouldn't have cared. Better to die in battle than to wither away in old age. But it wasn't just his life and if his weakness got one of his people killed, he wouldn't be able to live with himself.

Thus his new career, a sort of paid retirement if he was being honest. Put out to pasture overseeing a bunch of barely competent sell swords. Kind of sad when you thought about it. On the other hand, Lord Shenk's generosity in offering him a position of any sort came as a bit of a surprise. His lord wasn't known for sentimentality. Perhaps he really did think Hans could make a difference in the mansion's security. In any case, Hans intended to do his best to thank Lord Shenk for his kindness.

He adjusted the rucksack slung over his shoulder. All his worldly possessions fit inside with room to spare. Best not to think too hard about that.

When he left the business district and entered Gold Ward, it felt like the world changed. There were fewer people walking around and the ones he did see wore more gold than Hans made in a decade. Not that they were ostentatious about it. The rings were small, and well made; the necklaces partially hidden by silk tunics. The wealth was just visible enough to remind you that it was there without rubbing your nose in it. Thoughtful of them.

When the gates of Franken Manor finally appeared ahead of him, Hans let out a sigh. He felt totally out of place on the streets of Gold Ward.

The two guards on duty outside straightened as he approached. The man on the right—much like in the military, it seemed that the guards here also stationed their senior man on the right—said, "Sergeant Hans, welcome. Lord Shenk said you might be joining us today. It's an honor to have you leading the team."

Hans smiled. It seemed he was expected. "It's my honor to join you. Lord Shenk mentioned his wish that I do what I can to improve security. I'm sure that if we work together, we'll be able to fulfill his desire."

"We'll all do our best, Sergeant. If there's one thing none of us wants, it's to disappoint Lord Shenk. The commander's quarters in the barracks have been cleaned out and made ready for your use. Do you require a guide?"

Hans shook his head. "I've been here plenty of times. I know the way. And you don't have to call me Sergeant. I'm a civilian now, the same as you."

"You're also our new commander, sir. Just calling you Hans would be disrespectful. At a minimum we should call you commander."

"That's fine. I'm going to get settled in then take a walk around the grounds to see what I can see."

"Understood, sir. You should also speak to Timothy—he's the new head butler—at the main house and let him know you've arrived. It's not a huge deal, but the cooks need to know to make you supper."

Hans grinned. "I certainly don't want to miss supper. Thanks for letting me know."

The guards pulled the iron gate open and Hans strode through. As he crunched up the gravel path he looked left and right at the perfectly manicured grounds. If this was to be his new home, he could certainly do worse. All the trees and shrubs were beautiful, though they also provided plenty of places for a potential intruder to hide. Somehow he doubted that a suggestion to cut them all down would be met with a positive response.

The path forked after about fifty paces and he debated whether to approach the main house first or unpack his meager possessions. If he didn't want to miss out on supper, the mansion came first. Turning down the path, he made his way to the front door. Partway there he paused and cocked his head.

In the distance he heard the crack of wood followed by a high-pitched shout. He knew that sound. Someone was training with wooden swords. Curiosity beat out hunger and he changed directions. Soon enough he found himself near a training circle. One of the guards, a man not much younger than Hans if the gray hair was any indication, was sparring with a blond teenage girl. He'd seen Abby enough times to recognize her and even if he hadn't he doubted there was more than one little blond girl living here.

Lord Shenk did mention something about Abby wanting to learn the sword. Looked like she finally got her wish.

He watched as she flailed around, swinging the wooden sword with a good deal more enthusiasm than skill. Her instructor patiently dodged or deflected every strike, easily avoiding her clumsy efforts. What he didn't do was offer any suggestions for improvement. In fact, if she was just getting started, sparring was a waste of time. She needed to practice forms and work on building muscle.

Since he had no doubt that training her would fall to him eventually, Hans figured he might as well get started now. He took a few strides closer and the guard finally noticed him.

"That's enough for now, my lady."

Abby stopped and frowned. "I'm just getting warmed up."

"We have company."

Abby spun and flashed a smile that would no doubt turn the boys' heads in a few years. "Hans! Is Dad with you? I thought he was going home to Grandpa Shenk's funeral. I wish I could've gone, but Mom said there was no way."

Hans had briefly met Lord Shenk's eldest brother and wholeheartedly approved of keeping Abby as far away from him as possible. "Your father has indeed gone to Shenk Barony. I'm here because I've been reassigned as commander of the manor guards. I'll also be overseeing your training."

Abby brightened at that, but the guard scowled. "Lady Shenk asked me to begin the young lady's training."

Hans nodded. "If you wish to explain that to Lord Shenk when he returns, I'll be happy to step aside."

All the blood drained from the guard's face. "No! No, I would never question Lord Shenk's orders. Please don't mention that I said anything."

"I won't. In exchange, could you let the head butler know that I've arrived and will be eating with the guards going forward?"

"Certainly, sir. I'll see to it at once." The guard fled as if he feared the lord of the manor might appear at any moment.

"Everyone acts like that when they hear Dad's name. Seems excessive to me."

"Lord Shenk is not the most patient of men. When he gives an order, he expects it to be obeyed. Questioning him is not a route to a long, happy career." Or a long, happy life, he didn't add.

"Are you and Dad friends? He seems not to have many."

"I would never be so presumptuous as to claim to be his friend, but I do have tremendous respect for your father. He's saved my life on many occasions."

Abby still looked troubled, so Hans said, "Let's get started on your training."

She seemed to shake off her troubled thoughts. "You don't have a sword."

"You shouldn't have one either. You need to build up your strength and stamina first. Start by running twenty laps around the grounds followed by twenty push-ups and thirty sit-ups. When you can do that without getting out of breath, we'll move on to something more difficult."

"That doesn't sound like much fun."

"It's not supposed to be. Learning to fight isn't a game. At the end of the day, what you're learning is how to kill people.

And if you're in a position that you need to kill someone, being fast and strong will be a big advantage. In fact, until you've had a couple years of proper training, the best thing you can do is run from an attacker."

"Isn't that cowardly?"

Hans blew out a sigh. She sounded like some of the young noble boys he'd met over the years. They all had their heads filled with honor and glory and how they were going to fight in whatever war sprang up next. Idiots, every last one of them. Happily, the ones that lived generally grew out of it.

"Who filled your head with such a notion?"

She looked away, her cheeks slightly red. "Some of my friends. I heard them say they thought Dad was a coward because he fought with magic instead of a sword. I thought if I learned to fight, I could challenge them to a duel. Dad basically created the empire. Even Uncle Wolfric says so. No one should talk about him like that."

Hans wasn't sure what he found more amusing, the idea of Abby defending Lord Shenk's honor or that she imagined he'd care what some noble brat thought about him. Just to be on the safe side he asked, "You didn't mention what they said to your father, did you?"

Her gaze snapped back to him, eyes wide. "No. I was afraid he might take it badly. And, while I don't like what they said, they're still my friends. You won't tell Dad, right?"

"No. Lord Shenk has enough on his mind without me bothering him about that. If you're serious, you'd best get running. I'm not going to teach you anything else until you can finish your calisthenics without getting exhausted."

"Fine, it wouldn't hurt to get in better shape I guess. Then I can have cake with Grandpa and not get fat." She took off running, wooden sword still in hand.

Hans rubbed the bridge of his nose. What in heaven's name could the nobles be thinking? Those kids had to have heard their parents, or their fathers at least, calling Lord Shenk a coward. Saying such things in the privacy of their homes was bad enough, but if they should be so foolish as to ever say it where Lord Shenk might hear, he'd have no choice but to call them out to defend his honor. And Branik help any noble that did that.

"Hans."

A soft voice from the house drew his attention. Lady Shenk stood in the open doorway. She was an absolute vision in her white dress, her long blond hair trailing down her back.

He went over and offered a bow. "Lady Shenk."

"Did Otto send you to teach Abby?"

"Not exactly. He sent me to take over command of the house guard. Seems I'm getting too long in the tooth for the field. Teaching Abby is just a side task."

"You two had quite a chat. Did she tell you what prompted this foolishness?"

"She didn't tell you?"

"No. One day she came home and declared that she wanted to learn to fight. She's never shown a bit of interest in such things before. I was completely baffled."

"Guess it couldn't hurt to tell you." Hans repeated what Abby had told him. "I don't know what sort of idiot nobles she's hanging around with, but talk like that is a good way to earn a one-way trip to the Straken mines. Assuming you catch Lord Shenk on a good day."

Annamaria had a hand to her mouth. "She wants to protect Otto's honor?"

"Yup. Damnedest thing I ever heard, begging your pardon."

"You're sure she didn't tell him?" Lady Shenk's voice was tight, like she could barely get the question out.

"I'm sure. Abby seemed to realize telling Lord Shenk about that sort of thing wouldn't be healthy for her friends. Though if she plans to fight some of them in a duel, I can't imagine why she'd care."

"She has no idea what she's talking about," Annamaria said. "Fighting, duels, and all that are just words to Abby. She's never seen real violence. Real bloodshed. My guess is she just wants to force whoever said it to apologize. Heaven help me." That last sentence was muttered so softly Hans barely heard it.

"Don't worry yourself too much, Lady Shenk. I'll work her until she either gives up or is strong enough to actually win should someone take her up on the duel."

"You're very kind, Hans. Thank you. It'll be good to have you around the house. The guards are loyal, but jumpy. Always afraid of saying something that Otto wouldn't like. As if he actually cared what they said. You should be a steadying influence."

"I'll do my best, ma'am. If you'll excuse me, I need to get settled."

"Of course. I appreciate you indulging me. Good afternoon." She stepped back and closed the door.

Hans wiped the sweat from his brow. It seemed his time in Franken Manor wouldn't be as simple as he'd hoped.

CHAPTER SEVEN

Lady White sat in her casting chamber and let the energy from Astaroth's hell flow through her undead body. As the unique corruption flooded her senses, she meditated on what the demon said, or more precisely what it didn't say. What could her master be planning that he didn't want her to know about? Keeping secrets from a loyal servant made no sense. Astaroth should have either cut her off from his hell as a traitor and heretic or revealed what he planned on her world.

At least that was how it seemed to her. She couldn't help smiling at her arrogance. How did a speck like her dare to guess at the thoughts of a demon lord? It was ludicrous and yet she couldn't deny her obsession with finding out what her master wished to hide from her. Maybe he meant this as a challenge. A way to test her determination.

Either that or it was a way to see how skilled she was at mental gymnastics.

She was about to end her meditation session when a powerful surge of corruption rocked her magical senses. The power was a perfect match for Astaroth's and it came from somewhere in the city.

Lady White leapt from the floor and sprinted out of her casting chamber. She didn't know what might have caused such a burst of dark power, but if she hadn't summoned it—and she wasn't arrogant enough to imagine she was powerful enough to do so in the first place—then a priest even stronger than her must have been responsible.

That meant only one person, Lord of the Dead. Her former master and a deadly enemy.

But even he wasn't strong enough to cast a spell as powerful as what she sensed. As she ran through the halls toward her private exit, some of the pieces began to fall into place. Lord of the Dead had to be up to something. And Astaroth had to favor him if their master refused to share the details with Lady White.

She ground her teeth. This was the problem with different factions serving the same master. To save herself, she had to oppose Lord of the Dead. But if Astaroth favored him, then she risked losing her master's goodwill.

Astaroth, please, what do you want me to do?

As expected, the Lord of the Undead remained silent.

The massive source of corruption quickly faded. When she burst through the door, one weaker, but still strong source along with an uncertain number of far-smaller sources remained. As she both feared and expected, the powerful source was headed right this way. Any doubt she'd had that Lord of the Dead was responsible vanished when she confirmed that.

"Lady White?"

She spun and found one of Otto's soldiers—she couldn't recall the man's name—headed her way. It wasn't one of the house guards. She recognized them at this point, which meant it had to be one of the regular soldiers despite his lack of uniform.

"Is everything alright?" he asked.

She'd been so distracted she didn't realize she'd been staring at him. "No, everything is not alright. A powerful, dangerous source of corruption is rapidly approaching. It's likely either an undead or a warbeast. I know Otto has supplied you with mithril weapons. You'd best get them ready as ordinary steel isn't going to help you."

"That's considerably worse than what I feared. None of the guards here have mithril weapons and I left mine at the warehouse. Can you get a message to Lord Shenk? I suspect we'll be needing his help."

"No, my magic doesn't work that way. Do you not have some way to contact him?"

"No, he didn't leave me with one of those message sticks of his. I can ask the emperor to alert him that there's trouble, but I can't contact him directly."

"Then I suggest you do it." A roar shattered the air and it was close. "We have little time."

"I'll get the defenders organized and head straight for the palace."

The soldier ran off, leaving Lady White with a decision of her own. Did she fight or flee? The obvious answer came a moment later. She had nowhere else to go. Either she fought here and won or she'd stand before Astaroth and accept his judgement.

Hans sprinted across the lawn toward the front gate, bellowing for every guard to muster there. He had no idea what sort of horrible monster was coming, but from the look on Lady White's face, it was going to be bad. He cursed himself for not taking his mithril sword along with his old reliable. Lord Shenk would no doubt call him a fool for such a simple oversight. In his defense, Hans had thought his days of serious fighting were over. This was supposed to be a soft, cushy retirement job.

He smiled a little despite the situation. He was still serving Lord Shenk. That meant soft and cushy were almost certainly off the table.

"Hans!" Abby's shout brought him to a skidding halt. He'd been so focused on the immediate problem that he'd forgotten she was still running laps.

She reached him as soon as he came to a full stop. "What's going on? Can I help?"

"I'm not sure what's going on." Another roar, louder this time, shook the air. "And no, you can't help. Get inside and have everyone move to the deepest part of the mansion. Somewhere with a sturdy door that you can bar from the inside."

"Sure, the safe room. Dad ordered it built a few years ago. I'll tell Mom and Grandpa." She turned to run, paused, and turned back. "Be careful."

And with that she was gone, running toward the mansion as fast as her slender legs could carry her. Hans resumed his mad dash for the gate, relieved that he hadn't had to argue with the girl. He'd feared she might want to show off how tough she was. Thank Branik he'd been wrong about that.

Halfway to the gate a pair of guards fell in beside him. "What's going on, sir?"

"Something unpleasant is coming for a visit. What, exactly, I fear we'll find out all too soon. Once we get organized, I need to reach the palace and alert the emperor. He can contact Lord Shenk."

One of the guards grinned suddenly, looking far too young. "When his Lordship returns, he'll make short work of whatever's coming."

Hans dearly hoped the man's confidence wasn't misplaced. But in his years of service to Lord Shenk, one thing had become absolutely clear; there were no guarantees.

They reached the gate and Hans blew out a breath when he found it closed and the heavy iron latch thrown. Ten guards had gathered and all of them were staring out into the street. They held their swords in trembling hands.

"What's going on out there?" Hans asked.

"Best take a look for yourself, sir," said the older guard that had greeted him this morning.

Hans shouldered past two of the guards and peered through the bars. His eyes nearly popped out of his head. There was a... something out in the street fighting the city guards. It had to stand at least seven feet tall and was covered in thick green scales. Its head had an elongated jaw that reminded him uncomfortably of the monster that ate Cord on the Island of Giant Beasts. Even worse were the glowing red eyes that glared hatefully at the half dozen soldiers brandishing halberds at it.

One of the soldiers swung, the ax blade of his halberd landing a solid hit only to bounce off the scales without leaving so much as a scratch.

The impact threw the soldier off balance and the monster lunged in. It grabbed him and hurled him across the street and through the side of a store.

The rest of the soldiers backed away, keeping the spear points of their weapons leveled at the creature.

"A warbeast, as I feared." Lady White's voice right beside his ear made Hans jump. "Though I've never seen a creature like this. Are you familiar with it?"

The question calmed Hans a fraction. "No, ma'am. There's nothing in the empire that looks like that thing. At least not that I've ever seen or heard of."

"That is as I feared. There's nothing like it in the Land of the Demon Binders either."

"Beg your pardon, ma'am, but then where the hell did it come from?"

"Hell is exactly where it came from, at least, the demon spirit came from there. As for the host body, I haven't the slightest idea."

A lightning bolt crackled into the monster only to fizzle against its scales. A young woman in war wizard robes stared, obviously shocked at her spell's failure. Hans was pretty shocked too. Usually when a wizard hit something with a blast like that, the fight was over.

"Magic resistant as well." Lady White said it as if she were in a parlor discussing the weather. "I wonder how he managed to bond the spirit to the corpse."

Hans knew a rhetorical question when he heard one. His biggest problem was that the monster was between him and the palace entrance. There was no way he could sneak past it, which meant reaching the emperor was out of the question.

A war wizard came running from the opposite direction. Hans loosed a piercing whistle and the man stopped to look. His eyes widened and he trotted over. "Sergeant Hans! Is Lord Shenk with you?"

"Unfortunately not. I wanted to get word to the emperor,

but as you can see, there's a bit of a problem. Can you use your magic to sneak past it?"

"I can turn invisible, but no one will let me talk to the emperor."

"Then tell Draken! He might have a way to reach Lord Shenk himself. Hurry. I don't know how long we have."

"Yes, sir." The air shimmered and the wizard vanished.

A moment later the monster roared again and sent the guards flying as it charged right toward the manor gates.

Hans offered a silent prayer that the wizard was speedy and Lord Shenk was speedier. He figured the gate might buy them half a minute, then they were in for a fight.

CHAPTER EIGHT

Since becoming Lord Shenk's second-in-command, Draken's workload had only grown. He was fairly sure that's why his hair had turned white and he got all the new wrinkles. The way things were going today, it would be a wonder if he had any hair left by the end of it. Soldiers and war wizards were running all over the place, commanders were shouting orders, and pretty much everyone was looking to him for leadership.

He shook his head. Of all the days for Lord Shenk to be out of the city, why did it have to be today? He'd sensed a powerful surge in the ether and not long after reports of strange monsters attacking the city started rolling in. He had ten confirmed battles so far and messengers were arriving all the time.

The emperor, thank all that was good in the universe, had been hustled to a secure room by the imperial guards. They would keep him safe and, most importantly, out of Draken's hair. Wolfric was a fair fighter and strategist, but in times like this it was easier if one person was in charge. And since the person Draken would've preferred to be in charge was absent, it fell to him to step up.

He had the necessary magic to contact Lord Shenk, but interrupting his father's funeral would win Draken no rewards. Better for everyone if he dealt with this mess himself then gave a report about his success when Lord Shenk returned.

"Commander Draken!" One of the many squires that had been pressed into running messages came sprinting toward him. "Unit commanders report that conventional weapons are ineffective against the enemy. Units armed with mithril are having better luck. War wizards report that their magic is effective, but that it's taking a lot out of them to defeat even one opponent."

That was better than he'd feared. "Did you get a look at what we're dealing with?"

The boy trembled and the whites around his eyes were visible. "I saw some… thing. It looked like a skeleton with red flames in its eyes. It carried no weapon, but a single blow from its claws sliced a soldier into four pieces. What sort of thing is it?"

Draken wished he knew, not that knowing would make them any easier to deal with. The skeleton suggested something undead, but the flaming eyes argued demon. Whatever they were, they needed to be killed and killed quickly.

"I'm not sure what it is. Take a message to the armory. I want all mithril weapons deployed as quickly as possible. Are they close to the palace?"

"As far as I can tell, all the attacks are scattered around Gold Ward. We've had no word from the outer wards."

Great, unknown monsters appearing out of nowhere

wreaking havoc on the richest part of the city. This was a nightmare.

"Very well, you have your orders, relay them quickly."

The boy touched fist to heart and sprinted away as quickly as he'd arrived.

Mithril weapons would help, but they were still going to lose plenty of soldiers. At least he hadn't received word of major civilian casualties. Property damage was bad enough, but if the rich and powerful started dying it would really be an issue.

"Master Draken!"

For the love of heaven, what now? He frowned. Where was the messenger?

A moment later a war wizard appeared out of nowhere. "Master, a huge, powerful monster is attacking Franken Manor. Sergeant Hans is there and he said Lord Shenk needed to be contacted at once. I've never seen such a creature, Master. It shrugged off spells and threw grown men like they were toy soldiers. How are we going to stop it?"

Draken had no answer for his subordinate. But one thing was clear: he couldn't put off contacting Lord Shenk any longer.

〇

Assuming he lived through the coming battle, the first recommendation Hans planned to make was to add spears to the guards' arsenal. Swords were great, but when you had a seven-foot-tall reptilian monster bearing down on you, a little extra reach wasn't a bad thing.

Hans had every guard on the grounds arrayed in a semicircle

in front of the iron gate. The men had their swords drawn, but Hans had no confidence that they would fare any better than the city guards out front. His only real hope was that they could delay the creature long enough for Lord Shenk to arrive.

Branik, please, let the war wizard be speedy in reaching Draken.

The monster tossed the last city guardsman out of its way, roared, and charged the gate.

The guards flinched back just from the volume of its cry.

"Steady," Hans said. "We just have to delay that thing, not beat it. All the servants as well as the Franken family are counting on us. If we fail, they will likely all die."

The men's backs stiffened a bit. At least they did until the monster hit the gate and bent it nearly in half. The thick iron slowed it not in the least.

Hans turned to Lady White. "If there's anything you can do magicwise, we'd be much obliged."

"That creature is a warbeast of Astaroth. My magic is more likely to strengthen it than hurt it. The best thing I could do is flee and hope it follows me instead of killing you."

"That sounds great. Why are you not doing it?"

"Because if I did, I'd have to fight it on my own. I much prefer having nearly a dozen men to distract it while I attempt to unravel the magic."

Another roar drowned out Hans's unkind mutters. Of course the undead priestess wasn't going to sacrifice herself to save them all.

The monster ripped the gate free and hurled it at the gathered guards. Three of them dove out of the way, but the fourth wasn't so lucky. He got crushed under it, the spikes at the top piercing his body in three places.

Seeing one of their comrades hurt galvanized the rest. The guards gave a roar of their own and charged the monster. Their swords struck hard but couldn't even scratch the creature's scales.

A backhand blow sent one of his men flying twenty feet.

"If you wish to live, I suggest you fall back." Lady White followed her own advice, working her way back toward the mansion, never taking her eyes off the creature.

The monster's glowing red gaze followed her movements. It ignored the blows raining down on it until one man moved a bit too slow. It grabbed his arm and yanked it out of the socket, sending out a spray of blood.

"Fall back to the mansion!" Hans shouted. He didn't know what they were going to do when they got there, but it had to be better than getting slaughtered here.

To their credit, the surviving guards didn't break and run. They made a steady, disciplined withdrawal, even managing to avoid a few halfhearted swipes of the monster's claws. It helped that it was still staring at the fleeing Lady White. Hans would've been insulted at being ignored if it weren't for the fact that the creature clearly had nothing to fear from their weapons.

When they had fully disengaged, the creature glared at them as if in warning then chased after Lady White.

"Get inside and reinforce the doors," Hans said. "Use whatever you can."

"What about you, sir?" one of the men asked.

"I'm going to follow it. If Lady White can distract the thing, maybe I can stab it in the eye or the mouth. Just hiding in the mansion and hoping Lord Shenk gets back before it smashes its way inside isn't much of a plan."

"You think trying to stab that thing in the eye is a better one?" somebody asked.

He had a point, but Hans didn't have many options. "Just get inside. If anyone survived, grab them and go."

So saying, he sheathed his sword and pulled his dagger. He hurried along behind the monster as quickly as stealth would allow. A roar sounded. It must have caught up with Lady White. If Hans didn't want to have to explain to Lord Shenk why his ally was dead, he'd best hurry.

Slipping around a shrub, he found the monster thrashing and trying to push forward while Lady White faced it, arms raised and face twisted in concentration. Her magic seemed barely adequate to slow it down. At least she seemed to have its full attention. That was the best he could hope for.

Steeling himself, Hans sprinted forward and leapt as high up on its back as he could. His dagger came down and around, straight at its right eye.

And skipped off something before plunging home.

A powerful hand grabbed him and hurled him across the lawn where he slammed into the side of the mansion. His body crumpled and the world spun around before darkness claimed him.

CHAPTER NINE

Otto sat between his mother and Axel on a pew in the first row in the Temple of Branik. He kept his head bowed as the priest droned on about Father's many dubious virtues. As for the focus of the proceedings, Father's body rested in a plain wooden coffin that would go on the pyre as soon as the prayers were finished. It was a Shenk family tradition, whose origin Otto neither knew nor cared about. What mainly interested him was getting this farce of a ritual over with so he could find somewhere more comfortable to sit than a hard wooden bench.

He wasn't looking forward to the gathering that would follow, either. All the minor nobles and merchants would want to talk to him. They'd have questions about the emperor. Questions about roads and the portals. Questions about things Otto hadn't even thought about yet. He knew this because even the higher-ranking nobles he had to occasionally deal with in the capital asked the same damn questions. It took a great deal of self-control not to blast them all and hope that the next generation was less annoying.

Hopefully Mother would want some quiet time and he could keep her company.

He was just beginning to debate separating his hearing from his brain when a familiar ripple ran through the ether. Otto had sensed this particular spell enough times to recognize it at once. A moment later a message spell appeared in his mind, speaking with Draken's voice.

The city is under attack. Franken Manor primary target. Need help at once.

Well, he'd wanted an excuse to avoid talking to the local nobles. An attack on Garen City certainly wouldn't be his first choice, but at least it would give him someone to vent his annoyance on.

Otto stood and every eye in the place stared at him.

"What is it?" Mother asked.

"An emergency in the capital. I don't know the details, but it sounds bad. I hate to leave under these circumstances, but the living come before the dead. I'll be back when I can."

Otto became one with the ether and a moment later appeared in the rune circle hidden in his closet at Franken Manor. The instant he did, a powerful source of corruption slapped him in the face. The mithril in his bones at least protected him from the illness that usually came from being this close to so much corruption. It felt stronger than Lady White. That couldn't be a good sign.

Unwilling to waste time running through the house, he shifted through the ether and appeared again outside. Hans lay in a crumpled heap beside the mansion, his life force weak but still present. Lady White was using her magic to hold off a scaled monster. The creature leaned forward as if into the wind and took a ponderous step toward her.

Otto took all this in the moment he appeared. A forty-thread lightning bolt lanced out, hammering into the creature's back.

The spell darkened its scales, but otherwise did no damage. Otto would have said that was impossible if the results of his attack weren't right before his eyes. A powerful, magic-resistant enemy was pretty close to Otto's worst nightmare. Fortunately, he did have other options.

As the beast turned to glare at him with burning red eyes, Otto drew his mithril sword and infused his body with every drop of ether it could handle. It felt like his very being was vibrating.

He rushed forward and thrust, his movements blindingly fast.

Even so, the monster shifted just enough that Otto missed its heart and only pierced its shoulder. At least his mithril sword cut the creature. Now he just had to figure out how to kill it.

Using his speed, Otto waded in, slashing and thrusting like mad. His opponent kept up, moving just enough to avoid a fatal hit. As the seconds ticked by, the strain of channeling so much ether began to take a toll. He needed to end this soon.

"I'll slow it down." Lady White's voice sounded drawn out and slightly garbled. "You have to destroy the demon spirit animating it."

Otto would get a proper explanation later. The monster froze and he struck. His sword traced an X across its chest, cutting it into quarters before splitting its skull in two. The corruption dissipated and he released his spell.

Reality wavered for a moment as his senses realigned with normal speed. He kept his feet at least. That was something.

"Your timing was excellent." Lady White stepped over the body and stood beside him. "I couldn't have held the creature back much longer."

Otto shook his head and strode over to Hans. "Not perfect enough. I need to get him to the Chamber, quickly. Once Hans is better, you and I need to have a serious discussion. Please tell everyone inside that the threat is dealt with."

An ethereal disk appeared under Hans's unmoving body and Otto set out for the palace. It was at times like these that he wished he could teleport more than just himself. Unfortunately, until he got powerful enough to open portals on his own, he had no choice but to transport Hans the old-fashioned way.

He passed through the ruined gate with barely a glance and turned down the street. Bodies littered the ground. It looked like they'd been tossed around by an oversized child having a tantrum. After experiencing the dead monster's power firsthand, he had no doubt these unfortunate men wouldn't have had a chance against it.

Dismissing the carnage as quickly as he had the ruined gate, Otto ran toward the palace. He reached his usual side entrance and found it guarded not by the usual two men, but by a full squad of ten, all armed with mithril swords.

Despite the seriousness of the threat, they hastened to get out of his way and open the portcullis. Otto pointed at a random soldier. "Run ahead and tell them to bring all the prisoners to my private room in the basement."

When he didn't immediately sprint away Otto shouted, "Now!"

The man ran as if he feared for his life.

"Is the danger past, my lord?" the guard Otto assumed was in charge asked.

"I'm not certain. Remain on full alert until someone tells you otherwise." With that he set out for the basement.

He passed servants and guards on his way, but no one tried to stop him. He must've had his grim face on as Wolfric called it. He was certainly feeling grim. He had no idea how many prisoners it would take to restore Hans to full health, but he'd use all of them without a second thought.

It took most of five minutes to reach the chamber. Otto maneuvered Hans into place then sealed it up again. A thread of ether connected him to the Heart of Alchemy and from there his awareness explored Hans's ill-used body. The damage was extensive, but by some miracle both his heart and lungs were undamaged. On the downside, they were about the only things that were undamaged. What really worried him was the blood he found in Hans's brain. While the bone and muscle would be simple to repair, the brain damage would push his control to the limit.

"Lord Shenk."

The voice dragged him out of his contemplation. Otto turned to find the dungeon guards standing at the door, behind them a line of eight manacled, and more importantly, gagged, criminals. Hopefully they'd be enough.

"Bring them in." Otto pointed to a spot about fifteen feet from the Chamber. "Line them up there."

The guards hastened to obey. This wasn't the first time they'd brought prisoners for one of his experiments and they knew better than to ask questions or dillydally. When they were in position the guards stood a couple of feet away and kept their weapons drawn lest the bound prisoners try and make a break for it.

Otto didn't bother to correct them. Having them close might be handy should the prisoners not provide enough life force. If it was a choice between sacrificing a couple of guards and losing Hans, then it was no choice at all.

When everything was in readiness, Otto began. First he reestablished his connection to the Heart, then a thread went into the nearest prisoner. Life force flowed out and he got to work. Otto totally lost himself in the process. When he ran out of energy, he moved on to the next prisoner. Hans's wounds quickly healed and even the damage to his brain ended up being easier to fix than Otto had feared. As long as he was at it, Otto also restored his body to a youthful state while leaving his external appearance unchanged.

He knew it wasn't necessarily Hans's wish, but once the mess was cleaned up, Otto meant to find out who was responsible for this outrage and when he did, he was going to make them pay. To have the best chance of success, he needed his reliable right-hand man at his side.

When the final repair was complete, Otto released the ether. He turned and was surprised to find two of the prisoners had survived the process. Perhaps he was getting more efficient with his magic.

"You can take them back to their cells," Otto said. "And take the empty clothes and manacles as well."

As always, the guards hastened to obey. When they were gone, Otto went to the Chamber and conjured the opening. He helped Hans out. His bloody uniform notwithstanding, he appeared unharmed.

Hans staggered a couple of steps then grew steadier. He

looked up at Otto. "Didn't expect to see you again, my lord. Or anyone else for that matter."

"It was a near thing," Otto said. "How are you feeling?"

"Good. Better than I have in a long time."

"I'm glad to hear it. As soon as I figure out who's responsible for attacking the city, I'll be counting on you to help me hunt them down."

"Counting on me?" Hans looked down at his gnarled hands. "Did you..."

"I kept your appearance the same, but yes, I restored your body to what it was at roughly thirty years old. Given the amount of life force I had to use to save your life, it was a negligible amount extra to finish the job. Whoever attacked us is strong. I can't go after them with less than my best and that means I need you in charge of the team."

"Count on me, my lord. And many thanks for saving my life once again."

Otto clapped him on the shoulder. "Return to the warehouse and make sure the guys are ready. I want everyone armed with mithril. Hopefully by the end of the week I'll know where we're headed."

"We'll be ready," Hans said.

Otto was certain they would be and when he caught up to whoever sent that monster, they'd wish they hadn't threatened Otto's peaceful empire.

CHAPTER TEN

With Hans healed and headed back to the warehouse, Otto made his way to the main floor of the palace. Draken would have an update for him. With any luck, now that he'd dealt with the main threat, the city guards and war wizards would be able to mop up any remaining enemies. Given how much power he had to use against the reptilian creature, he didn't want to get into another fight anytime soon. At least the Heart of Alchemy allowed him to heal Hans without exhausting himself further.

At the top of a flight of stone steps he turned left toward Draken's office. Step by step the traffic got thicker. Soldiers and war wizards ran here and there. An occasional servant carried messages and in one case a meal. To a person they made a path as Otto approached. Sometimes the constant fear most people felt for him seemed a bit excessive to Otto, but today it served his needs and he wasn't going to complain.

He reached Draken's nondescript office and pushed the

door open without knocking. Seated behind a paper-strewn desk, a half-eaten sandwich in his hand, was Draken. Judging by the white hair and dark eyes, the job of second-in-command was taking a toll.

Draken looked up from his lunch and practically sagged with relief. "Lord Shenk, thank heaven you're back. The monster—"

"Dealt with. Mention was made of other, weaker enemies scattered throughout Gold Ward. What about them?"

"The most recent report indicates that the final creature, a black skeleton armed with a sword made of ice..." Draken gave a little shake of his head. "Had been engaged by a combined force of war wizards and soldiers armed with mithril weapons. That combination has worked well and I'm confident that they'll be successful."

Otto nodded, well pleased. "Very good. I'll leave the cleanup details to you. I'm going to handle investigating the source of the attack myself. I want roving patrols of mithril-armed soldiers and war wizards on duty at all times until I tell you the threat is eliminated."

"Understood, my lord. Do you have any clues as to the source?"

"Lady White indicated that the magic involved belonged to Astaroth. That suggests the Land of the Demon Binders and her former master, Lord of the Dead. The how and why of the attack remain a mystery. And, if I'm being totally honest, even Lord of the Dead's involvement is pure speculation at this point. For all I know, there might be some other powerful, hidden servant of Astaroth that no one even knew existed. Until I have solid evidence, no possibility is off the table."

"I hesitate to suggest this, my lord, but perhaps Lady White herself is involved."

Otto shook his head. "That's extremely unlikely. I trust her only slightly less than I trust you. Plus, I have magic to ensure her loyalty, which she knows about. No, whatever the issue, I fear it lies well beyond the empire. Time will tell. Has Wolfric been kept up to date?"

"He knows about the disturbance, but I thought that, until we had all the details, it would be best to wait to make a full report. Since His Imperial Majesty has yet to summon me, I assume he's not upset."

"Where is he?"

"The safe room, protected by a heavy guard. He took his harem with him."

"That explains why he hasn't bothered you. Just as well since I prefer not to take the time to explain. While I doubt such an attack could be easily replicated, the sooner we get to the source of the problem, the better."

"I wholeheartedly agree. Should I be of any use, I am, as always, at your disposal."

"Good of you to say, but you'll be of more use where you are. Contact me at once via the speaking spell should anything happen."

Draken offered a seated bow. "Yes, Lord Shenk."

Otto became one with the ether and a moment later stood outside Franken Manor a few feet from the reptilian carcass. It hadn't gotten any prettier while he was gone. He knelt beside it and examined the body. The muscle looked normal if a bit denser than a human's. The scales were really interesting. Unlike a snake's they didn't look leathery and, when he touched them, he found the surface hard as stone.

He really didn't know what to make of it and that bothered him.

Otto sensed Lady White's approach a moment before she said, "I made a thorough examination of the body. The demon spirit used to animate it was far stronger than anything I could summon. In fact, if Lord of the Dead did send it, I'm surprised he had strength enough to bind such a spirit. Though he is more powerful than me, he isn't *that* much more powerful."

Sounded like her ego got a little bruised. "I'm more concerned with how he got this thing to Garen without anyone encountering it. It's not like they could've snuck it across half a continent then past two sets of gates without someone noticing. A giant, seven-foot-tall lizard man along with a bunch of undead-looking demons kind of stand out."

"There, at least, I can be of more help. Based on what I sensed, the creatures arrived via a portal through Astaroth's hell."

That was a sort of magic Otto had never heard of. "Does it work like our portals?"

"Not really. The Arcane Lords created tunnels through the ether itself. A hell portal lets creatures enter one of the hells at point A then emerge at point B in an instant. Only an insanely powerful hellpriest can open them. I can't. And the last I knew, Lord of the Dead couldn't either."

Otto tapped his chin. "The more I hear, the more I think we might be dealing with a third party. Is that possible?"

"Anything's possible, especially since Astaroth has ordered his servants not to answer my questions."

"Why would he do that?"

She laughed. "I can't begin to guess why a demon lord

would do anything. They act on a scale that would make even an Arcane Lord stare in awe."

"Great. Looks like I need to figure out where this thing came from. Once I know that, we'll know where to look for the one who sent it."

"Do you have access to that sort of information?"

"Yes, though how long it will take me to read through all the data is a problem. Is there any way to protect the city from another of those portals opening?"

"I'm sure there are barrier spells that would work, but creating one big enough to surround the entire city would take months if not years, assuming it was even possible. I've certainly never seen anything on that scale."

That was exactly what Otto figured, but he still hated it. They'd just have to remain vigilant and hope that now that they knew how to kill the things, it would go more smoothly next time. There was one obvious place to start, Lord Karonin. He hadn't visited the hidden tower in nearly a year. His work with Lord Colt's simulacrum had kept him plenty busy. She would probably be grouchy when he arrived, but it wasn't like she could go anywhere, not without breaking her link to the mirror that let her interact with this world.

He reached for the ether and winced. Even with his increased power, he still had limits and it felt like he was getting close to them. The danger seemed over for the moment. Best to get a good night's rest and set out fresh in the morning.

He'd learned to his detriment that when he pushed himself too far, it was easy to get overwhelmed. And given how powerful this new foe seemed to be, that could be a fatal mistake.

CHAPTER ELEVEN

When Otto appeared in the hidden tower's sole second-floor room he let out a soft sigh. If Lord Karonin had allowed him to come, then she couldn't be too upset. It had only been a year since his last visit after all and what was that to an immortal spirit?

He nodded to himself and slowly turned. The room looked the same as always. No furniture, and perfectly free of dust and dirt. It was one of the few places he could think of that simply never changed. He found it oddly comforting.

When he faced the mirror, he found Lord Karonin's slightly green-tinted face surrounded by a cloud of floating hair staring at him. She wasn't scowling, which was a good sign. Of course, she wasn't smiling either. But that wasn't a surprise. Otto could count on one hand the number of times he'd seen his master smile.

He bowed and moved closer to the mirror. "Master, it's good to see you again."

"And where have you been this past year?" She arched an eyebrow. "I assume you've encountered some problem beyond your meager understanding and require me to explain it."

On second thought, maybe she was in a worse mood than he first thought. Well, best to just dive in and hope for the best. "You're right, Master. Garen was attacked. Someone opened a portal through Astaroth's hell and sent an incredibly powerful monster along with some lesser demons through to attack us. Lady White believes Lord of the Dead was responsible, but the creature looked like nothing that existed in the Land of the Demon Binders. We've certainly seen nothing like it in the empire."

"Describe it in as much detail as you can." She sounded interested now rather than annoyed. That was a good sign.

"I can do better than that. I've been working on illusion magic a bit." Otto concentrated and an image of the lizard monster as it had been before he killed it appeared in the air in front of the mirror. It was as close to perfect as he could manage, right down to the height.

"An impressive illusion. I'm pleased to see that you've learned something despite not coming here for instruction. As for the creature itself, I know exactly what it is. What you had the misfortune to encounter was one of Azteca's dragonmen."

Otto had never heard of such a thing. Dragons were creatures of fiction and the idea of one that looked like a man struck him as absurd.

"You're certain it didn't have wings or a tail?"

Had he believed her capable of it, Otto might've thought she was joking. "No, Master, it looked exactly as you see."

"You were fortunate then. The one that attacked your city was a first-generation dragonman. Had it been a third-generation I doubt you would've done so well." Lord

Karonin paused for a moment then said, "Though I doubt a third-generation dragonman could be transformed into a warbeast. Their magic resistance is simply too high."

She stared at him for a second then laughed. Otto shuddered at the bitter, humorless sound. "From the vapid, disbelieving expression on your face, I'm guessing you have both questions and doubts. Ask what you will and I'll do my best to make you understand."

"Thank you for your consideration, Master. I must admit that this is all a shock. I didn't think dragons were real. As far as I know there are none in the empire."

"Dragons are very real and exceedingly dangerous. They are also, luckily for the humans of this world, rare. In truth, they tend to sleep most of the time. Amet slew the only two in his kingdom and used their corpses in his experiments. You should count yourself lucky that you didn't encounter the undead he created from them."

"I count myself extremely lucky, Master. I assume Lord Azteca killed one as well."

"No. She was a bit more ambitious. Working with the pig Valtan, Amet and myself, Azteca captured one alive and bound it under her palace. She used samples of its flesh and blood to create her dragonmen. We weren't especially friendly, but just before our betrayal, she claimed to be getting close to perfecting them. Whether she was talking about the third generation or something else, I can't say."

Otto frowned, his mind racing. "Then is it safe to assume that whoever sent the dragonman had to do so from Aztecaland?"

"Without a doubt. None of the rest of us wanted the wretched things in our territory. We could control them if we had to, but it was a constant struggle as their anti-magical nature constantly broke the spells we put on them. I still don't know how Azteca managed as many as she did."

Otto cleared his throat. Images of an army of magic-resistant draconic warbeasts raced through his mind. Considering how much effort it took to kill one of them, he didn't know how they'd manage more.

"How many are we talking about?" he asked at last.

"I'm uncertain about the exact number. Perhaps twenty of the first generation and less than half that of the second. As for the third, as far as I know she only made one."

Otto let out a breath. That wasn't ideal, but it was far better than an army. "It seems I need to travel to Aztecaland. Do you have any advice for when I arrive?"

"I wish I did. Over the centuries I only visited her territory a handful of times and other than the dragon hunt, I never left the capital. I know it's a savage place, filled with dangerous and bizarre creatures." Lord Karonin got a faraway look in her eye. "Azteca was nothing like the rest of us. She disdained civilization, thinking it weak, a way of coddling those unfit to survive. Whenever she created a new monster, she simply set it loose in the jungle. If it survived, then it deserved life. If some other creature killed it, then it didn't."

"That's a rather brutal worldview. Did she have no one that served her and worked in the capital?"

"She did. She created an entire race of servant creatures, beastfolk she called them. Far weaker than any of her other monsters, they wouldn't have survived fifteen minutes outside the capital. But they were obedient and useful, which was all she required."

Otto ran his fingers through his hair. The more he heard the worse it sounded. "She at least had a portal, right?"

"Only one, in the capital. Amet insisted, to allow for ease of travel. Why in heaven's name anyone would want to visit that hellhole is beyond me, but for some reason she and Amet were close."

Though it had no practical bearing on his situation, Otto's curiosity got the better of him. "Close like lovers or just two people with creepy tastes in magic?"

Lord Karonin barked a laugh, one of the first he'd heard from her that seemed to hold genuine mirth. "You should know by now that the word love has no bearing where Arcane Lords are involved. No, Azteca was a source of unique new bodies for Amet to use in his necromancy."

Otto nodded. That made sense. For someone like Lord Sur, the jungles of Aztecaland were no doubt a buffet of corpses just waiting to be collected. And if there was something he wanted that was still alive, Otto had no doubt the First Lord would have no trouble remedying the situation.

He had only two more questions, then it would be time to make plans to depart. "Is it possible for me to travel directly there via the portal?"

"No. I never bothered to connect mine to hers. As I said, we didn't get along."

Well, that would've been too easy. "I don't suppose you have a map of Aztecaland?"

"No. A map would serve no purpose as there are no towns or other areas of interest. Picture a vast jungle with a single city at the center. That's it. Use resonance magic and home in on the portal. That's the easiest way to find the capital. As for whoever attacked you, I have no idea where you might find them."

Otto bowed. "Thank you again for the instruction, Master. I'll try not to be such a stranger in the future."

She snorted again. "Spare me your flattery. You will do whatever increases your power the most. You may no longer be on the path of an Arcane Lord, but you are still like us in many ways."

Otto couldn't deny that, though he considered it less of a compliment than he once did. With nothing left to say, he became one with the ether.

It seemed he had another journey to plan.

CHAPTER TWELVE

An instant after becoming one with the ether, Otto reappeared in the courtyard of Castle Shenk. Nearly a full day had passed since his abrupt departure and he wanted to check in and reassure his mother that he was okay. For the moment at least. Axel should still be here as well which would be convenient. His scout unit would make up the bulk of the forces Otto planned to take to Aztecaland. His personal guards and Corina would make up the rest.

Such were the thoughts running through Otto's head as he strode across the dirt to the keep entrance. The guards on duty hastened to open the gate for him. Doors opened for him as if by magic. Being well known was tremendously convenient, especially considering he still looked like he was just twenty years old. That was unlikely to change unless he decided to let it.

He offered a little nod to the guards as he passed through and went straight into the great hall. It was unoccupied at the moment. Having no desire to hunt down a servant to question, Otto used a bit of magic to locate his mother's unique spiritual essence. That was a trick he could only use to find someone he knew well. Despite that limitation, it was useful.

As expected, she was upstairs in her sewing room. Her fingers remained nimble despite her age. And the subtle magical repairs Otto made at regular intervals would keep them that way. It was a small thing, but he was happy to do it for her. Heaven knew there was little enough to keep her entertained in Shenk Barony.

Otto took the stairs two at a time and soon stood before the partially closed door. He knocked and said, "Mother?"

"Otto! Thank goodness you're okay. Come in, dear."

He pushed the door the rest of the way open and found her seated in a rocking chair beside a modest-sized pile of socks in need of fixing. She looked better than he'd feared. The tightness around her eyes had faded to a shadow of what it was before the funeral. She started to stand but he waved her back, came in, and kissed her cheek.

"I apologize for my abrupt departure, but there was an attack on the capital."

"An attack, how?"

"Magic. I'm still working out all the details, but rest assured that I will find whoever was responsible and deal with them. I know I invited you to stay at Franken Manor, but until this matter is resolved to my satisfaction, I fear Shenk Barony will be safer for you."

She smiled up at him. "That's okay, dear. I planned to tell you after the funeral that I wasn't going to take you up on your offer. Shenk Barony is my home and if I can in some way improve Stephan's rulership by my presence, then as dowager baroness it is my responsibility."

"Heaven bless you, Mother. This backwater barony doesn't deserve your generosity." Otto swallowed a sigh. "I hate to leave again so soon, but I have a great deal to do. Is Axel around?"

"Your brothers went hunting together this morning."

"Axel went hunting with Stephan? That's… surprising."

"To me as well, but if they can somehow patch up their relationship, it would be a welcome change."

If they could patch up their relationship, it would be a minor miracle. Otto refrained from pointing that out. "I'll have to interrupt them as I need Axel for the new mission. It might be awhile before I can visit again. Do take care of yourself. If you need anything, just send a message to the capital. Everyone there has orders to provide you with anything you need."

"That's sweet, dear, but I'm an old woman whose time is fast approaching. No need to make a fuss over me."

Otto would happily keep that from happening forever if she wished it. Of course she'd made it clear she didn't and he would respect her choice. Much like Hans, his mother considered magic unnatural at the best of times. Using sacrificed life force to extend her life would certainly be a bridge too far for her.

"Fussing is my job as your son. Until next time. Love you."

"Love you too, dear. Try to be careful."

Otto seriously doubted that was possible given what Lord Karonin said. Not wanting to lie to his mother, he just smiled, turned, and walked back out of the sewing room. In the hall he took a moment to extend his senses through the ether. If Axel and Stephan were together, that would make it easier to find them and sure enough he soon located the pair about ten miles east of the castle. Based on the time of day and how far they rode, they were probably just setting up camp.

Perfect.

Becoming one with the ether, he shifted himself to his brother's location and sure enough he ended up in a forest clearing filled with servants that were busy getting a fire going and setting up portable furniture. A handful of soldiers were keeping watch, though given how peaceful Shenk Barony had been lately, they weren't doing an especially enthusiastic job of it. They'd best get better at pretending lest Stephan notice their laziness.

For their part, Axel and Stephan were sitting in a pair of heavy-duty folding chairs well away from where the work was going on. Stephan was taking a long pull from a steel flask. Judging from the look on his face, Axel would rather be just about anywhere else.

Otto strode over and when Axel spotted him he looked exactly like a drowning man thrown a rope. Stephan lowered his flask and snarled. "You certainly made yourself the center of attention at the funeral. Couldn't let me have one day? When we got back to the castle all anyone could talk about was why you left so suddenly. I was an afterthought. Me! The new baron."

"My heart bleeds for you, Stephan. If it makes you feel any better, the capital was attacked and I was summoned back to deal with it."

"Is the capital secure now?" Axel asked.

"As secure as I can make it. We were attacked by someone using unfamiliar magic. One that I have no way of fully stopping. For the empire to be secure, the threat needs to be eliminated at the source. I'll be counting on you and the scouts to help me with that."

"The men will be pleased. We haven't had a mission in far too long. A real mission I mean, not surveying roads."

Otto nodded. That was exactly the response he'd been hoping for. "Good. Get back to the capital and get ready. Mithril weapons and plenty of arrows. We're cutting no corners on this one. Once I'm finished, we'll travel by portal to Lux and find a ship."

"Where are we going?" Axel asked.

"Wait!" Stephan butted in. "We're not finished here."

"Your hunt is a good deal less important than securing the empire, Stephan."

Before Axel could stand to join him, Stephan continued. "It's not just the hunt. That was an excuse to get out of the castle. I wanted to offer Axel a position in the barony. He's a Shenk, he belongs here."

Otto and Axel both stared at Stephan. Otto couldn't believe what he'd just heard and from the look on his face, neither could Axel.

"Doing what?" Otto asked when the silence had grown uncomfortable.

"Captain of the guards. Graves retired when Father got sick. I need someone experienced and that I can trust. Axel fits the job better than anyone else I can think of."

"Generous of you," Otto said. He wasn't certain if Stephan was really dense enough not to know Axel hated him or if he thought now that he was a baron he could just bully him into doing what he wanted. "But I need him for this mission and the good of the empire comes before Shenk Barony. I'm sure you'll be able to find someone else to fill the position."

Otto said that last sentence in his "that's the end of the discussion" tone.

Axel finally stood. "I'll ride back to the castle, get my gear, and say goodbye. I should make it to the capital in a couple days."

Otto nodded. "That's fine. I still have a lot of preparations to make. Stephan, good afternoon."

Axel started back toward where the horses were tied up and gave a little nod like he wanted Otto to come along. Curious, he fell in beside his brother. Axel stayed silent until they were almost to the animals.

"Thanks for the rescue. Now that he's a baron, I wasn't sure if I could brush Stephan off like I used to."

"You can and if he gives you any trouble, tell him to direct his complaints to me. You and your squad work for the good of the empire. I'll not have a backwater baron, family or not, getting in the way. Speaking of your squad, are they combat ready?"

"Everyone's fit for duty, twelve veterans and three rookies, though some of the new recruits haven't seen combat. I wish Cobb hadn't retired, but after he broke his leg during one of our surveys in Straken, he wasn't the same."

"The healers—"

Axel shook his head. "The healers did a fine job. The problem was in his head. He lost confidence in his strength and finally said he'd had enough. Fixing an injury is easy, fixing mental issues is nearly impossible. Better to let him go than to see something else happen."

"Fair enough. I'll meet you at your barracks when I'm finished."

Axel touched fist to heart. "We'll be ready. It's good to have a mission, little brother."

"When you've seen what we're dealing with, I hope you feel the same way."

CHAPTER THIRTEEN

Otto's next trip through the ether brought him halfway around the world to Lord Colt's Workshop. He appeared in the special rune circle he'd prepared. Its magic easily allowed him to bypass the wards that protected the workshop. He glanced around at the room that served as his temporary home whenever he spent an extended period here and found everything exactly as he left it. Not that there was much, just a bed, two-drawer dresser, table and chair. He spent most of his time in the lab after all. This was just a place to sleep.

He pushed through the door and turned down the unadorned steel hall. He could sense Lord Colt's simulacrum like a glowing beacon in the ether. Even though he couldn't manipulate the ether, the construct that served as his body was connected to it and utilized it to power its various functions. Otto couldn't even begin to fully understand how it worked. Maybe if he lived another five hundred years.

He found Lord Colt, in the form of a giant metal scorpion

with the illusion of a man over its head, in the yard outside. Luckily, Illsa was there with him. That would save Otto the trouble of finding her after they spoke. It looked like they were in the middle of testing one of the new large-scale ethereal capacitors. He and Illsa had been trying to build one efficient enough to power the portals on a regular schedule. So far, they had been less than successful. In fact, the only thing even approaching a success that they'd managed was an improved version of the backpack model Illsa had used to travel from Audin to Garen eight years ago.

He smiled when he remembered how panicked the portal guards had been when the runes started to light up. It had been both a shock and a relief when Illsa's bedraggled figure had tumbled out. Her story about Audin's fall and her narrow escape had been a remarkable one. Even more remarkable had been Lord Colt's invitation to return with her and study at the workshop. Otto had learned a great deal about magical engineering over the following years. His primary takeaway being that while it was very useful for some things, it wasn't really the discipline for him.

Sparks began shooting out of the capacitor, signaling yet another unsuccessful test. A part of Otto was beginning to wonder if they'd ever create a working device. Not that Illsa would ever give up once she had a problem in front of her. It was one of the things he admired about her.

When the sparks finally stopped, he decided it was safe enough to approach. Lord Colt turned to face him at once. As the master of the workshop, he would've sensed Otto's arrival instantly. It took Illsa a moment to realize that Lord Colt wasn't paying any attention to the project. She gave a little start and spun in a swirl of blond hair to face him. She wore her white robes with their perpetual grease stains along with practical boots.

"Lord Shenk!" Illsa hurried over and gave him a hug. She was one of the few people he allowed to be so familiar with him. During their time studying together, he'd developed a soft spot for Illsa. "I didn't expect to see you again so soon."

"I didn't expect to return so soon. There have been some issues in the capital." He went on to tell them about the attack and his plan to visit Aztecaland. "Anyway, I didn't want to leave without letting you know that I was going to be gone for a while. I was also hoping, Lord Colt, that you might know a way to connect our portal to Lord Azteca's."

The shoulders of Colt's illusion heaved and Otto suspected that, had he been able to do so, he would've loosed a huge sigh. "I don't know why those two hated each other so much. They lived an ocean apart and had nothing in common. You'd think they'd be indifferent to each other at worst. It was completely irrational."

"Given that they were the only two women among the lords, I suppose it was inevitable," Otto said. "It's a nuisance for me, since I'd like to be able to return my people home without having to sail a couple thousand miles. So, can I fix it?"

"Of course you can," Lord Colt said. "Properly applied magic can accomplish anything if you're strong enough. What you want to do isn't even all that difficult in the grand scheme of things."

Otto slumped with relief.

"But, it is tricky."

His relief quickly vanished. "Tricky how?"

"Basically you need to overwrite two runes, one on your

portal and one on Azteca's. That means you'll lose the ability to travel between one of the existing targets."

Considering the state of Markane City, that wouldn't be a great loss. "I assume I use the mithril sheets, the same way I did before?"

"You use the sheets, but not the same way. Since there's no power running to the portals, you need to affix them manually. Basically you need to fuse it completely with the rune you want to replace. There can't be any gaps between the patch and the portal. That's absolutely vital or it won't work."

"I believe I can manage that. I just need to know Azteca's rune."

"I can show it to you," Lord Colt said. "But it would be better if you made the patches here, then I can check to make sure it's perfect."

Otto bowed. "I would be most grateful, Lord Colt. However, I do have a few more things I need to take care of before we begin."

"Take your time and do it right. I'm not going anywhere. Traveling to Aztecaland isn't something to be done lightly. Those dragonmen of hers are nasty things. I'm not sure whether turning them into warbeasts makes them tougher or weaker, but either way, they're nothing to take lightly."

"I never take my enemies lightly. That's one of the reasons I'm still alive." He glanced at Illsa. "I hope you won't be offended, but I'm not going to take you with me on this mission."

"I'm happy to remain behind. It sounds like a nightmare. Frankly, after my escape from Audin, I have no desire for more adventure."

"I have no desire for adventure either," Otto said. "But the world seems disinclined to leave me alone. I'll be back in a couple days. Until then."

As he became one with the ether Otto muttered, "Bloody adventures."

CHAPTER FOURTEEN

From Colt's Workshop, Otto went directly to his room in Franken Manor. When he appeared amidst the fine clothes he seldom wore, he took a deep breath and let it out in a long sigh. Was it really too much to ask to be left alone? It didn't seem like it to him, but clearly whoever ran the universe thought otherwise.

He shook off his doubts and complaints. Otto had defeated every enemy that had dared threaten his empire and this one would be no different. He also had to admit that a visit to Lord Azteca's territory held a certain appeal. It was the only one he didn't travel to during his search for the Immortality Engine. Though from what Lord Karonin said, it was hardly a surprise that she wasn't charged with protecting one of the pieces.

Of course, give his master's obvious hatred for the woman, her claims had to be taken with a grain of salt. Lord Azteca would no doubt turn out to be less terrible than she'd been made out to be. The again, she might be like Lord Sur and end up being worse than Otto could imagine. Either was possible and he wouldn't know for sure until he got there.

He left the closet and focused on the ether. Judging by the level of corruption, Lady White was in her area doing something magical. His stomach grumbled.

Right, a quick bite to eat while she finished her current project wouldn't hurt. Using so much magic combined with a light breakfast had left him famished. If he could avoid his family, that would be perfect.

As soon as he stepped out of his bedroom he heard familiar voices. His first thought was to turn invisible, then he recognized Wolfric. It wouldn't do to avoid the emperor and this would save him the trouble of seeking him out later. If there was food on the table, that would be a nice bonus.

He made the short walk to the staircase and started down. At the bottom, sure enough, the entire family along with Wolfric was seated around a laden table. Everyone looked up as he approached.

"Daddy!" Abby said. "I didn't know you were home."

"I just got here. I can't linger, but Lady White is busy with some sort of magic and I can't talk to her until she's done. I need to eat, then, if he has time, to talk to Wolfric."

"I've got the entire afternoon," Wolfric said. "Draken assured me that the threats in the city have been eliminated. The poor man finally left his post to get some sleep. You work him far too hard."

"All he does is shuffle paper most of the time." Otto grabbed a couple pieces of bread and threw some chicken in between them. "An occasional emergency will keep him on his toes."

Abby hopped to her feet and pulled a chair out for him. "No need to stand while you wait."

He grunted and sat. Otto thought he caught Annamaria smiling, but as long as she didn't comment he'd ignore her.

As he took a bite of his sandwich Wolfric said, "Draken's not the only one that needs to stay on his toes. I admit I panicked a little when the guards told me the city was under attack. It was not a pleasant feeling."

"I imagine not. Despite the best efforts of the war wizards and the army, there are no guarantees."

"Could it happen again?" Wolfric asked.

"I have no way of preventing it. On the positive side, my research indicates that both the magic used to transport the monsters here and the largest creature are hard to create. Hopefully I can get to the source and destroy it before another attempt is made."

"That would certainly be for the best." Wolfric took a sip of wine. "Where will your hunt take you?"

"Aztecaland. That's the only place lizard creatures like the one that attacked the mansion can be found." Otto had no intention of explaining that it was born from the blood of a dragon. He hadn't completely accepted the fact himself.

"That's halfway around the world!" Edwin said.

"It's not as far as the Celestial Empire, but it is a ways. If everything works out, we should be able to return by portal. Of course, I'll be able to come and go via magic, so even if there is another attack, I can be back in moments to deal with it."

"What about Hans?" Abby asked.

Otto cocked his head. "What about him?"

"Is he okay? I couldn't find him after the battle and none of the guards knew what happened to him."

"He's fine. I healed his injuries. He'll be going with me to Aztecaland. One of the other guards can continue your training." Otto ate the last of his sandwich and checked the ether. Lady White's spell had ended. "I have to go."

"Be sure to stop by the palace before your final departure," Wolfric said. "I can wish you luck if nothing else."

"I will. Any and all luck is welcome." Otto stood and nodded to everyone. "Good afternoon."

He hurried toward Lady White's wing of the mansion before anyone else could ask a question. He'd made it through with a minimum of fuss and that suited him fine. Maybe Lady White had finally gotten some useful information from her master. Not that he held out much hope given Astaroth's silence to date.

A little chill ran down his spine when he reached her wing. Probably some lingering effect from the spell she cast. He expected Jet to greet him, but there was no sign of the woman.

He didn't need a guide anyway. Following the strongest source of corruption brought him right to her. Not to the casting chamber though. Instead he ended up standing in front of one of the bedrooms. Since she didn't sleep, he couldn't imagine what she was doing.

One way to find out. He knocked and said, "Lady White?"

A long moment passed and she finally opened up. Physically she didn't look any different, but there was something about the way she held herself that made him think she looked tired. Maybe it was the slightly drooping eyelids.

"Are you well?"

"I used up a lot of energy investigating the corpse. Your mithril sword purified most of its corruption, but there was just enough left for me to learn a few interesting things."

"I've learned a few things as well. Shall we exchange notes? Maybe sit down before you fall down."

"Excellent idea. Please come in."

He followed her inside. The bedroom no longer had a bed, but there were chairs and a coffee table. Lady White dropped into the nearest chair and he sat opposite her. He glanced around the room while she composed herself. Not that there was much to see. Other than the sitting area, there was a chest of drawers and a two-shelf bookcase. The room felt more like something you'd find in a high-end inn than someone's home.

"Would you like me to go first?" Otto asked when she seemed to have herself sorted out.

"If you like. It's going to take me most of the day to recover. I'd offer you refreshments, but Jet is still healing."

"I just ate, but thank you. So, the reptilian man is actually a dragonman created by Lord Azteca. That means whoever sent it here is in her territory. I'll be traveling by ship as soon as my preparations are complete. Do you wish to join me? I intend to return by portal, but I know that's not possible for you."

"I will join you. Everything in me screams that this is Lord of the Dead's doing. If you mean to face him, then I will be with you. I intend to send his soul screaming back to Astaroth for daring to try and kill me."

"I'm far less knowledgeable about this subject than I like to admit, but do you not fear that your master will be angry if you interfere in a fellow priest's work? If I was Astaroth, I certainly would be."

She offered a faint smile. "No, you truly don't understand. If I oppose Lord of the Dead and win, it means that he was too weak and thus unworthy to serve our master. If he destroys me, then the opposite is true. That's what it means to serve a demon lord."

"Seems inefficient. But I suppose when you're omnipotent and immortal, efficiency is less of a concern. So what did you learn from the body?"

"Right, analysis of the remains indicates that he bound a tier-three demon to create the warbeast. I've never seen one before. They tend to be too hard to control. Also, the corpse itself tried to resist my magic. That's another thing I've never experienced before."

"That's likely because dragons are highly resistant to magic. I noticed my spells were considerably less effective when it was alive. My sources indicate that there are about thirty more of them in Aztecaland. Of course, the information is centuries old, so that may have changed."

Her smile widened. "As is always the case, we'll not know for sure until we arrive and face the danger head on."

"So it would seem. What about Jet? I doubt she'll want to be left behind."

Lady White's smile withered. "I had high hopes for Jet, but her pouting is getting tiresome. If a simple correction is enough to turn her into a useless whiner, she has no hope of becoming something of real value. This mission will be her last chance. Should she fail to prove useful, she will not be coming back."

And people claimed Otto was harsh. "When I finish my preparations, we'll be traveling to Lux via the portal. Do you have a method of getting there quickly?"

"Not that quickly, but when I'm recovered I'll create an undead mount. It will be able to run nonstop. Barring any issue, I should make it in three days."

"That's fine. I'll probably be at least a week." Otto stood. "Have a good rest. I'll see you in Lux."

CHAPTER FIFTEEN

Forging two perfectly matched mithril patches might not have been the most difficult thing Otto had ever done, but it was certainly one of the more tedious. And as much as he appreciated Lord Colt's guidance, having a giant metal scorpion standing behind you and watching your every move was a bit nerve-racking. On the plus side, after four days of effort, Otto had two patches that met Lord Colt's exacting standards. Now, if he failed, he'd only have his application technique to blame.

Otto rubbed his eyes and slid the patches into a leather holder, the same one he'd used on his trip to Colt's Land over a decade ago. That mission had gone reasonably well and, while he was far from superstitious, using the same case felt like the right thing to do.

He turned and bowed to Lord Colt. "Many thanks for your guidance, Master."

"You hardly needed it. I just gave you a pointer here and there. While you might lack the patience to make a first-rate magical engineer, you've got a talent for artificing. I've had apprentices with centuries more experience than you that would struggle with something like this. Take pride in that."

"I do, Master, thank you. Since I've already said goodbye to Illsa, I believe I'll depart directly. Do you have any advice about Aztecaland for me?"

"My only advice is to be careful. Everything there wants to kill you. Even the bugs are especially aggressive."

"That doesn't surprise me given everything I've learned about Lord Azteca. I found a few useful items in Lord Karonin's armories that should help with the local wildlife. Until I return, Master."

With that final sentence, Otto became one with the ether.

A long moment later he appeared in the converted warehouse in Garen. The rune circle he used was in an out-of-the-way corner and everyone knew to avoid it. He heard voices, though at this distance he couldn't make out what they were saying. Lux crystal lanterns provided a steady warm glow that revealed the space in all its dubious glory. It was tidy of course. He wouldn't stand for a mess, but there was still an industrial quality to it. Maybe it was the lack of swords and banners you generally associated with a barracks.

He shook the random thought away and stepped out of the alcove. A moment later Corina came running toward him. In some ways she really hadn't matured much. She reminded him of a puppy, always eager to see her master. She was dressed in her black war wizard robe. It always looked a bit oversized for her despite the fact that he knew she'd had it altered to fit. Probably her slender build had a lot to do with it.

"Is it finally time, Master?" she asked.

"Very soon. I'll affix the patch in the morning then we'll

head to Lux. Draken sent a message so the crew will be ready as soon as we arrive. You'll need to begin charging the capacitor immediately."

She nodded. "I've been practicing like you said to. I can do it."

"I'm sure you can. Is everyone ready?"

"Yup. Hans has been putting the guys through their paces. He seems a lot more energetic. You'd think almost getting killed would have the opposite effect."

"It's not the almost getting killed, it's the magical healing that has him in such good shape. In addition to his major wounds, I went ahead and fixed a number of non-life-threatening but still annoying injuries. He probably hasn't been this healthy in thirty years. Did Axel arrive?"

"Two days ago. He stopped by to let us know."

"Good. We should be all set then. Tell Hans we'll meet at the portal fort at noon."

"Yes, Master." Corina grinned. "Isn't this exciting? It's been so long since we've had a real mission."

Exciting wasn't the word Otto would use, but if she was happy, so much the better. He doubted they'd have much to be happy about once they reached Aztecaland.

"Lord Shenk!" Ulf was waving from the doorway that led to his alchemy lab.

"You'd best start charging. See you tomorrow."

Corina bowed and ran back the way she'd come. Otto put his former apprentice out of his mind and marched over to Ulf. "Did you finish it?"

Ulf nodded. Otto didn't know how old he was, but his hair was now more gray than brown and he had plenty of new wrinkles. At least his smile seemed undimmed.

"Five gallons of repellant, just as you requested. I'll have it packaged and ready when the team leaves in the morning." Ulf hesitated as if uncertain he should say whatever was on his mind.

"Is there something else?"

"The repellent is designed to work on normal insects and beasts. I have no idea if it will be effective on creatures that have been modified with magic. I wanted to be sure you understood."

"I do understand, thank you for the warning. I think we both know that when it comes to magic, the only real guarantee is that anything can happen. I'm sure there will be plenty of naturally occurring critters we can use the repellent on even if it is less effective on the magic ones."

"Thank you, Lord Shenk. I didn't want to seem like I was making excuses, but I also wanted to be sure you were clear on the potential limitations."

Otto was about to leave when curiosity got the best of him. "How are Allen and Sin? I haven't spoken to them in six months. That means all is quiet in the underworld, which suits me perfectly."

"They're well, my lord, thank you for asking. They spend most of their time running the tavern. Given how little time she puts into her criminal enterprises, Sin has almost gone legit. Though she still gets frequent reports." Ulf hastened to add that last bit lest Otto think they weren't doing their jobs.

"Calm down, I'm not upset. The less work they have to do, the fewer problems I have to deal with. And how is the alchemy lab? Not having any trouble getting supplies?"

"No trouble at all, my lord. Since you spoke to them, the quartermasters have been excellent about getting me the supplies I need. I've even taken on a couple of promising students chosen from the war wizards."

That was news to Otto, but at least it was good news for a change. The more types of magic they could field, the stronger Garen's army would be.

"If there's nothing else, I need a good night's sleep if I'm going to be at my best tomorrow."

"That was all, my lord. Good evening."

Otto nodded and left the warehouse. To conserve energy, he'd walk home tonight. Having heard Lord Colt's instructions, he suspected he'd need all his strength to attach the patch in the morning. If he failed here, they'd have no hope of using the portal to return.

CHAPTER SIXTEEN

Fully rested and ready to get to work, Otto strode out of Franken Manor just after dawn. This allowed him to avoid any final goodbyes. Jet was waiting for him out front. She wore a black robe with Astaroth's skull symbol on the chest. Subtle it was not, but no one they were apt to encounter would care. A laden pack sat on the ground in front of her. She looked fully recovered from Lady White's —what did she call it, correction?

"Good morning, Lord Shenk." She fell in beside him and they walked together toward the main gate.

Technically it wasn't a gate at the moment, just a gap in the fence. An iron smith was busy making them a replacement. The head butler had informed Otto, as if he cared, that the new gate would be finished and installed by the end of the week.

"I assumed you'd be riding north with your mistress," Otto said.

"She says I lack the stamina. Since I'm still human, riding nonstop for days is, unfortunately, beyond me."

Otto nodded to the guards in passing and turned up the street. "If it's any consolation, unlike Lady White, you can travel via the portal. So your humanity does have some value."

She glanced at him and he noted how deep and dark the circles under her eyes were. Jet wasn't an unattractive woman by any means, but decades as a demon worshipper hadn't done her any good. While he had no strong feelings one way or the other, Otto found he was rooting for Jet to get what she wanted. Anyone willing to devote as much time and energy to something as she was deserved some reward.

Pity the universe didn't work that way.

"I am grateful for your attempt to cheer me up, but Lady White made it clear that if I don't make myself useful on the mission, my only future is as dirt in the Eternal Graveyard."

"Do you want a piece of advice?"

"Certainly. At this point, what do I have to lose?"

"Until we get back, I recommend you forget about gaining the reward you seek and try your best to serve Lady White. Prove your loyalty and dedication and most importantly your willingness to serve with no promise of getting the reward you desire. Actions speak louder than words. If your prayers don't reach Astaroth, maybe your efforts will."

"I doubt that, given how little interest he's shown in my actions to date. But at the very least your advice is likely to get me back home alive."

Otto had never been overly interested in the tenants of Lady White's faith, but their walk would take at least a few more minutes. Assuming they were going up against the leader of the cult, it might not hurt to find out a bit more.

"Is there no way to become a priestess without killing everyone that knows your true name?"

"Yes, but they're all lesser paths. To become like Lady White, nothing else will do."

"And nothing less will suit you?"

"Nothing less will give me what I want, eternal life and beauty. Though I've lost a great deal of both on my quest." She sounded so bitter. "The irony of dying old and ugly while I search for eternal beauty is not lost on me. If only I'd been born in the Land of the Demon Binders. Everything would've been so much simpler. Just murder my parents and siblings and I'd be done. I don't even know how many people know my name!"

"If that's true and you'll never get what you want, why not give up and accept what you can have?"

"Would you?" she countered.

Otto smiled at the question. He'd already given up on his dream of becoming an Arcane Lord. The price was simply too high. As someone that valued practicality as the highest virtue, he doubted he'd ever understand Jet's obsession.

"I would've moved on to a new path as soon as it became clear that the first one wouldn't work." Otto shrugged. "But as a wizard, I have options that you don't. That's life in a nutshell, isn't it?"

"What, that it's miserable and unfair?"

"Exactly. I was born with advantages a commoner couldn't begin to imagine. And Wolfric was born with even more. And while I would never give up my power, there have been days when the simple life of an ordinary merchant looked pretty good."

Jet said nothing and the portal was just ahead in any case. As soon as the guard on duty saw them approaching he shouted for the gate to be opened. The portcullis clanked up in perfect time for Otto to pass under it without breaking stride.

A little ways further in, the fortress commander bowed. A little sweat covered his brow despite the cool morning. Otto was pretty sure the man had served here for most of a decade. It seemed like he should've been more used to dealing with this sort of thing. Maybe he just had a nervous disposition.

"Welcome, Lord Shenk. Do you have any orders for us?"

"Nothing in particular. Two more groups will be arriving around noon. You can let them in without issue. I'll be focused on the portal, so I'd appreciate it if no one approaches until I'm finished. Other than that, go ahead and perform your duties as usual."

"Understood, my lord." The commander bowed again and hurried away. Had Otto given it any thought, he might have been insulted by how quickly the man wanted to escape his company.

"That's what I want," Jet said. "When I show up somewhere, I want everyone to be terrified of upsetting me."

"It's overrated. While I don't deny that I found the bowing and scraping amusing for a year or two, now I just want everyone to do their jobs properly and not cause me trouble. You'd be amazed how often terrified people screw things up. Their minds aren't properly clear. I need to get to work. Excuse me." Otto turned to go.

"One question, please."

He paused and turned back. "Go ahead."

"Why are you being nice to me? I'm a worthless failure."

"I'm being polite. You'd be amazed how many people mistake being strong for being a shit-heel. Many of the nobility especially. You gain absolutely nothing by treating people badly. You don't have to be sweet, but basic politeness costs nothing. Was there anything else?"

"No, thank you for indulging me."

He nodded and strode toward the portal. As he went, he pulled the mithril sheet he'd forged with Lord Colt out of his satchel. He'd been told that this would be difficult and had no reason to doubt it. Unlike when he'd replaced the master rune, he had to replace the one that led to Markane City. That alone would prevent it from happening automatically even if there was the power to do it, which there wasn't.

First things first. He found the proper rune and used four threads to carry the patch into position. It took twenty-five threads and every drop of concentration he could muster, but slowly the mithril began to fuse.

Otto lost all track of time as he worked. It didn't matter if it took hours as long as he got the right result. At least that's what he told himself as the pain built in the back of his head. Grimacing against the growing discomfort, he maintained his concentration.

He would succeed.

No matter what, he would succeed.

CHAPTER SEVENTEEN

"Let's get going," Corina said.

She had her gear packed, but one of the guys was carrying it. Beside her sat the fully charged ethereal capacitor. She grinned when she thought about it. Lord Shenk would be so proud of her. Not that the process had been especially difficult, but she'd never done it on her own before.

"Calm down." Hans ambled over, his own pack over his shoulder. "We've got another hour until noon. I swear you're worse than a rookie on his first mission."

"Sorry, it's just been so long since we all went on a mission and I'm excited. I haven't gotten to spend much time with Lord Shenk since he declared my training complete." She looked around to make sure no one was close enough to hear. "I know I'm a full war wizard now, but I think I preferred being an apprentice."

Hans chuckled. "You mean you preferred being *his* apprentice."

Corina's cheeks warmed. "Is that so bad?"

"No, but if you imagine he's suddenly going to fall head over heels in love with you on this trip, I fear you're going to be disappointed."

"I'm not an idiot. But if we're together, at least there's a chance."

"If you throw a boulder in the ocean there's a chance it will float, but not a good one."

Corina grimaced. Hans was right, she knew that, but deep down she couldn't help being a little optimistic. Even though the magic had burned away most of his human emotions, Lord Shenk was still a man. As far as she knew he had no one special in his life. She looked down at herself. She'd filled out a bit, though compared to some of the ladies around him, she was far from beautiful. But she was a wizard and that gave them something in common.

Hans snapped his fingers under her nose and Corina gave a start. "You still with me, kid?"

"Sorry, my mind wandered. Don't worry, I won't do anything foolish."

"That's good. We're all ready. Let's head out."

Corina grinned and shouldered the capacitor. The damn thing had to weigh over thirty pounds. How did a skinny little thing like Illsa carry it? She'd seen the brilliant magical engineer with Lord Shenk a few times. She'd been a bit jealous at first, then it became clear that he treated her exactly the same as he treated everyone he considered an ally, polite but impersonal. She was a valuable asset for the empire, no more and no less.

Corina swallowed a little growl and focused on the matter at hand. If she couldn't keep her head on straight, she'd be less than useless, she'd be a liability and Lord Shenk would leave her behind. There were many things Corina didn't want, but she wanted that least of all.

The guys were waiting by the main door, each of them burdened by packs that made Corina's look like a lady's handbag in comparison. She turned to Hans. "Why don't we take a wagon?"

"Because there are no roads where we're going. This is a test. If we can't carry the load here, under perfect conditions, we'll have no hope in the jungle. Worst comes to worst, we can leave some of the nonessential gear on the ship."

She hadn't even thought about that. "Did you learn about this sort of thing during your training?"

"Nah, experience. I've been on enough campaigns and shlepped enough crap over the years to know what to do."

The team set out with Corina and Hans in the lead. As soon as they left the warehouse behind, the sounds of clanging hammers and roaring furnaces assaulted their ears. The forges and foundries made an awful racket, though it would quiet soon when the lunch hour arrived.

They hurried to put the noise behind them and soon reached the gate to Gold Ward. The guards on duty just waved them through, which likely meant Lord Shenk had visited to let them know they were coming.

The few members of the rich and powerful that they passed only glanced at them before crossing to the opposite side of the street. You'd think they were thugs looking to steal someone's jewelry. Everyone was dressed in their uniforms for heaven's sake. They should be cheering the people in charge of keeping them safe, not looking down on them like riffraff.

She put the ingrates out of her mind as they got closer to the portal. There were sparks flying off of it as Lord Shenk worked to fuse the patch into place. Corina shifted her vision to the ether and marveled at the amount of power he was wielding. She couldn't begin to do something like that.

There was no time to study it now, not if she didn't want to get left behind. Corina hurried to catch up and followed them through the gate. Just inside, the fortress commander was waiting with a slightly nervous expression. The group strode into the yard, but made sure to keep well away from Lord Shenk and his magic. No one wanted to get too close and disturb him. That would be an excellent way to end up in the mines. Assuming you didn't get blasted on the spot.

The fortress commander smoothed his uniform and walked toward them doing a reasonable impression of confidence. Only the sweat on his brow and slight trembling of his hands gave him away.

They all straightened and offered a salute.

"Morning, sir," Hans said. Corina wasn't sure if the commander actually outranked Hans, but since they were in his fort, it made sense to be polite.

The commander returned his salute. "Good morning. Lord Shenk let us know you'd be coming. Please, make yourselves comfortable."

"Much obliged, sir." Hans lowered his pack to the ground and everyone else followed his lead. "Did he have any order for us?"

"Not that he shared with me. All he said was to make sure everyone kept their distance while he was working." The commander looked around and added, "It was an unnecessary order. My men would sooner cut their own arms off than approach Lord Shenk when he's doing magic."

Hans nodded. "He can be a bit intimidating, but if there's a fight, you wouldn't want anyone else on your side. Has

Captain Shenk sent word about his arrival? I expected to find him waiting already."

"No one sent word to me. It's still half an hour before noon and it's a short walk from Franken Manor."

Corina spotted something dark moving in the keep shadows. A moment later Jet strode into the yard. What was she doing here? Usually the woman stuck to Lady White like glue. Bad enough the beautiful undead priestess seemed closer to her master than she was, but Jet was pretty as well. Though less so than when they first met. She took comfort in the fact that Lord Shenk seemed no more interested in them than he was in her.

When Jet was close enough Corina said, "I didn't expect to see you here."

Jet frowned, making her look even older. "Lady White said it would be easier for me to travel with Lord Shenk. We spoke a bit and he offered me some words of advice. Given his youth, he's surprisingly wise. I am most grateful for his consideration."

"Given all he's seen and done, it's only natural for him to be wise. Though I kind of wish he looked a bit older. I mean, I'm a year younger than him yet he still looks like a teenager."

"An effect of the magic I'm sure," Jet said. "I've been watching him work. Whatever he's doing, he's been at it for hours without a break. I'm not even sure Lady White has that much stamina and she's dead."

Corina beamed as if the compliment had been offered to her instead of her master. She often felt that the people of the empire took Lord Shenk for granted. His power and determination were what made all this possible in the first place. He should get credit for it.

"Soldiers approaching!" the lookout called from his place on the wall.

"That'll be Axel and his scouts," Corina said. "I'm glad he's here. When Lord Shenk is finished, he'll be anxious to leave."

Jet nodded and turned back to watch Lord Shenk work. That struck Corina as a good idea. Though she wasn't nearly strong enough to do what he was doing, maybe if she watched closely, she could pick up a few tips. At the very least, if he asked her, she could tell him what she saw.

She smiled at the prospect of a one-on-one discussion. The truth was, she was probably the only one in the empire, outside of Wolfric of course, that would look forward to such a thing.

It was a shame, but then so was much of life.

○

Hans blew out a sigh of relief when the lookout announced Axel's arrival. He didn't imagine for a moment that the scouts would be late, but if they had been, Hans really didn't want to be the one that had to tell Lord Shenk.

Twenty scouts marched through the gate with Axel at their head. He looked a bit older than the last time Hans saw him. His hair had receded a bit more and gone gray at the temples. And he was only around thirty. How did the saying go? It wasn't the years, it was the wear and tear.

Axel gave his men some orders then broke off to join Hans. They shook hands and Hans said, "Captain Shenk. It's good to see you. My condolences on the loss of your father."

"He was an ill-tempered bastard, but I appreciate the thought. Do you have any details about what we're walking into? My brother was a bit light on the intel."

"What did he tell you?" Hans asked.

"That we were going to a monster-filled jungle to hunt down whoever sent the creatures that attacked the capital. He said to bring plenty of mithril weapons and we did. That's about it."

"I can't tell you much more about our destination, but I can tell you that the monster I fought at Franken Manor was strong enough to twist the iron gate out of shape and send me flying like I was a boy. Without Lord Shenk's intervention, I'd be dead right now."

"You sound less pleased by that than I would've expected."

"Don't misunderstand, I'm delighted to be alive, I just know what he had to do to keep me this way and it's not nice."

Axel snorted. "'Not nice' describes a great deal of what Otto does. I try my best not to think about it."

"A fine policy. Anyway, I don't think he's keeping secrets. As far as I can tell, he doesn't exactly know what we're dealing with either."

"That worries me more than if he was keeping secrets. Still, it's not like this is the first time we've walked into trouble blind."

Hans nodded. "That's a fact."

"He's done!" Corina's excited shout brought the conversation to an end.

"Looks like I didn't get here any too soon," Axel said.

"Shall we go see what our next move is going to be?"

Axel nodded for him to take the lead and the two men strode over to where a pale, gasping Lord Shenk waited. He looked as worn out as Hans had ever seen him, but at least he was on his feet and conscious.

"Orders, Lord Shenk?" Hans asked.

"Make yourselves comfortable. Even with the enhanced capacitor it's going to take half an hour to charge the portal."

Otto turned to Corina. "Let's get the capacitor set up and the charge flowing. You had no issues preparing it?"

"No, Master."

"Good." That was it. One word of praise. Not much, but more than he sometimes gave. From her smile, Corina seemed pleased at least.

The two wizards got to work doing whatever they did.

After a few seconds Otto shifted his attention to his brother. "Did you get the manor's guards squared away?"

"Everyone's got a mithril weapon. You should've seen the looks on their faces when I handed them out. I've seen less nervous men on the way to the gallows. You'd think I was handing out poisonous snakes."

Lord Shenk's smile was thin and humorless. "It's not every day you get handed a weapon more valuable than the combined income of a working-class block. Though I consider the likelihood low, those weapons give them the best chance of protecting the mansion should more monsters show up."

"What are the odds?" Axel asked.

"Slim. Our working theory is that the one that sent them was targeting Lady White. If she's with us, then the city should be safe."

"What about our safety?" Corina asked.

"We're sailing to a monster-filled jungle to hunt down possibly the most powerful priest of Astaroth on the planet. Worrying about our safety is pointless."

CHAPTER EIGHTEEN

The cry of gulls and the smell of saltwater filled the air of Lux. Crystal City was every bit as beautiful as Otto remembered, at least the tops of the towers visible over the portal fort's walls were. Out of all the former kingdoms and current provinces, Lux seemed to be thriving the most. A competent imperial governor combined with a populace more interested in commerce than fighting combined to create a model province. If only Straken were equally obliging.

It had taken closer to an hour for the portal to fully charge and even though Otto was eager to get underway, he hadn't been upset about the extra recovery time. Fusing the mithril patch to the portal counted among the most difficult things he'd done. Not in terms of raw power involved—he'd only needed about sixty percent of his maximum—but duration. He'd never sustained a spell of that power for that long.

He considered it a point of pride that he didn't pass out at the end, though it had been a near thing. The half hour of rest had allowed him to walk through the activated portal without assistance. It didn't make an especially good impression when the leader of the mission had to be carried to the transport.

"Ah, Lord Shenk!" The fortress commander hurried over. "Welcome to Lux. Is there any way my command and I can be of use?"

"We're just passing through, Commander. Open the gates and we'll be on our way."

Otto pretended not to notice the man sagging with relief. With a few shouted orders, the soldiers on duty got busy pushing the gate open. As soon as they finished, Otto strode through, heading straight for the docks. Hopefully Lady White would be in the area waiting for them.

"Did you have any trouble finding a ship?" Axel asked.

"Not at all. When Captain Wainwright retired, I bought the *Sea Star* and had it transferred to the empire. It's kept ready to sail on a day's notice. All the crew needs to do is load it up with supplies. Which they should have done several days ago."

Axel winced. "How much did that cost?"

Otto shook his head. "I don't recall, but it didn't put a dent in the imperial budget. Besides, having a reasonably comfortable and convenient ship on call is far from a luxury. Given the things we need to deal with, it's a wonder we haven't needed it before now."

"I suppose that's true."

Otto and his team drew plenty of nervous looks from the locals as they marched down the main street to the harbor. Since no one was stupid enough to make a move in their direction, Otto ignored them. Hans and the other members of his personal guard, on the other hand, kept their heads on a swivel as if expecting an attack any moment. He said nothing about their overprotectiveness. They were just doing their jobs after all and it was useful for them to get back into practice. He hadn't gone anywhere that required a full team of bodyguards in a long time.

Halfway to the harbor he sensed a faint but rapidly approaching source of corruption coming from behind them. "Hold up a moment."

"Is there trouble, Lord Shenk?" Hans asked, hand resting on the hilt of his mithril sword.

"No, the final member of the team is on her way and I wanted to let her catch up."

A few seconds later Lady White seemed to appear out of nowhere. She wore her usual black robe and aside from a modest satchel over her shoulder carried no supplies. Being undead she probably had no need of them.

"I figured you'd meet us near the harbor," Otto said.

"I considered that, but then I remembered you had to activate the portal. I find the ethereal waves that come off the mithril uncomfortable, so I waited outside the city. It wasn't difficult to figure out when you arrived."

That was certainly true. The portal activating was about as subtle as a sledgehammer to the forehead.

"Well, you're here and that's the main thing." Otto started walking again and Lady White fell in beside him. "Did you have any trouble on your ride north?"

"Not a bit. I can say with confidence that the empire between Garen and Crystal City is quiet and peaceful. I avoided anything resembling civilization. Less open-minded people have trouble dealing with individuals like me."

Ignorant people were certainly not hard to come by. After all, this was still the generation that made wizards into virtual slaves. Who could expect them to deal rationally with an undead priestess? Otto still had high hopes for the next generation. Whether he was being prudent or foolish only time would tell.

They reached the harbor without incident and he led the group to *Sea Star*'s berth. While Otto wasn't much of a judge when it came to ships, the three-masted vessel appeared to be in good shape. The crew was busy on deck and the gang plank had been set out for them.

One of the sailors noticed them and hurried over to the top of the plank. "Lord Shenk?"

"Correct. Fetch Captain Coleman, the time of our departure has arrived."

The sailor's eyes widened a bit but he nodded and said, "Understood, sir. Please come aboard. I'll find the captain for you straight away."

The young man seemed a solid fellow if a bit nervous. Otto strode up the plank and everyone followed along. "Axel, Hans, get everyone settled. I need to talk to Coleman about our route."

Hans saluted and everybody made their way toward the steps that led to the lower decks.

"Lord Shenk, welcome aboard." Captain Coleman was a big, burly fellow that wouldn't have looked out of place in Straken, with his black-and-gold uniform straining at the seams. The general effect was ruined by a smooth-shaved baby face that made him look about half his actual age.

"Captain. Have you had time to study the charts I provided?"

"Yes, my lord. Though they were a bit vague. Our port of destination being the main item missing."

"The reason for that is simple. There are no known ports

in Aztecaland. You'll need to get us close to the coast then we'll land via rowboat. I won't be able to give you a more accurate destination until we're within sight of land. Oh, before I forget, did the special food get delivered? We can't leave without it."

"It did, just yesterday. Will it truly last us all for a year? There weren't that many crates."

"According to an alchemist I trust, if we eat at the correct times and consume the right amount of water, it will. I've also learned some spells that will make it easy to catch large quantities of fish should that prove necessary."

"That's reassuring, my lord. We can set sail as soon as the tide turns. If there's nothing else, I'll begin final preparations to depart."

"By all means, Captain. I'll be in my cabin."

As Otto descended the stairs to the second level, he couldn't quite believe that he was heading out into unknown danger once more. He'd hoped and indeed believed that this sort of thing was in the past. He really should've known better.

CHAPTER NINETEEN

Lord of the Dead rubbed his temples. He'd thought his days of feeling pain had ended centuries ago, but when his warbeast died, even though it was thousands of miles away, he felt the killing blow as if he'd been struck himself. The shock of it had almost rendered him unconscious. And that could've been a disaster.

Since arriving in Aztecaland, he'd found nothing beyond jungle, aggressive mutants, horrible, twisted beasts, and barely intact stone structures. There was nothing even vaguely resembling civilization. Though given the size of the empire, he assumed there was a city or cities somewhere in the sprawling jungle. An Arcane Lord wouldn't want to live like a savage after all. She'd need labs and libraries. A place for her apprentices to live and work. And a portal. There had to be at least one around here somewhere.

Pity the damn thing was made of mithril. It was the one thing he couldn't use resonance magic to find. On a stump beside him rested the Rod of Terror, a black iron rod covered in spikes and featuring an open hand at the end.

That hand had once gripped a black orb. According to Lord Astaroth, the orb was supposed to be red. Hours of meditation and study had allowed Lord of the Dead to connect with the rod's magic enough to determine that the red orb was in Aztecaland. But now that he'd arrived, something was blocking him from homing in on its exact location. Some magic of the late Arcane Lord he had no doubt.

And so he and his servants were reduced to searching the seemingly endless jungle on foot. It was a tedious process made more so by the fact that Aztecaland consisted of an entire continent. Searching the whole thing might take centuries.

The only good thing he could say about the place was that the endless attacks by aggressive animals had given him an excellent supply of warbeasts. Ten of them were out searching even now while another six were guarding the clearing he'd chosen as his temporary camp. They were a motley collection of monsters. Two looked like giant, long-legged crocodiles, one resembled a gorilla with a mouth full of shark teeth, and the last were all variations on big cats. Some of the ones he'd sent scouting were feline in form as well. Perhaps Lord Azteca had a fondness for them.

He smiled to himself. Even incomplete, the rod had increased his power by nearly double. He'd never been able to control this many warbeasts and his magic was even more lethal. The rod corrupted the ether with its mere presence, making Lord of the Dead's magic that much easier to use. Interestingly, it hadn't done that while gripping the black orb. Something about the orb's magic had prevented the effect.

Even if he didn't find the red orb, he could build a new empire of the dead in this abandoned land. It wasn't like the wild beasts, strong as they were, had any hope of stopping him.

Another stab of pain shot through him. This one with a different flavor.

Right, his master wanted the artifact restored. Best not to even think about failing to find the missing piece. Maybe it would take years or decades to find the red orb. And if it did, that was fine. One thing about being an immortal undead priest, you never had to worry about time. Even if it took a century, he'd be no worse off.

One of his vulture-headed slave beasts slowly approached. What could the useless thing want? They weren't good for much more than fetching and carrying. He honestly wasn't sure why he'd bothered bringing them with him from the Land of the Demon Binders. Because leaving them behind would've been a waste seemed a poor reason.

"What is it?" The slave beast flinched when he snapped at it. They really were pitiful.

"Something's sniffing around, Master."

He grimaced. He still hadn't recovered from the loss of his most powerful warbeast. Killing whatever was prowling around out there wouldn't be a problem, but it would delay his full recovery. For now it would be best to leave it alone as long as it remained peaceful.

"Don't bother it, but don't lose track of it either."

"Yes, Master." The slave beast hurried back to its post.

Lord of the Dead put the threat out of his mind and focused on drawing corrupt ether into his body. The sooner he got back to full strength, the better.

One thing was certain, he wasn't going to send another monster to kill Lady White. That had taken far too much out of him and accomplished absolutely nothing. Let her rot in the human empire. It's where the traitor belonged.

᠊ᠥ

A few hours passed but finally Lord of the Dead got the pain in his head under control. It wasn't completely gone, but it was down to little more than an annoyance. He wished he knew what he did to cause it in the first place. He'd had plenty of warbeasts die over the years and he never felt anything like that. Perhaps it had something to do with the higher-tier demon he used. Not that he'd had a choice. The lower-tier demons couldn't even bond to the corpse. It was like it rejected them, though how a corpse had such an ability was beyond him.

Done was done. He put the riddle out of his mind and stood. It was time to resume his search. He'd barely taken a step toward the tree line when one of the warbeasts he'd sent to scout reached out to him. The creatures weren't exactly sentient, but they did have a basic level of intelligence. If they didn't, they'd be totally useless for anything besides battle.

Drawing corrupt ether into his body, Lord of the Dead strengthened his connection to the warbeast. It stood on a trail about half a mile north of the clearing. It was too wide and regular for a game trail. Was it an ancient road?

If Lord of the Dead's heart had still beat, it would've raced at the news. This was the first sign of anything resembling civilization that he'd found in the months since he arrived. With a psychic command, he ordered his servants to form a circle around him.

He spotted the slave spirit and motioned it over. The

vulture-headed creature quavered as it approached. "Is the creature you sensed still out there?"

"No, Master. It wandered out of my range half an hour ago, heading roughly east."

"Good. Be sure to keep alert in case it doubles back."

It bowed. "Yes, Master."

Hopefully the creature would find easier prey. With any luck, now that they were moving in different directions, they wouldn't encounter it again. Lord of the Dead had no doubt that he'd be able to kill it, but he didn't want to waste the time or energy.

Ten minutes of walking brought them to the warbeast. This one had the body of a black leopard with tentacles growing out of its shoulder. The tentacles ended in bone spikes that were hard enough to pierce steel. He couldn't help wondering about what sort of person not only thought up such a creature, but made it a reality. The time and effort required for such an undertaking boggled the mind.

One thing he'd determined was that the Arcane Lords, for all their undeniable power, weren't fully in their right minds.

Setting the useless thoughts aside, he studied the path. It was about six feet wide and ran in a straight line from north to south as far as he could see in either direction. There were no markers. Certainly no sign with an arrow that said "Three hundred miles to the capital."

Time to make another attempt to connect with the orb. Closing his eyes, he focused on the Rod of Terror. "Merge your essence with the corruption," his master had said. It sounded easy when you said it, but to fully merge his corrupted essence with that of the rod, he had to give up part of his awareness. No easy task, especially when you were in the middle of dangerous territory. But failure meant he would just have to guess again. And so far his luck had been terrible.

Okay, draw corruption in and mingle it with his essence. He pictured the rod's energy as a black mist and breathed it in. His own essence was a black ball at the center of his body. He mingled the two together and then breathed the combined corruption back out into the rod. In and out, over and over, he repeated the process. Soon a tendril formed to connect them. When it did, he felt a tug to the north and a little west.

A moment of excitement snapped the link but he didn't care. He had a direction now and that was all that mattered. After weeks of flailing around, having a real direction felt amazing. With his entourage around him, Lord of the Dead set out. He would find the orb soon, he knew it.

CHAPTER TWENTY

Ten days of walking brought Lord of the Dead exactly nowhere. At least nowhere interesting. He'd been following the path his warbeast found north without stopping. His best guess was that he'd put at least three hundred miles between them and their starting point. Even so, this section of jungle looked exactly the same as where they left. Same tall palm trees, same dense shade, same hot, humid air. The only difference was the lack of insects. He could see them buzzing around at the edge of the path, but it seemed they couldn't cross it.

Time to see if they were getting any closer to their destination. He stopped and his guardians stopped as well. Taking a firm grip on the rod he repeated the psychic ritual that would connect his essence. It took less time for the connection to form. That had to be a good sign.

Focusing on the orb, he soon sensed that it was now more west than north. He turned slowly then opened his eyes. If they wanted to take a direct route, they'd need to leave the path. Moving through the jungle wouldn't be that much slower given the lack of undergrowth. His gaze darted back and forth from the path to the jungle.

He could wait until they were directly across from the orb then cut west. It wouldn't take them that far out of their way. In addition to the extra speed, nothing had attacked them since they started traveling on the path. There was no magic involved, not that he could sense at least. The lack of cover might have had something to do with it. Lord of the Dead knew a great deal about many things, but he was no wilderness expert.

To Astaroth with it. He turned off the path and strode into the jungle. He'd make a straight line for the orb and kill anything that dared get in his way. A mental command sent six of his strongest warbeasts ahead of the group. They'd either chase off or eliminate anything that approached. One advantage to this place was that there were no allies to worry about. When everything was an enemy, indiscriminate killing was easy. And that was Lord of the Dead's favorite kind.

As he'd hoped, the walking proved easy and aside from dodging around the occasional tree trunk, he was able to keep a straight course. Other than a distant growl, there was no sign of wildlife.

He was just starting to think he'd made the correct choice when one of his warbeasts vanished from his awareness. Nothing less than its destruction would cause that.

"Defensive positions." His guards formed a circle around him and he sent a psychic recall to the other warbeasts he'd sent ahead.

Five of them came running back, but one of the feline beasts was missing. He knew there were powerful creatures living in the jungle, but to find something capable of so easily slaying one of his warbeasts was a surprise.

He was still debating what to do next when the mangled carcass of his warbeast came flying in out of nowhere to land a few feet from him. He heard and saw nothing. Even his magical senses were blind to the beast.

Perhaps leaving the path wasn't the best idea after all.

He turned and made a strategic withdrawal. Not fleeing, certainly not. Just getting back to a known safe location to reassess his decision. These things happened after all and it was important not to let your pride keep you from making the right decision.

Half an hour of quick-marching, his every sense alert for an attack, left Lord of the Dead in a poor mental state. On the plus side, they reached the path without getting attacked by any monsters. That was a more than acceptable result. Maybe there was some magic on the path that prevented the savage creatures from attacking them after all. He wasn't so foolish as to think that an Arcane Lord would be incapable of hiding such an enchantment from him.

"Did anyone see what killed the warbeast?"

Most of his servants were incapable of speech, but he sensed their negative responses. Even the ones that had been on advance patrol had seen nothing. Only powerful magic would be able to hide the attacker from their enhanced senses. That led him to believe that he faced something smarter and thus more dangerous than a merely cunning beast.

The prospect didn't excite Lord of the Dead in the least. He knew some of his fellow priests reveled in showing off their strength and challenging powerful foes; the worshippers of the Horned One were the worst for that kind of thing. But when you served a master dedicated to strength, that was the price you paid.

As far as Lord of the Dead was concerned, the best way to gain power was to send expendable lackeys in to collect artifacts or to summon and bind demonic servants. Before his recent fall from grace, he hadn't even left the Land of the Demon Binders for centuries. And that was fine with him. It made no sense to have eternal life if you were going to go out and put yourself at risk all the time.

But look at him now, out in the field, fighting monsters, at least one of which seemed like a real threat. This situation represented an absolute failure of everything he believed in. Not that his master cared. If he failed to restore the artifact, all that awaited him was an eternity of agony in the Endless Graveyard. A dismal prospect if ever there was one.

"Master?" One of the slave spirits cautiously approached, knocking him out of his gloomy thoughts.

"I was plotting out our new strategy. What's the problem?"

"No problem, Master. You've just been standing there for most of an hour staring at nothing. I grew concerned that you'd been struck by some sort of psychic attack."

Had he truly lost track of time that badly? He'd thought only moments had passed. "I'm fine. The situation requires careful planning. For now, let's keep moving north. A better opportunity is bound to present itself."

He said that, but he had no real idea if a better opportunity would present itself. At some point, they were going to have to turn west. When that moment arrived, all he could do was hope that the thing that killed his warbeast wasn't waiting in ambush.

〜

A week of steady, peaceful marching brought Lord of the Dead and his group to a crossroads. Just as he hoped, the intersecting path ran east to west. It looked exactly like the path they'd been following, which continued north as far as he could see. For all he knew, this path might lead all the way to the border of Colt's Land. Lord of the Dead wasn't confident enough in his geographic knowledge to say for sure.

He felt certain that this new path would lead to wherever the orb had been hidden. Just to make sure, he decided to check its location once more. When he focused on the Rod of Terror, the connection came much more quickly. Not allowing his pleasure to distract him, he focused on the orb. Sure enough, it was almost due west and not that far. At least it didn't feel like it was that far. His sense of distance was a bit shaky when it came to using the rod.

But no matter. They were on the right track now. Staying on the path was the correct move. The more he thought about it, the more he felt like a fool for leaving it in the first place. Safe and steady was the way. How many times had he laughed at others' stupidity when they ran into the unknown? To make the same mistake himself was just pitiful.

He turned west and set out with his guardians around him. The jungle was largely silent save for the incessant buzzing of insects. That never went away. He couldn't imagine having to sleep in a place like this. Thank Astaroth that weakness had been removed from him. The fact that he didn't need to eat also helped.

They made good time and as the sun began to set the jungle finally opened up into a huge clearing. In the middle of it was a city made of stone and filled with simple square buildings. At the center sat a step-sided, flat-topped pyramid that towered above every other building in the city. The one thing it didn't tower over was the mithril hoop that stood a little ways to the east of the pyramid. Though he'd never seen one firsthand, Lord of the Dead knew enough to recognize one of the Arcane Lords' portals.

This had to be the capital. As he suspected, the path led right to the front gate. The wide-open front gate. Strange. Was the city abandoned?

It was hard to judge from a distance, but he could definitely sense life forms down there. Not totally abandoned then. Perhaps some of the local wildlife had settled in the city. Surely nothing intelligent remained behind. He'd certainly seen nothing so far to indicate that the local wildlife had more than the crude intelligence of an animal.

Well, whatever. If he had to kill every living thing between him and the orb, he'd do so. Claiming Astaroth's prize was all that mattered.

CHAPTER TWENTY-ONE

From where he had stood overlooking the city, it hadn't seemed that far away, but when Lord of the Dead finally reached the walls, the half-moon had risen high in the sky. Placing a hand on the cool stone, he concentrated, searching for wards that might harm him or his servants. As far as he could tell, there was nothing. Perhaps time had done the work of erasing them for him. Nearly three-quarters of a millennia was a long time after all.

Once he'd completed a thorough search, he was confident that there was no danger, at least no magical danger, if they entered. He led the way around the wall until they reached the open entrance. Other than a few shards of rotten wood and rusted, barely intact giant hinges, there was no sign of the gate. So, it wasn't that they'd been left open, but rather the horrid environment had claimed them. That was fine as far as he was concerned.

Lord of the Dead strode through the opening, shoulders back and head up, corrupt power radiating off him in waves. It was a direct challenge to anyone that wanted to try and stop him. If there was to be a fight, he'd just as soon have it immediately.

He walked past block after block of stone buildings as he made a beeline for the central pyramid. That had to be where he'd find the orb and even if he was wrong, it was still the best place to start looking.

"Master." As soon as the slave spirit spoke, Lord of the Dead felt it too. A large concentration of powerful life force not that far ahead.

"I sense them. It seems the city's keepers are waiting for us."

Lord of the Dead turned to the nearest building and smashed through the rotten front door. Nothing about the building interested him beyond having walls of stone between him and whatever was out there. When all of his servants had entered the building, he selected one of his warbeasts, weaker, but fastest of them all, and sent it scouting.

Keeping his mind merged with it, he rode along for a few more blocks until it stopped just outside of a huge open courtyard that surrounded the pyramid. It didn't take long to spot the source of the life force. There were a dozen of the humanoid reptile beasts like the one he sent after Lady White. There were also a few others. Five with tails, and one giant brute with both a tail and wings. He didn't know what to make of the new variants, but suspected they were more powerful versions of the one he'd fought previously.

Considering how strong a single tailless monster was, he shuddered to think what would happen if he had to fight all of them at once. Though he had great faith in his strength, Lord of the Dead wasn't so foolish as to think he had a hope in hell of beating all of them.

The biggest one, the one with the wings, stopped its pacing and glared right at his warbeast.

Lord of the Dead had seen enough. A mental command sent the warbeast fleeing into the city. Not directly back to his hiding place. The enemy didn't seem overly interested in attacking, but why take chances?

He blinked a few times to clear his mind and focus. He'd known, of course he had, that the odds of him simply walking into an empty city and claiming the orb were beyond slim. Nevertheless, finding such a formidable force between him and his goal far exceeded his worst fears.

None of his options were appealing. A direct attack, even with all his warbeasts, would be suicide. He tapped his chin. Those things, whatever else they might be, were alive. He could sense the teeming life force within them, more than he'd ever felt in any living thing he'd encountered previously. And if they were alive, that meant they needed to eat, sleep, and drink. Assuming they didn't have a huge stash of food in the pyramid, eventually they'd need to hunt. Picking off a small hunting party would be no easy feat, but it would certainly be more doable than taking on all of them at once.

He nodded to himself as a plan slowly came together. First, he'd need a way, a safe way, to keep an eye on the gathering. His warbeasts were a bit much for such a simple task. An imp would do. As far as an expendable pair of eyes went, the minor demons were perfect. They were also smart enough to understand what the enemy was doing and make an intelligent report. He wished he could extend his sight the way a wizard did, but his magic didn't allow that.

Using corrupt ether from the rod, he opened a one-foot-diameter portal to Astaroth's hell and sent a mental summons. It didn't take long for a hideous, rotten humanoid figure to emerge. The imp stood two feet tall. Bits of flesh constantly dripped off it to plop onto the floor. He knew his master's demons weren't any weaker than any of the other demon lords' creations, but even so, sometimes Astaroth's aesthetic disgusted even him. But as long as the imp got the job done, nothing else mattered.

Lord of the Dead sealed the portal and focused his considerable will on the imp. It must have recognized him for what he was as it didn't bother with the usual bluster and threats most demons gave when summoned. That was well, as he had no time for such foolishness.

"How may I serve, Master?" the imp asked.

"There is a gathering of powerful enemies not far from here. Can you sense them?"

The imp cocked its rotten head for a moment then nodded. "Yes, Master."

"Good. I want you to observe them and when any leave the courtyard, alert me at once."

"Understood, Master." The imp turned invisible and flew out of the building.

Lord of the Dead set two of his warbeasts to guarding the entrance. It was a waiting game now and if there was one thing an undead was good at, it was waiting.

CHAPTER TWENTY-TWO

The wait ended up being shorter than Lord of the Dead had feared. Only three days after setting his imp to watch, he felt a faint psychic tingle in the back of his mind. An effort of will completed the connection.

Four of the tailless ones and one with a tail just left the courtyard, Master. They're headed for another gate to the west. The rest are holding their position.

Good, keep watching.

He severed the connection and considered his options. Defeating five of them was a big task given the forces at his disposal. Even if he won, Lord of the Dead estimated that he'd lose half of his warbeasts at a minimum. And given his recent experience using the reptile men, he wasn't eager to make them into replacements.

A little snarl twisted his lips. If he did nothing, he'd never get any closer to his goal. This was a risk he had to take. Leaving the slave spirits behind, he set out with his entire force of warbeasts. They made their way south through the silent city. Though far from a brilliant strategist, Lord of the

Dead knew enough to plan a simple ambush. He'd flank the hunters and take them by surprise. If they'd be kind enough to split up before he arrived, that would be okay with him as well.

All he sensed from his warbeasts was bloodthirst and eagerness to kill. They weren't smart enough to be afraid and even if they were destroyed, they'd just reappear in Astaroth's hell ready to be summoned again. For a moment, Lord of the Dead envied them. How nice it must be not to have to worry about plotting and scheming. Just do as you're told and if you die have the satisfaction of knowing nothing bad would happen to you.

Should Lord of the Dead die without completing his mission, the fate awaiting him in the Endless Graveyard didn't bear consideration. But he wasn't going to fail. One way or another, he was going to defeat the foes standing in his way and claim the orb. Thinking any other way would only weaken his resolve.

They slipped out of the city without issue and started making their way around it through the jungle. It was louder here, but he ignored the distractions. There was no issue with finding their targets. They were the most powerful sources of life force out here and thus easy to home in on. After about an hour it felt like the group broke apart with one especially strong individual going one way and the other four sticking together.

The explanation came to him a moment later. The leader must have sent its underlings out to do the actual work while it waited somewhere comfortable. It was the same everywhere, even in the jungle.

Lord of the Dead grinned. If you cut the head off, the body would be easy pickings.

He set their course for the solitary presence. As they drew nearer it gave no indication that it was aware of the danger approaching. His warbeasts dispersed, making a circle around the clueless monster. When they were all in place, Lord of the Dead peeked through a gap in the trees and spotted the tailed monster standing, arms crossed, with its ugly face twisted in what he assumed was a scowl. It was bigger than he first thought, though not as big as the one with wings.

It was also alone.

He took a tighter grip on the Rod of Terror.

Attack!

Warbeasts came roaring in from every direction.

Lord of the Dead felt a moment of exultation. It died as quickly as it came when one of the warbeasts got caught midleap and casually torn in half.

A swing of the creature's stout tail crushed another warbeast's skull like a chicken's egg.

A third warbeast clamped onto the monster's arm.

Lord of the Dead chose that moment to strike. A stream of corrupt energy shot out and slammed into the monster's back only to fizzle against its scales without doing any damage. This one was even more resistant to magic than the one Lord of the Dead had killed.

Grimacing, he focused on the warbeasts. If he couldn't attack directly, he could at least strengthen his servants. Dark energy flowed into them, making them faster and stronger. He focused, adding sharpness to their fangs and claws. Despite the occasional successful strike, the warbeasts' natural weapons were just scraping off the monster's scales.

The monster roared when one of the enhanced warbeasts sank its fangs into its scaly thigh. That was the only blow the warbeast made as a moment later it was ripped free and torn in half. Lord of the Dead took some satisfaction from the thick, crimson blood oozing out of the wound. They'd hurt it at least. And if it bled, they could kill it.

He glanced at the six remaining warbeasts as they circled the monster. They *could* kill it, right?

He'd barely begun to debate his next move when he sensed a dozen more life forces approaching. Reinforcements? No, while they were strong, they weren't as strong as the reptile men.

"Human." Lord of the Dead started and looked up to find some sort of monkey with an extra hand at the end of its tail hanging directly above him. It was about two feet tall and covered with gray fur. "If you want to live, come with me. My master wishes to speak with you and my brothers can't hold the dragonmen off for long."

He had so many questions, but one thing was clear: he had no chance of winning this fight. "Very well, lead on."

The monkey scrambled up into the tree and started swinging through the branches due north. Lord of the Dead hastened to follow. A psychic command recalled his two strongest warbeasts while the rest continued to keep the dragonman busy.

He shook his head at that. More bloody dragons. It must be his fate to deal with them. First a dragon brought him the Rod of Terror and now these things were trying to keep him from completing it. There was a certain balance to the situation that he appreciated on one level and hated on another. Perhaps the dragon had known that more of its kind were waiting so he didn't fear handing over the incomplete rod. The only one that could say for sure was many thousands of miles from here and no doubt disinclined to answer his questions.

When they'd put a couple of miles between themselves and the dragonmen the monkey stopped and said, "Do you need to rest, human?"

"Hardly. And I'm only barely more human than you. How far is it to your master?"

"Why do you lie to me?" the monkey asked. "You look as human as all the other humans."

"I was human once, but now I'm undead. Did you not notice that I only breathe when I talk?"

The monkey's furry muzzle scrunched up. "The master said to bring the human that just arrived. I thought that was you. But maybe you're the wrong one. Are there any other humans that have recently arrived?"

"Not that I'm aware of. If your master saw me somehow, it is possible that he mistook me for a still-living human. I would like to talk with him if possible."

"If I go back with no one, I'm in trouble. If I go back with the wrong person, I might also be in trouble, but maybe less than if I have nothing." The monkey scratched its head and occasionally picked out a bug to eat as it thought.

Lord of the Dead concentrated, but sensed no sign that the dragonmen were pursuing. He also no longer sensed his warbeasts. It seemed they had all been destroyed. That put him in an extremely tenuous position. Making a deal with this thing's master might be his only chance of success.

Time to hasten things along. "I don't mean to rush you, but should the dragonmen catch up, we'll be in bad shape with only four of us."

The monkey gave a little squeak. "Good point. I'll take

you and the master can decide for himself if you're the human he wants."

With his guide once again swinging through the trees above, Lord of the Dead set out. He didn't know what sort of master the monkey served. Perhaps some other, more horrific monstrosity. Or maybe one of Lord Azteca's apprentices that somehow survived to the current day.

Whoever it was, if they were an enemy of the dragonmen, Lord of the Dead was determined to do everything he could, short of offering the crimson orb, to secure their help.

CHAPTER TWENTY-THREE

Lord of the Dead followed his furry guide for the rest of the day. Nothing troubled them as they hurried through the jungle. Whether because their guide knew a safe path or because the local wildlife sensed their power and didn't wish to fight, he didn't know. All that mattered was that they were getting further away from the dragonmen and closer to a potential ally.

When the sun had nearly set the monkey stopped and climbed down to a limb about even with Lord of the Dead's face. "This is a good place to stop for the night."

He looked around the little patch of jungle, but couldn't see anything that made it different than any other patch. "If you say so. I'm content to keep going if you'd prefer."

The monkey shook its head. "I need to sleep. There's also some tasty fruit in the top of this tree. That's what makes it a good place to stop."

"As you wish. When you're ready to continue, let me know."

Lord of the Dead closed his eyes and concentrated on his connection to the imp.

Report.

Nothing has changed since you departed. They continue to guard the courtyard. No more have left and none have returned. I assume that's because you killed them all.

You assume incorrectly. I'm on my way to hopefully arrange an alliance with a mutual enemy. Keep me apprised of any changes.

He severed the connection. There was no way that dragonman hadn't survived its minor wounds. That being the case, it simply must not have arrived at the temple yet. Well, no matter. Assuming he couldn't make a deal with the monkey's master, Lord of the Dead didn't know what he'd do. Having seen the power of the tailed dragonman, it was clear he had no hope of besting one, much less the five of them guarding the temple. And if the winged one was more powerful yet, he shuddered to think what it might be capable of.

He couldn't worry about that. Best to stay optimistic. If the master went to all the trouble of dispatching a guide, clearly it was as eager for help as Lord of the Dead.

The night was long and tedious, but nothing bothered them and at first light the group set out again behind their furry guide. Marching through the jungle had little to recommend it but as with the previous day, none of the local wildlife troubled them.

Curious, he asked, "How come there are no aggressive wild animals around here? It seemed when we were further from the city, we couldn't take a step without some mutated horror trying to kill us."

"We are in my master's territory. He sends out regular

patrols to keep the local predators in check. Though far from brilliant, they have learned to avoid this part of the jungle."

"I've seen nothing for the past day. Are there any patrols in the area now?"

The monkey paused and let out a few noises that were a cross between a hoot and a howl. It cocked its head and listened for a moment then said, "It seems not. Don't worry, we're still in no danger here."

Lord of the Dead wasn't remotely worried. As long as no dragonmen showed up, there was little that he feared in this jungle. In fact, he was going to need to hunt down some of the local predators to replenish his stock of warbeasts. The two he had left weren't nearly enough.

They spent one more night in the jungle then around noon the next day the monkey said, "We're getting close."

Lord of the Dead closed his eyes and concentrated. He sensed a few powerful life forces not that far away. Strong as they were, none of them came even close to matching the dragonman they fought a couple of days ago.

If they were that weak, would they really be of any help?

He shook off the pointless question. He didn't have so many allies that he could afford to turn even one away. Even if it wasn't as strong as he would've preferred, inferior help was still better than no help at all.

They went another half a mile or so before the monkey stopped and said, "Wait here while I let the master know we've arrived."

Lord of the Dead had no time to reply before the monkey vanished into the jungle. He looked all around, but saw nothing resembling civilization. Had he been led into a trap?

No, that made no sense. If whoever this mysterious master was wanted them dead, the dragonman would've been more than capable of handling it. Guiding them to safety only to kill them now would be beyond foolish. He let out a little growl. Speculation was pointless. He just needed to be ready to deal with whatever came next. Trying to guess what it would be was a fool's errand.

After a mercifully short delay, their guide came swinging back. "The master is pleased that you're still alive and arrived so quickly. He wishes to speak with you at once."

"That suits me perfectly well. Please lead the way."

Without further discussion their guide began to retrace its steps, more slowly this time so Lord of the Dead had no trouble keeping up. The undergrowth grew gradually thicker then suddenly vanished. Ahead of them was a clearing in the center of which sat a collection of the largest monkeys he'd ever seen. And they were all different. In the center was what he assumed to be the leader, a massive gray brute that easily stood eight feet tall and had a silver band of hair running around its middle and down its back.

Flanking the gray monkey on the left sat an orange one with long hair and four arms, both sets of which were crossed over a massive belly. On the right was a smaller one with a lithe but still muscular build and black hair covering its body.

Giant monkeys, well, he shouldn't be surprised given that they sent a monkey for a guide. The trio certainly looked strong, though he could see nothing special about them in his magical vision. No doubt their considerable muscle was more than enough to deal with most problems they faced.

Lord of the Dead offered a polite nod and introduced himself. "Your servant tells me that you wish to make an alliance against the dragonmen. They're my enemies as well, so I'm happy to consider your proposal."

"You are well spoken for a human," the huge gray one said. "The tales passed down through our tribes say that humans are arrogant and foolish beings that look down on others as less than themselves. I am Throng, the leader of the Simeon Coalition."

"Pleasure to make your acquaintance." Lord of the Dead decided against pointing out that Throng spoke well for an oversized monkey. "If I may ask, when did your people last encounter humans?"

"It was many generations ago," Throng said. "Not long after the Goddess of Life gave birth to our people."

Lord of the Dead nodded. So, they thought of Lord Azteca as a goddess. Given the power of an Arcane Lord, that wasn't a hard mistake to make. "I see. It is true that some humans think less of those that look different from themselves. As you can see, I'm used to working with nonhumans, so that won't be an issue. May I ask a question?"

"Please do," Throng said.

"Thank you." It seemed that if Lord of the Dead wanted to recruit this battle fodder, he'd need to play the polite, humble part. He could do that. There were plenty of demons that liked to be flattered similarly. "I was wondering why you want to fight the dragonmen. You were both created by the Goddess of Life, were you not?"

"We were, but we came first and our legends say that the goddess said to the first of our kind that we were her finest creations. The dragonmen came after she sent us into the wild to build our tribes. They were the only strong ones to remain behind and serve her directly. It was an insult, but if that was her will, we could do nothing. Then the goddess vanished and the dragonmen claimed the city as their own, driving out the beastfolk slaves and preventing any others from approaching. Even we, the greatest of her creations, were denied access to the holy city."

"Did you not try to negotiate with them?" Lord of the Dead asked.

"We did. Many attempts at reason were made, but Skar would hear none of it. He said none but the dragonmen would be allowed to approach the holy temple." Throng gave a slow shake of his massive head. "And so it was decided by the tribes that our only choice was war."

"Unfortunate," Lord of the Dead said, trying to sound like he cared. "Please don't be offended, but it seems clear to me that your war isn't going especially well."

"No. The dragonmen are strong, stronger than us, though we have the advantage of numbers. It's a stalemate and has been for many generations. But with your help, perhaps that can change."

"In what way can I help?" Lord of the Dead asked.

"Your magic can make us stronger, can it not? With our numbers, even a small increase in our strength might be enough to turn the tide."

Lord of the Dead nodded. "I know some techniques that could make you stronger in battle. However, there's something I want in return."

"We assumed that this would be the case. What do you desire?"

"Somewhere in the city is a crimson orb." He held up the Rod of Terror for them to see. "It is the companion piece to the one I hold. I'll help you in exchange for that item."

"That is acceptable," Throng said at once. "None of us can use magic, so it will be of no value."

Lord of the Dead smiled. What wonderfully practical people. "Splendid. Do you have a plan for our assault?"

"You will make us stronger and we will attack."

Lord of the Dead stared for a moment. It seemed he was serious. "Even with my magic, taking on the entire group might not be wise. Is there some way we might separate them?"

"Skar is no fool. When my people intervened to allow you to escape, he will know that we are allies and will probably suspect a trap."

"Perhaps an attack and quick withdrawal, just to test the effectiveness of my magic. I noticed during the battle that dragonmen are good at resisting spells."

"That is not a bad idea. I would not have more of my people die than necessary. It is agreed. We will move closer to the city then you will make us stronger."

"Agreed."

Lord of the Dead smiled to himself. If he could use these creatures to gain access to the temple, or whatever the pyramid was, he would be happy to do so. Should most of them die in the process, so much the better. They would make fine warbeasts.

CHAPTER TWENTY-FOUR

Skar paced and snarled to himself. As leader of the dragonmen, he had a responsibility to protect Lord Azteca's palace, or more specifically, his bound father inside. Knowing his duty did nothing to make it easier to wait. The force he dispatched should have been more than enough to deal with the undead creature that infiltrated the city. Even Father didn't know where that thing came from. It just appeared one day out of nowhere.

It was beyond Skar's comprehension and what he didn't understand he... didn't fear exactly, Skar feared nothing, but it did make him nervous. Despite his current situation, there were few things Father didn't know. This was one of them.

He paused, turned, and looked over his troops. The lesser dragonmen lacked the intellect to speak, but they could carry out reasonably complex orders. They were also extremely durable, as expected of Lord Azteca's elite troops. All the same, he had trouble thinking of them as true brothers.

Not that his anger at losing one of them was in any way lessened. To think that the undead creature had strength enough to kill one of them. It had been a shock, no mistake about that.

Skar snapped his wings then forced himself to relax. Getting tense and angry would help nothing. The team would return when they returned.

He caught the scent of blood in the air. Speaking of, here they come now. The thought had barely formed when the team came running into the courtyard. At least they were all alive, though the greater dragonman he'd put in charge had a fairly deep wound on its thigh.

The squad leader, Gorr, hurried over to Skar and bowed, an awkward move with his thick, stubby tail. "The undead and its monsters followed us just as you said, Skar. I killed many of its beasts, but it fled before I could finish the job. Also, the Simeon Coalition helped them escape."

Skar snarled at that last bit. Just what he didn't need, his two greatest enemies joining forces. "What happened to your leg?"

"One of the undead's monsters bit through my scales. The wound is annoying at worst. I can still fight."

Skar nodded and clapped his subordinate on the shoulder. Gorr had done well under the circumstances. The fact that one of the undead's monsters somehow pierced his scales was a greater concern. The dragonmen's scales were so hard that a steel sword would slide right off without leaving a mark. The powerful defense allowed them to fight freely, confident that they were protected. But now, not only had one of them died, but even Gorr had been injured, though not seriously. It was a troubling turn of events.

"I'll speak with Father. Did you see which way the undead went?"

Gorr hung his head. "No, I was too busy fighting. Apologies, Skar."

"It is of no concern. I only hoped you might confirm my guess that it fled into Coalition territory. If those wretched apes interfered on its behalf, there's really nowhere else it might have gone."

"I will do better next time, Skar, I swear it."

"Don't be too hard on yourself. You brought your team back alive, that's the main thing. Keep an eye on your wound. If there's any trouble, we'll ask Father to take a look at it."

Gorr's tail quivered, a sure sign of anxiety. "I would not trouble Father over such a small thing."

Skar smiled. The others worshipped and feared Father in equal measure. Only Skar had spoken to him enough times to understand that while Father felt little for his children, he did want the best for them.

With a final pat on Gorr's shoulder, he left the courtyard. The palace door swung open at his approach and he immediately felt Father's regard moving over him. It was an unsettling feeling. Certainly he understood why the others felt like they were being observed by a god.

He stalked down undecorated stone passages, through rooms big enough to hold a battle, and finally descended a set of stairs to the lower level. With each step, the weight of Father's presence grew heavier.

At the bottom of the stairs, he turned right and took a short hall that ended at a black metal door. Skar steadied himself, wrapped his wings around his body like a cloak, and pushed the door open. Beyond it was a domed chamber nearly as big as the entire courtyard outside.

Father lay in the center, his green-scaled body fifty paces long not counting his tail. His wings were tight to his body.

Most remarkable of all, his massive form was bound to the floor by bands of silver metal. Despite his tremendous strength, Father couldn't break free. In truth, it was only in the last couple hundred years that he'd been able to speak directly to Skar's mind.

You have news?

Though he couldn't actually hear it, Father's voice felt deep and powerful in his mind. Like he could crush Skar flat with nothing else.

"Yes, Father. It seems the undead creature has gone to join forces with Throng."

Father let out a deep bass growl. *That is not the news I was hoping for but I suppose it is to be expected. Though far less than us, Throng is no fool. He will use the undead without hesitation if it gives him a chance at victory. Together they will be a threat far greater than any you have yet faced.*

Skar swallowed hard. "Can you offer me any advice, Father?"

Not with the information we currently have. Be cautious until you better understand their plans. You have led my children well, Skar, and I'm confident that you will see them safely through this crisis.

Father's confidence and warm regard filled Skar to bursting. He would succeed in this task. There was no question in his mind.

CHAPTER TWENTY-FIVE

Three days of traveling through the jungle with Throng's army—well, army might be overly generous given that the force numbered less than a hundred giant, mutated monkeys—brought them within a couple hour's march of the city. It was evening when they stopped. Since none of the creatures could see especially well in the dark, Throng said it was best to attack in the morning. That was fine with Lord of the Dead. Unlike vampires and certain sorts of lesser undead, his power remained undiminished in daylight.

Since they had some time before dark, Lord of the Dead picked his way through the giant monkeys relaxing under the trees as they ate some sort of fruit the size of his head. He'd never seen anything like it, but the monkeys seemed to thoroughly enjoy it. Better yet, it was common. Half the trees they passed under had clusters of it hanging from them like giant grapes. Foraging, at least, wouldn't be a problem.

He found Throng at the center of the gathering, stuffing his face with fruit. For something so big, it probably took a lot to keep his energy up. Beside him were the same two monkeys that were there for the first meeting. He'd come to think of them as a sort of honor guard.

Throng finished his final piece of fruit and said, "We will attack tomorrow. Have you decided how to use your magic to make us stronger?"

"That's what I wanted to talk to you about. In order to use my power to the best advantage, I need to understand more about how you fight."

Throng cocked his head as if he didn't understand the question. "We charge in and rip our enemies to pieces."

"You don't use any sort of weapons? Claws, for example."

Throng held up a hand so big it could've wrapped all the way around Lord of the Dead's head. The fingers were long and thick, but blunt with short fingernails much like a human's. Clearly Lord Azteca had been less than generous when handing out natural weapons to her so-called greatest creations.

"All are different, but none have claws," Throng said. "Is that a problem?"

"No, not at all. There are spells to make claws sharper and tougher, but that obviously won't work in your case. I should probably focus on making you stronger and faster. Maybe a defensive spell to make your hide tougher to penetrate."

"That all sounds useful," Throng said. "With your help, I will find Skar and rip his head from his body."

Lord of the Dead doubted it would go quite that smoothly, but he said nothing. No sense being negative before they even made the first strike. Maybe they'd get lucky and completely wipe out the dragonmen in the first attack. He certainly wouldn't complain about such a result.

"I'll need to apply the spells shortly before the battle and I can't cast them on everyone. You'll need to select your twenty favorites."

"So few?" Throng said. "I had hoped you could enhance everyone."

"Despite my considerable power, I'm still only one person. If I were to try and enhance everyone, I would end up doing so little for each individual that it would make no difference."

"I suppose that makes sense. Very well, when we reach the city wall, I will bring my best warriors to you."

Lord of the Dead nodded. "I will do my best to be worthy of them."

Throng's lips peeled back in what Lord of the Dead had come to recognize as a smile. "That is well. You are a good ally. The Goddess of Life smiled when she brought you to our territory."

He offered a polite bow in return. It was good that these naive fools lived in the jungle. No one so trusting would last a week in the real world.

The next morning Lord of the Dead and his allies of convenience reached the city wall. No one made any attempt to stop them at the ruined gate. Could the dragonmen be unaware of their arrival? It seemed impossible, but just to be sure he made contact with his imp.

Has there been any change?

No, Master. A small group arrived a few days ago. They were likely the survivors of your battle. Other than that, nothing of interest has happened.

Are they all in the courtyard?

Yes, Master.

You've done well. Continue to watch.

He severed the connection as Throng and his chosen twenty approached. It seemed the time had come to keep his end of the agreement. At the very least, Throng had chosen some exceedingly large specimens. Several had extra arms. One was completely hairless and looked a bit like an over-sized, exceptionally stupid human. They were a motley, but still-imposing group.

"We will attack as soon as you're finished," Throng said.

"Perfect. My spy says that all the dragonmen are gathered in the courtyard. It's possible that they don't even know we're here."

Throng shook his head. "They know. I don't know how, but they always know. No matter how quiet we are or how small a party approaches, Skar is always ready for us. My biggest hope is that even if he knows we're coming, he might not know about you."

Lord of the Dead considered that extremely unlikely. But whatever, it was time to start. "I settled on strength enhancements as well as vampiric healing. Whenever you kill an enemy, all your wounds will close."

Throng's deep-set eyes widened at that. "You didn't mention that ability. That will be a huge help."

Lord of the Dead didn't bother to point out that the way he planned to do this was to bind minor vampiric demons to their bodies and that when the time was right, they would do far more than perform the minor magic he just described.

He'd leave that as a surprise for later.

Drawing on the Rod of Terror's corrupt ether, he began the spells. Shadowy figures appeared and flew through Throng and his companions, settling into their bodies. He sensed the magic take hold and as far as he could tell, nothing about their souls had been damaged or altered.

"It's done."

"That was unpleasant. It felt like something cold and slimy wriggled into my body." Throng gave a full-body shudder.

That was a fairly accurate description of what had actually happened. "All power comes with a price. As such things go, you got off light. Now hurry and attack before the spell wears off."

Throng roared and pounded his chest so hard it sounded like war drums. Lord of the Dead turned away and put a hand over his face to hide the grimace. If the dragonmen hadn't known the enemy had arrived, they certainly knew now.

The giant monkeys charged through the gate roaring and hooting and raising an awful ruckus. Lord of the Dead followed at a more sedate pace. He had no intention of putting his life on the line to help the stupid creatures. If they won, great. If not, hopefully they at least took plenty of the dragonmen with them.

He sensed a faint life force approaching a moment before the monkey that served as his guide landed on his shoulder. "You should hurry and help."

"I've done all I can. It took every bit of power I could muster to enhance Throng and the warriors. If I tried to fight as I am now, I'd only get in the way. Why don't you go help?"

The monkey squeaked in a way Lord of the Dead took for a laugh. "Do I look like I'd be of any use in battle?"

It certainly had a point. "Then do you serve only as a guide?"

"I am Throng's herald," it said with considerable pride in its voice. "I am the only other one of our kind that has mastered speech."

"Why is that?"

"What do you mean, why?"

"I mean, surely it would be convenient for more of your people to speak."

"I see, you don't understand how it works. We are all born with different skills. No one taught me how to speak. I heard Throng and within days I could speak as well as him. That is the way the goddess made us."

That seemed rather arbitrary for an Arcane Lord, but clearly Azteca did what she did on purpose. As to why, he doubted anyone living could tell him.

A roar and a crash sounded from up ahead.

"It's begun," the little monkey said. "Hurry! There might be something we can do to help."

The last thing Lord of the Dead planned to do was hurry onto a battlefield. He only had two warbeasts left and was in no rush to lose them. "Go ahead if you wish. As I said, right now I'd be useless in battle."

"At least I can bear witness." The monkey leapt off his shoulder, climbed to the nearest roof, and leapt to the next one.

"Yes, I wish you much joy," he said to the creature's rapidly vanishing back. "Still, bearing witness might not be a bad idea."

He smashed his way into a convenient house and sat. "Keep watch."

His warbeasts went into guard mode and he focused on his imp. It took little effort to link their minds so he could observe as the battle unfolded.

CHAPTER TWENTY-SIX

Throng charged through the holy city at the head of his army. It was his duty to lead his people well and he tried his best. Sometimes he wasn't sure what the right decision was, like trusting the human. The strange, slimy magic still writhed around in his body. He did feel a bit stronger, but it was hard to tell just running.

He set his doubts aside. They were always there, but he couldn't let them be a distraction during the fight. He'd made his choice and he and his people would live or die with it. That was what it meant to be leader. How he wished the goddess hadn't bestowed the blessing of speech on him.

Ahead, the courtyard loomed. As always, Skar and his dragonmen would wait for Throng and his warriors to arrive. It was as if the rest of the holy city didn't matter to them. Throng felt certain that if he and his clan moved into the stone houses, Skar wouldn't care. But the holy temple, the place of their birth, that was where he drew the line.

Familiar rage filled Throng. What right did the dragonmen have to deny his people access to the place they were born? It was their right! He believed that with all his might. And Throng would use that might to force Skar to give way.

He found the dragonmen waiting, just as he knew he would.

Roaring, Throng leapt at the nearest enemy, a tailless lesser, and swung with all his might. His fist crashed into the dragonman's head and sent it flying across the courtyard.

All around him, Throng's warriors were battling the hated enemy. Roars and shrieks loud enough to deafen anyone with the misfortune of listening filled the air.

Throng's blood ran hot and he looked for Skar. If he could take out the enemy leader, it would make the battle much easier. His momentary lapse in concentration cost him. One of the lesser dragonmen leapt on Throng and ripped its claws down his back, shredding muscle, fur, and skin with equal ease.

Howling in pain, Throng grabbed the dragonman by the neck and slammed it to the ground. A sharp twist snapped its neck. A moment later energy flowed into him and the pain in his back vanished. For all his doubts, it seemed the human's magic did what he claimed. In fact, beyond being healed, Throng felt even stronger than before. As if a piece of the dragonman he'd killed stayed behind and lent him its power.

They could do this. He would do this.

A blast of heat washed over him as flames bathed the battlefield. He traced them back to the source and found Skar breathing orange fire across the battlefield. The dragonmen were unbothered by the heat, but Throng's people howled and thrashed as they burned. And there wasn't a thing Throng could do to help them.

Aside from killing Skar.

As soon as the flames stopped, Throng charged across the

battlefield, his enhanced strength sending anything that got in his way flying.

"Skar!"

He leapt and caught a hard blow from Skar's tail for his trouble.

Staggering from the unexpected blow, he wasn't ready for the slashing claw that opened his chest. Blood flowed from the shallow wound.

Enraged, Throng swung a heavy fist at Skar's head.

The dragonman ducked under it and slashed again, opening a deeper wound in Throng's side. Skar looked at him with pity in his eyes.

Pity! He dared to look down on Throng and his people, the greatest of the goddess's creations. He would suffer for his arrogance.

Throng swung both fists.

And Skar caught them with ease. Struggle as he might, Throng couldn't free his hands.

"Why must we do this every generation?" Skar sounded both sad and tired. "You can't beat my dragonmen. It's a pointless exercise that accomplishes nothing beyond ending the lives of both our peoples."

"We are the goddess's greatest creation," Throng panted through the pain. "Yet you deny us access to her holy temple. It's wrong."

"You poor, stupid monkey. Your kind weren't her greatest creation. You were her greatest creation at the time. And when she was finished with you, she discarded you, took what she learned, and made us. You were never more than a step in the process."

Throng's heart lurched. Skar's words hurt worse than any wound. All the more so because they held the ring of truth.

Did the goddess truly think of his people as no more than trash to be discarded? It certainly explained why she sent them out into the jungle but kept the dragonmen with her in the holy city.

"I see you have accepted the truth," Skar said. "It's a hard thing. Take comfort in knowing that you won't have to live with the knowledge for long."

Skar opened his mouth and flames came roaring out into Throng's face. Through the pain he thought maybe death wouldn't be such a bad thing. Even burning alive hurt less than knowing what the goddess truly thought about his people.

Something small and furred slammed into Skar from the side, jarring his grip loose. "Go, Throng! Survive and avenge our people."

"Herald?"

"Go!"

The tiny one scrabbled all over Skar's face and neck, his tiny fingers useless against the dragonman's impenetrable scales.

Fighting through his pain, Throng turned and ran. He couldn't help his dead and dying soldiers. Flames and claws had done them in, just as they always did. He'd been a fool to bring them here to die, fighting to claim a temple to one that thought nothing of them.

Throng made it out of the courtyard and half ran, half stumbled into the city. He had no idea where he was going, but he was determined to survive. He had lost one purpose and gained another. If he wasn't worthy of the goddess's love, he would see the entire miserable city reduced to rubble.

〇

Skar finally got ahold of the tiny monkey crawling all over him and twisted its head off. He tossed the corpse aside and surveyed the battlefield. His dragonmen had emerged victorious, just as they always did. The enemies were simply too weak to have a chance of defeating them. The battle was a useless, pointless waste of time and life. His gaze landed on the unmoving form of one of his dragonmen.

So they'd managed to kill one. It happened once in a while. He'd now lost five lesser dragonmen over the centuries of his watch. It was a great loss, especially since dragonmen, unlike all of Lord Azteca's other creations, couldn't reproduce on their own. Much like Father, only fate and the whim of the ether allowed a dragonman to produce an egg. In all of his long life, Skar had only seen it happen twice, both times with lesser forms of his people. And while he wouldn't mind increasing their numbers, having seen the excruciating pain involved, he wasn't eager to do his part.

Gorr came trotting over. He'd acquired a couple more minor wounds during the battle, but nothing that wouldn't heal in a few days. "It's over, Skar. The last of the invaders is slain."

Skar looked around and frowned. There was no sign of Throng's massive form. Despite the wounds and burns, somehow he'd escaped. The monkeys were exceptionally durable if not terribly bright. He couldn't have gotten far. Best to hunt him down and end it once and for all.

"Take two of the lesser dragonmen and hunt Throng down. He can't have gotten far."

"I'll bring you back his head." Gorr hurried away, eager as always to prove his loyalty and worth. He was a useful subordinate, but as limited in his own way as Throng and his people.

Skar's frown twisted into a bitter smile. Did Father feel this way when he was forced to deal with Skar, someone so much less than he was? The thought twisted his guts, but it felt like the truth all the same.

He took some small comfort in the fact that, no matter what he might have thought, Father never treated him with contempt. He didn't treat him as an equal either, but then Skar wasn't arrogant enough to imagine he was Father's equal, so that didn't bother him much.

Shaking off the useless thoughts he said, "Let's get this mess cleaned up. There's enough meat for a while here, so get it into storage."

The others hastened to get to work. They were incredibly tough and nothing less than a thorough maiming would keep them down for long. It never ceased to amaze him.

It seemed they'd barely gotten started when one of the lesser dragonmen gave a shout and staggered away from the body he was dragging.

Curious, Skar strode over. "What is it?"

He asked out of reflex. The lesser dragonmen couldn't speak after all. When he reached the corpse, he looked down. There didn't seem to be anything remarkable about it. The orange fur was charred from Skar's fire and one of its four arms had been ripped off, but other than that it seemed perfectly ordinary.

Or so he thought until it moved. The arms and legs twitched though the face remained completely lifeless. Unsteady hands grasped his ankles and when Skar tried to pull away, he found the thing's grip even stronger than when it was alive.

Another roar of surprise sounded and when Skar glanced that way he found more of the corpses rising. One of the lesser dragonmen was dragged to the ground and three of the bodies leapt on him.

Skar finally freed himself and shouted, "Fall back to the palace!"

The others hastened to obey his command. When they'd all gathered in front of the entrance, one of the greater dragonmen, Skar didn't catch which, asked, "What do we do? They're already dead."

The usually unflappable dragonmen were panicking and if Skar didn't come up with a plan soon, he'd lose any chance he had of counterattacking.

Calm yourselves, my children. Father's voice rang in Skar's and he assumed the others' heads. *You need to dismember the bodies so they can't move anymore. Once that's done you can burn them to ash.*

Father's timely intervention calmed everyone. Across the courtyard, twenty out of the hundred dead had risen and they stood facing Skar. Now that he knew what to do, he could lead the others.

Whatever evil magic had caused this, they couldn't lose to it.

CHAPTER TWENTY-SEVEN

Lord of the Dead watched the failed assault through his imp's eyes. He wasn't especially surprised the oversized monkeys had lost. Most of them were little stronger than his warbeasts and they'd failed miserably against just one of the tailed dragonmen. When the last of them fell, he sent a surge of corrupt ether out into the spirits he'd bound to the chosen twenty. Warbeasts had already proven useless. It was time to try Astaroth's specialty: undead.

It would take a couple of minutes for the transformation to complete. The shock of seeing the corpses move would hopefully buy them enough time to finish.

He sensed a single, faltering life force headed his way. Curious, he left the magic to run its course and stepped out into the street. A badly charred and wounded Throng was stumbling along toward him.

The leader of the monkeys staggered to his knees a few feet from Lord of the Dead. "Friend. Can you help me?"

"I can't," Lord of the Dead said, a new plan already forming. "But my master can. Tell me what you desire."

"I want power! Power enough to slaughter Skar and his cursed dragonmen. Power enough to reduce this city to gravel."

Lord of the Dead smiled. This was perfect. The desperate fool had no idea what he was asking for. "Astaroth will be pleased with your desire. Know that power has a price. Are you willing to pay it?"

"I will pay any price your master requires."

"Even your soul?"

"Any price."

Throng was gasping, his words slurred. They didn't have long now.

"Then we will pray together. When you hear Astaroth's voice, pledge your soul to him and you will have the power you desire." Though certainly not in the form he might desire.

Lord of the Dead bowed his head and drew on the rod's magic. "Great Astaroth, I bring you the soul of one who would serve you for all eternity. Grant him the power he seeks that we may work together to destroy those who stand in the way of us completing your great task."

The full weight of Astaroth's regard fell on them and even Lord of the Dead felt a moment of fear. It passed quickly and when Throng said, "My soul is yours, Great One," he was ready.

To get something from Hell, you needed to make a sacrifice and few things were as powerful as a soul freely given.

When Astaroth's power came streaming through, Lord of the Dead seized control of it. First he used the bulk of the corrupt energy to turn Throng into something far more useful than the broken husk he'd been reduced to. The remainder he sent out into the city, raising the fallen as zombies.

He'd barely used up the last of Astaroth's power when he sensed three potent sources of life force approaching. A group of dragonmen rounded the corner. There were two of the tailless ones led by one with a tail. Was it the same one he'd found earlier? Possible, but in the end they all looked the same to Lord of the Dead.

"Throng!" the tailed dragonman said. "Your life ends here."

Little did the fool know that Throng's life had already ended a few minutes ago.

"You wanted to kill them all," Lord of the Dead said. "Here's your chance to get started."

Throng roared, beat his chest just like he'd done when he was alive and charged. Now that he was undead, Lord of the Dead had many more options when it came to enhancement magic. He increased Throng's strength and also surrounded his fists with a necrotic aura. How effective the latter would be he didn't know, but it couldn't hurt.

Throng hit the dragonmen like a battering ram, sending them flying in all directions. A single blow from a massive black fist crushed the skull of a tailless dragonman. The necrotic aura absorbed his departing life force and made Throng even stronger.

As his newest servant slaughtered the dragonmen, Lord of the Dead studied his new form. While it was unique, it did have a lot in common with an undead juggernaut, a powerful sort of undead that he'd never succeeded in creating. Truly Astaroth had guided his hand this day.

"You!" the tailed dragonman shouted as he stared at Lord

of the Dead. "You're responsible for all this, aren't you? I'll kill you!"

The dragonman charged at Lord of the Dead. His warbeasts shifted to block its attack. For all the good they did. The monster was only slowed for the half a second it took to throw them out of the way.

But that was enough for Throng to come up behind it and crush its skull with a two-fisted overhead smash. More life force was absorbed by the spell Lord of the Dead had cast.

Now that the threat had been dealt with, he took the extra strength as well as the captured life force back. It would be an excellent resource as he built up his forces.

Speaking of, he should check on the new thralls. Following the link to his imp, he soon found his gaze filled with the courtyard. His thralls were facing down the dragon-men, who had reformed their ranks in front of the palace door. Pity they hadn't broken completely, but that had probably been too much to hope for.

"What have I become?" Throng asked, the confusion in his voice clear.

Lord of the Dead didn't have time to discuss it at the moment. "Something of greater use to Astaroth. Now be quiet, I need to concentrate."

Drawing on the stolen life force, Lord of the Dead sent corrupt ether out into the dead bodies, completing their resurrection as zombies. Slow, weak, and stupid, zombies were some of the most useless undead, but they did look just like proper thralls. Eighty more foes would hopefully be enough to break the enemy's will.

○

Any second Skar expected to be attacked by the creatures—he refused to think of them as honorable if foolish enemies at this point. He hastened to get his surviving warriors in order. Twenty enemies, even if they were stronger now, would still be no match for his dragonmen.

"Skar, look."

Someone interrupted his planning. He spun and his heart sank. The rest of the dead were rising. One after another they stood until Skar faced not twenty but one hundred of these new enemies. It was too much, even for them.

"We can't win, Father."

Bring everyone inside. Azteca's wards will protect us for now. Once everyone is inside, come see me. There's much we must discuss.

Skar hastened to obey. He yanked the palace gate open. "Everyone inside."

They hesitated. Usually only Skar was allowed into the palace.

"Now!"

He grabbed the nearest lesser dragonman and shoved him through the gate. When he wasn't immediately struck down, the rest rushed to follow.

Skar was about to join them when he remembered Gorr was still out in the city.

He's already dead. Hurry and seal the palace.

Skar winced as he stepped inside and threw a heavy beam across the gate. Gorr had been a good soldier and the closest thing Skar had to a friend. Losing him was a blow, both to the palace's defense and to Skar personally.

He shoved the pain aside for now. "Everyone stay here. I need to talk to Father."

"What about those things?" one of the greater dragonmen asked.

"Father says Azteca's magic will keep them out. Have no fear. As long as you stay calm and don't try to go outside, we'll be fine."

He didn't know if they believed him, but no one else spoke. Leaving them in the entry hall, Skar made the familiar journey to the underground chamber where Father waited. The bound dragon shifted as much as his silver chains would allow and focused his yellow eye on Skar.

The threat ended up being worse than I feared. You will have to take shelter here until help arrives.

Skar stared for a moment, uncomprehending. "Help? I don't understand."

Soon one will arrive in this land with the power to free me from my bonds. The price will be high, I'm sure, but whatever he wants, we will give it to him.

"Who is it? And how do you know this person will free you?"

I don't know who he is, but I have sensed the approach of a powerful wizard, the strongest I've encountered since Azteca and her fellows bound me here. The only reason I can imagine for such a person to come here is a desire to claim her magic. Since we are the guardians of that magic, he will have no choice but to bargain with us for access. He will also have to help defeat our enemies if he wants to safely come and go.

"What if you're wrong? Is there some other way to defeat the creatures outside?"

Father blew out a breath. *If I'm wrong, it likely means the one I sense is an ally of the ones outside. If that's the case, we're doomed. As for defeating them on our own, we lack the necessary resources. Azteca never kept much in the way of weapons around, unfortunately for us.*

Skar didn't like the idea of having to rely on others, but having seen the strength of the creatures outside, he had no choice but to accept Father's words.

"Very well. What must I do?"

Behind me there's a passage you've never explored. Follow it. It's quite large, but at the far end, it's been sealed. You need to open it up and bring the wizard in that way so you can avoid the enemy. Have your brothers begin digging it out so it will be ready when you get back.

Skar's throat tightened. "Where am I going?"

To guide the wizard here. You're the only one intelligent enough to speak with him and be convincing. None of your brothers have what it takes to get him to agree.

He'd been afraid that was what Father planned. Much as he hated leaving the others behind, they should be okay as long as all they needed to do was dig out a tunnel. "Will the meat stockpile last long enough?"

You ask that like there's some other option. You are all of my blood. Dragons can go a long time without food when necessary. You lot should be able to as well.

It seemed there was no getting around it. "I will, of course, do as you command. But is there some way for me to get past the enemies surrounding the palace?"

There is no easy way. You will have to sneak out the servants' exit. I can make you invisible to the undead for a short time. Be sure you're well away when the magic wears off. Get the others ready. They have never seen me, so when you bring them here, it will likely be a shock. The best time for you to leave will be high sun. So you have until then to make preparations.

Skar hated to keep pestering Father with questions, but

there was one more thing he needed to know. "How will I find this wizard?"

You will have to figure that out on your own. He will likely be headed toward the city from the east. At least I assume so based on where I sense he'll arrive. Unfortunately, while I can get a vague sense of his location, that's not something I can share with you. As the greatest of my children, I'm confident that you'll succeed.

Skar very much appreciated Father's confidence in him, he just wished he shared it.

CHAPTER TWENTY-EIGHT

Lord of the Dead strode through the silent city with the undead juggernaut version of Throng stomping along behind him. He'd watched the dragonmen retreat into Azteca's palace through his imp's eyes. His undead now fully controlled the courtyard and had the palace surrounded. Since they didn't need to eat or sleep, starving out the living dragonmen should be a simple, if tedious process. Assuming that Lord of the Dead couldn't hasten the process a bit.

The pair reached the courtyard without issue and the undead parted to let them pass. When he reached the closed gate, Lord of the Dead shifted his vision to the ether and sure enough found a powerful ward in effect. The complexity of it defied his effort at analysis. Sometimes it was easiest to get answers directly.

He reached out and rested a single finger on the gate.

An instant later his finger was shorter by half an inch and pain like he hadn't felt in centuries racked his body.

Luckily only for a second, then he was back to normal,

minus some of his finger of course. Drawing on the corrupt power of the rod he regenerated the damage in an instant.

"So, definitely an anti-undead ward," he muttered to himself.

And it was as powerful as only magic cast by an Arcane Lord could be. Even with the rod boosting his power, there was no way Lord of the Dead was forcing himself through there. No, it was the long, sure path for them.

"What now?" Throng asked.

"Now, I'm going to upgrade all my zombies into something actually useful. Once that's done, you will show me to your people's villages. Once they've been transformed into undead, we'll have an excellent start on my army."

"My people must be left in peace," Throng said. "It is the warriors' duty to fight. The rest must be safe so they can raise the next generation."

Lord of the Dead shook his head. Did this fool truly not understand what becoming a servant of Astaroth meant?

"No. You see, it is Astaroth's will that I build an empire of the dead in this place. Your tribes will only be the beginning. Before we're finished, every living thing will die and rise again as a minion of our master."

He felt Throng's rage and desire to smash him flat. Of course, he couldn't do that. The process that transformed him also left him incapable of defying Lord of the Dead's will. Poor stupid beast, letting his anger overwhelm his intellect, limited as it might be. Still, Lord of the Dead wouldn't complain about gaining such a powerful new servant.

Putting Throng and his foolishness out of his mind, Lord of the Dead got to work. He had enough life force stored in the rod to transform about half the zombies into proper thralls. That should be plenty to keep the dragonmen in check, especially since he doubted they could tell one from the other.

He smiled to himself as he began to cast. It felt good to finally be making real progress on his mission.

☾

Skar had never been afraid of anything, other than Father of course, but the thought of sneaking out of the palace and avoiding all the monsters guarding the area terrified him. Not so much the danger, but the fact that likely all of his brothers and maybe even Father would die if he failed in his mission. That was something he couldn't live with. Not that he imagined he'd live very long should he be caught by the hoard of creatures outside.

And so he paced and fretted in Father's chambers as he waited for the appointed hour to arrive. The only minor distractions were Father's deep breaths and the crunching of the workers as they dug out the tunnel. How Skar had missed the massive passage all these years was another matter, one he preferred not think about. Just getting past the encircling force would be a challenge, even if he was invisible. They were bound to see the servant's door open after all.

Calm yourself. I will arrange a distraction when it's time for you to go. Just focus on finding the wizard and bringing him to the tunnel.

"Yes, Father." Skar hesitated before asking, "Can you not give me some hint as to what he looks like? I would hate to bring the wrong person."

He's human. In that regard he's probably the rarest individual in Aztecaland. Should you find a male human wizard,

170

bring him. The odds of you finding the wrong one hardly bear consideration.

What Father said was true, though Skar had never thought about it before. Azteca hadn't allowed normal humans to live here. Or maybe it was more accurate to say that normal humans couldn't live here. They were just too weak to survive.

Time seemed to drag on forever. Anxious as he was, at this point, Skar wanted to get it over with. When Father said he was ready, the announcement came as a great relief.

Do not open the door until I tell you. Good luck, my son.

A tingle ran through Skar as Father's magic settled over him. He looked down at himself, but there was no change in his appearance. He swallowed hard and made his way back up to the first floor of the palace. The few orders he had to give had been given. The others would obey Father without question so there was no need to worry on that account.

He passed through the palace's massive kitchen and sniffed. Even from a distance he could smell the meat that filled the cold room. It was always kept filled for emergencies just like this one. It would take months for them to get into serious food trouble. Skar offered a silent prayer to any watching archangel that he'd be back with the wizard long before that happened.

An explosion shook the palace.

GO!

Father's voice slammed into his mind with such force he had no time to even think about what he was about to do. Skar slipped out the door, closed it tightly behind him, and sprinted across the courtyard.

A few yards from the wall he leapt and snapped his wings. He cleared the top with inches to spare before gliding down out of the city. When he landed he stopped to listen. No sign of pursuit. Good. Father's distraction must have kept them busy.

Now to put as much distance between himself and the city as possible before dark. Then it was just a matter of finding a single human somewhere in Aztecaland. It sounded like a far more daunting task all of a sudden.

But he would complete it no matter what.

CHAPTER TWENTY-NINE

Crossing the Eastern Ocean for the second time turned out to be every bit as tedious and mind-numbing as it was the first. Otto at least had some books to occupy his mind. He also enjoyed a number of pleasant conversations with Lady White. Corina divided her time between playing cards with the guys and practicing her magic. Otto never asked, but he felt certain his comment about a wizard's training never truly ending spurred her to resume her studies. The biggest surprise had been Jet. She had been an ideal servant, never uttering a word of complaint. Lady White was both surprised and pleased.

But now they had come to the end of the nearly three-month journey and land was in sight. It was time for Otto to find them a place to go ashore. The first part of the job was fairly easy. He dug the scrying crystal out of its padded storage box, and settled down with it on his lap. That was far from his preferred way of using it, but there was nowhere else secure enough to place it on the constantly rocking ship.

He charged the crystal with ether then stared into the

smooth surface. Soon a distorted image of the ship appeared as if from a bird's point of view. Okay, now to check the coast.

An effort of will shifted the view east until he was looking down at the bleakest stretch of cliffs and jungle he'd ever seen. There was no way the team could land around here. Mountain goats would have trouble climbing that cliff.

He shifted south and found nothing but miles and miles of the same wilderness. And then the cliff vanished and he found a modest cove. Nothing huge, certainly compared to Crystal City's port, but there was a dock and a small village. He poured more ether into the crystal in the hopes that he might get a clearer view of the tiny figures moving around. When it started to vibrate he stopped. It seemed this was the best the long-range scrying crystal could do.

Frowning, Otto pulled the ether back out and the image vanished. Everything he'd read indicated that Aztecaland had no settlements and certainly no ports. And while he wasn't sure the tiny village counted as a port, it was a settlement of sorts. As always it seemed his many-centuries-old information was less up to date than he would've liked.

When the crystal was once more secure in its case, he stood and stepped out into the narrow hall outside his cabin. He'd barely taken a step when Corina came running out of the hold. Either she had excellent hearing, or she'd been listening for him.

"Do you need anything, Master?"

"No. I'm going to speak with the captain. I found us a place to land."

"That's great. Everyone wants off the ship in the worst way."

"I estimate we'll be in sight of it in a day or so. Let them know if there's anything they need to pack up, they should think about doing it soon."

"Yes, Master."

She ran back the way she'd come and Otto continued on the staircase that led up to the main deck. Sailors were busy attending to their duties, many of which were less comprehensible to Otto than a complex magical ritual. Captain Coleman was manning the helm himself. Otto angled that way, enjoying the fresh sea breeze as he walked.

The trip had been remarkably issue free. A couple of modest storms being the main problems and even they didn't cause any noticeable damage beyond a couple severed lines. The trip had gone so well that, if Otto had been a superstitious man, he would've feared they'd have to pay for it on land. There'd be plenty of problems on land, he felt certain, they just wouldn't have anything to do with the good weather.

He reached the helm and Captain Coleman offered a nod of greeting. "Lord Shenk. Is all well?"

"Indeed, I found a place for us to go ashore. A small village with a dock. I'm uncertain if it's big enough for the *Sea Star*. When we get within sight, I'll let you make the call. With any luck, we can make a deal with whoever's in charge to allow you to stay in port until we finish our mission."

"That would be welcome. A bit of shore leave would do the men good and fresh food wouldn't go amiss. Your preserved magic food will keep a man alive and working, but it gets monotonous."

Otto couldn't argue with that. After weeks of eating nothing save the slightly sweet biscuits, he'd begun to envy Lady White's undead nature. "You'll need to bear a bit further south. I estimate the port will be visible tomorrow."

The captain adjusted his course a fraction. "That soon? Praise heaven. Do you want us to sail right in, assuming it looks viable?"

"No, better if I take a smaller group ashore to speak with whoever's in charge. The entire village didn't look like it could muster a defense that would trouble me, but peaceful contact is preferable." It might also net him some valuable information, which couldn't be overlooked.

"I second that, my lord. We'll heave to well offshore. Close enough so they can see us, but not so close they might think we're a threat."

"I leave that to your discretion. Send someone down to get me when we're almost ready. I need to make some final plans and pack up."

Coleman nodded again. "Yes, my lord."

Otto turned back toward the stairs but only made it halfway across the deck when Lady White called out, "Otto, do you have a moment?"

He hadn't even noticed her on deck, but quickly spotted her crossing over to join him. "Of course. What's on your mind? Somehow I doubt you're up here to enjoy the fresh air."

"No, fresh air is a good deal less interesting to someone that doesn't need to breathe. I came up because I could sense, distantly, Astaroth's power. We're pretty close to the secret he's keeping from me."

"Is it Lord of the Dead?"

"Impossible to tell from here. His magic is no different, at least in how it feels, from any other priest. I won't be able to tell anything for sure until I'm within about a mile or so. Still, I can't imagine it being anyone else. What I'm most curious about is how he got the power boost. I shouldn't be able to sense his magic at all from this distance."

"I suppose you're hoping to seize it for yourself."

She smiled a dazzling white smile. An undead shouldn't be that beautiful. "Naturally. It would be of no use to anyone save a priest of Astaroth, so it's not like you could use it even if you wanted to."

"Don't misunderstand, I'm not complaining. Anything that makes my allies stronger, makes me stronger as well. That's not a bad thing."

"You would still trust me even if my strength increased?" She sounded doubtful, but in the end, Otto knew her true name and had the amulet Lord Karonin had helped him prepare on the off chance she found a way to betray him despite her oath.

"I do. You made your oath to me on your true name. In all the time we've been together, you've done nothing to make me doubt your loyalty. I can't see that changing if you get stronger."

She put a cool hand on his shoulder. "You are so different from the other priests in the Land of the Demon Binders. I'm reminded once again why I'm glad I left."

Otto nodded. He was glad she left as well. Lady White had proven a useful member of the team as well as an interesting partner for conversation. Her understanding of magic and how it worked was very different from his. He valued the change of perspective.

"We should reach a small port village sometime tomorrow. If you have preparations to make, you should get started."

"I need very little. Fifteen minutes' notice and I'll be ready."

"Excellent. If you'll excuse me, I need to talk to my brother."

Otto left Lady White on deck and resumed his walk to the stairs. He found Corina waiting, a little frown creasing her face.

"Something on your mind?" he asked.

"She's trying to seduce you. Did you notice the way she smiled and put her hand on your shoulder? I don't trust her."

"She's not trying to seduce me. Lady White is undead. I doubt such a thing is even possible. As far as I can tell she simply appreciates being treated with a bit of kindness. It seems rare enough in the circles she used to travel in. Did you let everyone know we were getting close to our destination?"

Corina shot one more venomous look at Lady White then said, "Yeah, everyone was thrilled."

"We'll see how long that lasts when we enter the jungle." Otto stepped past Corina. "I need to talk to Axel."

"I'll come along." When Otto didn't object, she fell in beside him.

It wasn't a long walk to the hold. The large, open space had been converted into a barracks filled with hammocks rather than cots. Hundreds of crates and casks filled with water and supplies covered the floor. A bunch of the crates had been pushed together to make tables where the men were playing cards.

Hans spotted him as he entered and hastened to stand. "Lord Shenk. Corina said we were close to our destination. Do you have any orders for us?"

"Only to make whatever preparations you need to." Otto caught Axel's eye and motioned him over. "Hans, you can join us as well."

The four of them moved a little ways away and Axel asked, "What's on your mind?"

"It seems there's a village built around a modest port. My hope is to make peaceful contact and get a feel for the local situation. I had no expectation of finding anything even vaguely like civilization. My thought was to take a small advance team to make contact. Hans, you and the guys will handle security. Axel, I want you with me when we talk to whoever's in charge. I doubt magic will be an issue, but Corina will join us as well to help me keep an eye out for any wizardly mischief."

Corina lit up when he said she'd be coming along. He'd have thought at this point she'd be over the whole eager-to-please stage, but it seemed he was mistaken.

"We'll be ready," Hans said. "Should we leave our gear behind?"

"Everything but your weapons. Axel's scouts can bring our stuff once we've completed the negotiations."

"Think they'll be reasonable?" Axel asked.

"I hope so, for their sake. I didn't come all this way to wipe out a piddling village, but if that's what needs to happen to secure us a landing..." Otto shrugged. Keeping the empire safe was all that mattered to him. The wellbeing of the rest of the world didn't interest him in the least.

CHAPTER THIRTY

Midmorning the day after discovering the port village found Otto standing on deck staring out over the water. He had his mithril sword as well as the black iron dagger that he always wore. All his other gear was packed up and in the hold with Axel's scouts.

If he squinted, he could just make out the buildings not far from the water's edge. Captain Coleman was guiding the ship closer, but soon enough they would drop anchor then it would be up to Otto and his companions to make arrangements for their safe approach.

Otto had been thinking off and on how best to manage that, but in the end, until he found out what sort of people called the village home, there was no way to say for sure. It would please him tremendously to find a group of calm, good-natured people eager to meet with others from the outside world. If they were generous with their information, that wouldn't hurt his feelings either.

His lips twisted in a faint, humorless smile. It would be equally nice if he could learn how to fly so he could soar over the miserable jungle right to the capital. But neither seemed likely.

The ship changed course and Coleman bellowed orders to take down the sails. Their progress slowed until they stopped, then the anchor splashed into the water. It seemed this was as close as the good captain wanted to get. That was fine with Otto. He put them at about half a mile from shore. Rowing that far shouldn't be an issue. Not that he would be the one doing the rowing.

As the sailors worked, Coleman left his post at the helm and headed for Otto. When he arrived Otto quirked an eyebrow. "Captain?"

"Will you be needing a rowing crew, my lord?"

"No, my guards can manage that. If there's danger, the fewer people they need to protect, the better."

"Understood." Coleman visibly relaxed. "There was one other thing. If you could gauge the depth of the water as you approach the dock, it will help me know whether it's safe to take the ship in. There's a sounding line on the dinghy already."

"I'm unfamiliar with the process."

"It's simple. The line is knotted every three feet and has a weight on one end. You just need to drop the weight over the side and see how deep the water is. Checking it every couple hundred yards is fine. If it's deeper than our draft, we can go in. If it's not, we can't. Simple."

"I don't intend to stop multiple times on our way in, but if all goes well, we can do it on the way back."

"Perfect. Many thanks, my lord."

Otto nodded absently as he noticed Hans and the others emerging from below. Good, it was time to get this mission started. He left the rear castle and strode across the deck to where the others had gathered beside the dinghy.

"Climb in, we're leaving. Hans, pick four men to row." Otto motioned the others to get aboard.

They'd barely settled in when a quartet of sailors arrived to man the ropes that would lower them to the water.

"What should I do?" Corina asked as they descended.

"Watch the water. Lord Azteca was well known for creating mutated beasts. I have no idea if she worked on aquatic creatures, but I'd just as soon not have any of them take us by surprise. Everyone not rowing should keep watch as well."

Axel snorted a laugh. "After you mentioned water beasts, I can assure you, no one is going to be looking anywhere else."

That was just fine with Otto. He hadn't been kidding about the potential danger and he really didn't know what might be swimming around here. Hopefully nothing eager to make a meal of them, but damned if he was going to lose anyone this early in the mission.

They hit the water and Hans's chosen men got busy rowing. Otto closed his eyes and spread a ring of threads around the boat. If anything bigger than a trout passed through it, he'd know at once. The steady splashing of the oars and the creak of wood heralded the passage of time.

Otto was only vaguely aware of anything beyond the magic until Corina touched his shoulder. "We're about a hundred feet out, Master."

He let the spell fade and opened his eyes. The dock was only a little ways away and no welcoming committee awaited them. That was disappointing. He'd hoped that at least one person would have the guts to talk with them. On the plus side, at least there wasn't an armed force waiting to try and stop them from tying up at the dock. That would've been an even bigger problem.

The front of the dinghy thunked into the piling and Axel leapt out. He quickly tied the boat up with a heavy rope and everyone climbed onto the pier. Otto wobbled for a moment as he got used to standing on a surface that wasn't moving. Yet another thing he hated about ocean travel.

"Well, let's go knock on someone's door." Otto took a step toward the village and the guys immediately fell in around him with Hans at his right hand. At least they didn't draw their weapons. He was trying to make peaceful contact here after all.

The nearest building was little more than a hut made of timbers and mud. The roof was covered with some sort of large, thick leaves and the door consisted of a curtain hung across the opening.

"Hello?" Otto called. "Is anyone here? I'd like to speak with your leader if possible."

A minute passed with no response. He debated pulling the curtain open and taking a look, but decided against it. That was the sort of thing that could lead to a serious misunderstanding.

He left the first hut and moved deeper into the village. It was dead silent.

"Why don't they have a wall?" Axel asked. "If the jungle is so dangerous, you'd think they'd want something to keep the local critters out."

Otto hadn't given it much thought, but Axel had a point. Very little about the situation made sense. Whoever lived here couldn't be so foolish as to think Otto would just leave if they ignored him. Of course, if there was no wall and no guards, they could just go on their way, but Otto really wanted some intel and permission for the sailors to come ashore.

They reached an open space in the middle of town that he took as the village square. Looked like as good a place as any.

"You might want to cover your ears." After drawing ether into his throat and mouth Otto took a deep breath. "We're not leaving! We mean you no harm! Come out so we can talk!"

The words thundered through the village and Otto wouldn't have been surprised if they were heard on the ship. He didn't care. One way or another, he meant to get someone's attention.

"Subtle, little brother," Axel said.

"I tried subtle already and it didn't work. It's time to be a bit more aggressive."

"Lord Shenk," Hans said.

He turned to find the doorway of one of the nearby huts open and a wizened, bent-over figure shuffling out. The villager wore only a crude shift of rough, coarse cloth. What really caught Otto's attention was the slightly elongated muzzle and furry, rounded ears poking up out of his... her... he wasn't sure's head. This person, assuming that was the right word, had to be descended from one of Lord Azteca's creations.

The villager stopped a few feet away and stared at them with large, rather yellow eyes. "No human has ever visited our village. Why have you come?"

"Someone from Aztecaland sent a monster to attack our homeland," Otto said. "We've come to find whoever is responsible and make sure they don't do it again."

"I assure you no one from our village is capable of such a thing."

Otto smiled at that. "I have no doubt. The only reason we came to your village is because I spotted it when I was looking for a good place to make landfall. Also, my research indicated that there were no settlements beyond Lord Azteca's capital. When I saw the village, my curiosity got the better of me. Would it be possible for us to talk? You must have a fascinating story to tell."

The ancient villager's face scrunched up. At last it said, "Ours is a tale of abandonment and woe. It is clear to me that you are no threat to the village. If you wish to hear our story, I will tell you. I am Dhumoc, chosen leader of this settlement."

"Otto Shenk." He introduced his companions. "There are others on my ship that would enjoy a bit of time on land. Would it be okay if they came ashore? Everyone will be on their best behavior, I promise."

Dhumoc blew out a breath. "That would be fine, but we have no food or supplies to spare. The village is barely hanging on as it is."

"That's fine, though a source of fresh water would be welcome."

"Water we have in abundance. Take all that you wish."

Otto offered a nod of respect. "Thank you. Is there somewhere we can speak more comfortably?"

"We can talk in my hut, though you won't all fit."

"Not a problem. Hans, Axel, and Corina, you're with me. The rest of you take the dinghy back and be sure to make those depth measurements Captain Coleman wanted on your way. Tell him shore leave has been approved and that if anyone causes these people any trouble, they'll answer to me. Clear?"

A chorus of, "Yes, Lord Shenk," followed his question.

Hans flicked a glance at Dhumoc, moving only his eyes. "Are you certain it's safe, my lord?"

"Given where we are, I doubt anywhere is perfectly safe, but I think we'll be fine for however long it takes them to get back." Otto turned back to the guards. "Off you go."

They darted quick looks at Hans but were smart enough not to question Otto's order. That wouldn't have gone well for them. Hans was a worrywart, which Otto generally appreciated, but there were times it got annoying.

With that bit of business taken care of, Otto turned back to Dhumoc. "Sorry for the delay. After you."

"You are concerned about your safety. There is no need to be. My people know nothing about fighting and the beasts of the jungle can't enter the village. This may be the only truly safe place in Aztecaland."

The group followed Dhumoc toward his hut. A few tentative faces appeared, peeking out from behind various tarps. It seemed curiosity had overcome fear, at least to a certain extent.

"Your people seem awfully nervous considering that you said this is the only safe place in Aztecaland."

Without looking back Dhumoc said, "It is our nature to be fearful. It was bred into us by Lord Azteca along with obedience of course. We are all descended from her palace servants and the commands run deep. Even after all this time, if she were to appear and give us an order, we would have no choice but to obey."

"Do you even know what she looks like?" Axel asked.

Dhumoc pulled the curtain aside. "It doesn't matter. The

magic in us would answer to her magic. I'm no wizard, so don't ask me how I know, I just do. We all do. It's as much a part of us as our hair and blood. Now, let us exchange stories and see how we might help each other."

So she created an entire race of servants. Otto couldn't say anything an Arcane Lord had done surprised him, though this was certainly as remarkable as any of the feats he'd heard about. Now he just had to hope they'd be as useful to him as they were to her.

CHAPTER THIRTY-ONE

humoc's hut didn't have furniture as such, but there was a single mat made of woven leaves. Their host offered it to Otto, but he declined. It wouldn't do anything to soften the dirt floor anyway. The pad of ether Otto conjured as he sat, on the other hand, helped a great deal. Axel, Hans, and Corina had to make do sitting directly on the ground.

When they were all as comfortable as the setting would allow, Dhumoc said, "I will tell you my story. It isn't a long one and please understand that it has been passed down from generation to generation. Some things may have been exaggerated."

"That's fine," Otto said. "Please go ahead."

Taking a deep breath, Dhumoc began. "My people, the beastfolk, were made to serve Lord Azteca, as I said. We are among the few of her creations capable of speech. For many generations we handled all the menial tasks in the capital. Then one day she vanished. We all waited, expecting her to return, but eventually Skar came to us and said she wasn't coming back."

"Skar?" Otto asked.

"Leader of Lord Azteca's personal guards, the dragonmen. We handled labor and the dragonmen slaughtered any creature foolish enough to enter the city. They were our protectors. That's why what Skar said next came as such a shock. He told us we had to leave the city and that four dragonmen would escort us somewhere safe. Our ancestors didn't understand why, but in the end, a single dragonman could have killed us all had he wished to do so. Fighting and arguing would accomplish nothing, so we left."

"And came here?" Corina asked.

"Not directly. They wandered for over a year before finding this place. Skar is kind and didn't send us away without protection. He gave us one of Lord Azteca's artifacts. It protects the village, driving away any of her mindless creations that comes within a mile of it. We have just enough room to forage and fish. It's not a life of abundance, but we've survived all this time."

That seemed to be the end of the story. "And you have no idea why Skar forced you to leave?"

Dhumoc shook his head. "He said only that it was his father's order and that they wouldn't be able to protect us should we stay. Why and what that means, I have no idea."

Otto had no idea what it meant either, but it sounded like there were a bunch of dragonmen still in the city. "What's the city called? I've never heard its name."

"We called it Home."

Somehow Otto doubted that was what Lord Azteca named it, but the more he learned about the eccentric Arcane Lord, the more he wondered if she even gave the city a name.

"Will you tell me how you ended up here?" Dhumoc asked.

Otto couldn't see any harm in it, so he gave a brief overview of the attack on Garen and how Lady White sensed Astaroth's activity in this part of the world. He didn't mention his discussion with Lord Karonin. No one else knew about her and the hidden tower and he preferred to keep it that way.

"So our hope is to find the responsible party and make sure they can't attack our home again."

"Someone killed a dragonman?" Dhumoc sounded incredulous. "They are the mightiest of our master's creations. I would say it was impossible, but I can't imagine why you'd lie to me. Someone capable of killing a dragonman…"

He trailed off, sounding troubled.

Otto understood how he felt. The sooner Lord of the Dead, assuming he was responsible, was dealt with, the happier he'd be.

At last Dhumoc said, "Such a dangerous person is a threat to us as well. While we can't fight, you are welcome to use our village as a base. Forage in the jungle and take all the water you need. I will answer any questions you might have."

"I appreciate your willingness to cooperate. The water will be welcome. Other than that, all I really need is directions to the city. If that's where the dragonmen are, I have to assume our enemy will be nearby."

"That is simple enough. There are trails through the jungle, enchanted by allies of Lord Azteca to keep the beasts away. All of them lead to the city."

"Is that the same magic that protects your village?" Otto

asked. He'd been curious about the lack of a wall and some sort of forbiddance magic would explain it.

"I know nothing about magic. Skar gave us an item when we left Home. He said it would keep us safe from mindless beasts. Our village has never been attacked, so I assume it works."

Otto hadn't noticed anything in the ether, but if the magic was diffused enough, he might have missed it. "We'll spend one night here and make our preparations. Thank you for your hospitality."

"If you deal with the threat, I will consider it a fair trade."

Otto and his companions stood and walked out of the hut. Dhumoc didn't bother to join them.

When they'd moved a little ways away Axel asked, "What do you think?"

"He told no lies," Otto said. "And his fear of whatever killed the dragonman was honest. Frankly, a safe place for the ship along with water was about all I was hoping for. If the trails he mentioned are really safe, it should speed up our journey a great deal. That said, I have no intention of letting my guard down. When the scouts get here, take Corina and have a look around. Hans and I are going to take a look at the water supply he mentioned. Just because it's safe for them to drink doesn't mean it'll be safe for us."

"Will you offer them something for their hospitality?" Corina asked.

"Yes. With any luck, a dead priest of Astaroth."

○

Skar ran through the jungle, ducking branches, leaping logs, and generally moving as quickly as he could to the east. He avoided the paths that ran throughout the nation as they made him too easy to find. None of the local predators were stupid enough to take on a dragonman and the ones hunting him were unaffected by the paths' magic.

And he was being hunted. Every once in a while he'd pause and listen. Without fail he heard faint, distant sounds of something large thrashing through the jungle behind him. The only good thing he could say about the transformed giant monkeys was they lacked their former skill at stealth. These things just charged through the undergrowth, heedless of the noise or damage. Whatever they were now, it wasn't technically alive, though they did retain some small amount of intellect.

The worst thing about them, besides their greater durability, was that they didn't seem to sleep. Skar had been running nonstop for two days and was getting close to the limit of his endurance. Soon he would have to turn and fight or risk being so exhausted that he'd be helpless when they eventually caught up. The danger, of course, was that if he did turn to fight, he might lose. And if he lost, he'd fail to complete the task Father had set him. Heaven only knew what would happen then.

He burst through a wall of brush and into a clearing. In the center of it, a cluster of tall, jagged boulders jutted from the earth. If he put his back to those, at least they wouldn't be able to come at him from behind.

Skar doubted he'd find anywhere better for his inevitable battle.

Quickly making up his mind, he ran over then spun, putting his back to the central boulder. His muscles burned from the long run and he shook them out in the hopes that they'd get a little stronger.

And that was all he had time for. A couple of minutes after his arrival, four giant, transformed monkeys rushed into the clearing. There was a four-armed orange one and three grays that looked like slightly smaller versions of Throng. They stopped for a second and glared at Skar with glowing red eyes.

The transformation hadn't helped their appearance any. Patches of hair were falling out of their bodies. The lower right arm of the orange one looked only half connected to its body. Though it still seemed to move freely. All in all, they were among the ugliest enemies Skar had ever fought and that was saying something given some of the mutated beasts that roamed the jungle.

The four-armed monster roared and that was the signal for the others. They all charged at Skar.

As soon as they were in range, he breathed out a gout of flame.

That proved to be a mistake. He lost sight of his foes for a moment and soon found them leaping at him through the fire, singed but otherwise unfazed.

He caught a gray one by the ankle and hammered it down into the four-armed brute, sending both tumbling off to one side.

The second airborne monster slammed its fist into his shoulder, driving Skar to one knee.

He barely blocked a kick from the monster on the ground.

Surging to his feet, Skar drove his right hand through the nearest monster's chest.

It just snarled and swatted him upside the head, rattling Skar's brain in the process. If he'd needed any more proof that these things weren't truly still alive, this would've been enough.

He hurled the impaled monster at the now-recovered duo to his left, sending them sprawling into the dirt once more. A second blow from the still-standing monster staggered him a stride away from the boulder. The tang of blood filled Skar's mouth and he roared.

A spinning blow from his tail sent the monster flying into the boulder.

Skar leapt after it, grabbing it by the chin and forehead.

Muscles clenched as he twisted and yanked, ripping its head free of its body. The creature finally dropped to the ground and didn't move.

So that was how you killed these things.

The thought barely crossed his mind when the three survivors slammed into him from the side and drove him to the ground. Using his legs and momentum, he sent the four-armed monster flying halfway across the clearing.

Pain shot through him when one of the grays grabbed his wing and wrenched it to the side. There was no crunch, but he suspected at least one bone had broken.

Skar lashed out, slicing the nearest monster's face to ribbons with the claws on his right hand. It barely flinched before countering with a heavy fist to Skar's head.

There was no hope of dodging, not with the other one still hanging on to his wing. He did manage to turn his head just enough to make it a glancing blow. The power of even that made the world turn black for a moment.

Snarling through the pain, Skar reached back, wrenched the one off his wing, and hurled it away. Judging from the pain, he'd done more damage in the process, but at least he could move freely.

The one that struck him reared back for a second swing. Skar had no intention of letting him take it.

As the oversized fist came toward him, Skar surged forward to meet it. Evading the blow, he drove his straightened fingers into the monster's throat. Razor-sharp claws punched through and he ripped to the side, sending its head flying.

That was two down. And now he had a much more efficient means of killing them.

Focusing on the remaining enemies, he found they'd separated. The four-armed monster was coming in from his right and the gray one from his left. That was about the worst situation he could find himself in.

Not wanting to get pincered, he leapt straight up and landed on the lowest boulder, grimacing in pain as his damaged wing tried to beat and failed.

The two monsters roared their frustration and started climbing. Their nimble fingers found many holds. It wouldn't take long for them to reach his position. Not wanting to face both of them at once, Skar sent a blast of fire roaring down at the four-armed brute. He doubted the flames did much damage, but they did send it crashing to the ground.

And not a moment too soon. The last gray reached his perch and charged.

This time Skar was ready. He caught the monster's wrist, twisted, and sent it slamming into the boulder. He lashed out with his claws and chopped its head most of the way off. A wrench to the side finished the job and he tossed both head and body off the boulder.

The four-armed survivor stared up at Skar and he stared back. One on one he felt confident that he'd be able to defeat his opponent. The creature must have agreed as it turn to flee back into the jungle.

No way could Skar let it escape. Constant fear of ambushes would make his journey even more intolerable.

He sprang from the boulder and tackled the four-armed monster to the ground. Hard elbows slammed into his ribs drawing a hiss of pain. Claws and muscle quickly separated its head from its body. When it finally went still, Skar stood and took stock of his condition. What he found didn't encourage him. His damaged wing could barely move, his face throbbed from the blows he took, and his ribs ached with every breath. He couldn't quite make up his mind whether some of them were broken or just bruised, but either way, they hurt.

A few hours' sleep would be welcome and this clearing was as good a place as any. The smell of the dying monsters might bring scavengers, but they wouldn't trouble Skar when easy meat was right there.

He returned to the boulders, put his back to them, and closed his eyes. Sleep was not long in coming.

CHAPTER THIRTY-TWO

The beastfolk village was bustling with activity. Otto watched the sailors walking around, stretching their legs, and generally enjoying not being on a ship. Everyone had been informed in no uncertain terms that they'd better behave themselves. He made it clear that should anyone make trouble for the locals, they'd answer to him. From the looks on their faces, he felt confident that his message had been received.

The only downside he could see to using the village as a base was that Captain Coleman had decided it was just too shallow to risk bringing the ship in. That meant leaving a skeleton crew aboard the *Sea Star* to make sure the ship was safe. The first group wasn't thrilled to be left behind, but they'd rotate out in a couple of days.

Axel, his scouts, and Corina had already left to explore the jungle. They were hunting for fresh meat, which would be a welcome change for everyone. Hopefully they could find enough for the villagers as well.

And speaking of tasks, Otto needed to head out to the

spring where the villagers got their water. He had alchemy supplies that would ensure it was safe to drink, but he'd prefer to save that for when they really needed it. Hopefully the water would be as pure as Dhumoc claimed.

He turned to Hans who was hovering a few feet away as was his habit. "Care to take a walk?"

"Ready when you are, my lord."

Otto nodded and set out for the edge of the village. According to Dhumoc there was a well-worn trail that led to the spring. Otto figured they would have no trouble finding it.

The rest of the guys formed up around them and Otto headed for the western edge of the village. Sure enough they found a dirt path that had been well worn by many feet. As they passed under the canopy, the sounds of birds grew louder. He couldn't see any of them, but given how thick the leaves were, that was no surprise.

"Do you trust these... people, my lord?" Hans asked.

"You know me better than that. However, I do believe that they are what they say they are. According to my research, Lord Azteca did create a race of servants, and they certainly fit the description. I'm confident that the sailors will have no trouble while we're gone. Why, are you worried about them?"

"I'm mostly concerned that if they end up getting killed, we'll have no way back home."

Otto smiled at that. "A perfectly valid concern. If it makes you feel better, this is still safer than having them sail around until we get back. At least the ship is close enough to benefit from the same magic that protects the village."

"I suppose that's something," Hans muttered.

Otto appreciated his faithful bodyguard's concern, but he

still had high hopes that he'd be able to seize control of Lord Azteca's portal and travel home that way.

"What the bloody hell is that?" one of the guys said, knocking Otto out of his musing.

"That" turned out to be a cat the size of a horse with eight legs and two tails that ended in bone spikes. It prowled around just beyond a clear pool of water and stared at them with slightly glowing yellow eyes. It hissed and bared four-inch-long fangs.

Hans and his men hastened to draw their mithril swords. Otto didn't stop them, but he didn't want them to attack either. "Steady. Let's see what it does."

Hans stared at him for a moment, but as always did as he was told.

With everyone on full alert, Otto shifted his vision to the ether. The very edge of the protective magical effect was visible as a sparkly wall about a foot in front of the cat creature. Interesting that he wasn't able to see the magic in the village itself, but out here it was clear as day. Did the monster's presence have something to do with that? Impossible to say for sure, but he had to assume so. Otherwise Otto would've noticed the other side when the ship passed through it.

The cat took a couple steps and growled.

"Lord Shenk?" Hans asked.

"Relax, it can't get to us. There's a wall of magic between that thing and the spring. Still, I don't like having it this close with Axel out hunting."

Otto sent out a targeting thread, but it couldn't pass through the barrier. Interesting; it not only stopped anything from coming in, it stopped magic from going out as well.

"Does anyone have a bow?" Otto asked.

"Sorry, my lord," Hans said. "We're all armed for close combat."

"A mithril dagger then?" Otto looked from one man to the next and they all just shook their heads.

"Do you wish us to go kill it?" Hans asked.

"No, that's not what I want to test." He shook his head. "It doesn't matter anyway."

Ignoring the still-prowling monster, Otto sent a thread of ether into the water. As he'd hoped, there were no contaminants.

"It's safe. Start filling the skins." They hesitated, clearly not wanting to take their eyes off the monster. "I'll watch the kitty cat. Get to work."

As he hoped, mocking their fear got everyone moving. It took about ten minutes, but they finally had all the skins they'd brought with them filled. They wouldn't last long in this heat, but hopefully Otto would have little trouble finding more. Emphasis on hopefully. He was hardly an expert on jungle survival after all.

The group headed back toward the village. If the cat was able to attack, this would be the perfect time. Their backs were turned and their weapons sheathed. But it didn't and they soon left it behind.

Otto had so many questions about how the magic worked. Unfortunately, he doubted Dhumoc had even a clue to share with him. He doubted anyone living did. His only real hope for learning more was to find some of Lord Azteca's books in the city.

When they reached the village, Dhumoc was waiting. The man had a little smile on his face. "Did you see the stinger cat?"

"We saw some sort of cat. Is it a friend of yours?"

"It likes to watch us collect water. I'm not sure why since it can't reach us."

"When I was younger, my mother had a pet cat that never left the castle. It liked to stare out the arrow slits at the birds. This is probably something similar. Are the stinger cats edible?"

Dhumoc shrugged. "The entire village working together couldn't kill one, so I have no idea. Did it look appetizing to you?"

"Not especially, but in a pinch it would be nice to know what we can eat and what's unsafe."

"I wish I could tell you. Lord Azteca changed their physical appearance, but I don't know if she changed their toxicity as well. With her, it would be impossible to guess. She might well do it just to see if she could."

"That would be a very Arcane Lord thing to do. Guess I'll just have to check each one individually."

"Wise decision."

Otto yawned. Speaking of food, it was time for lunch. Hopefully Axel wasn't having any problems on his hunt.

⌒

Axel checked the mithril-tipped arrow set on his bow for the tenth time. He hated the jungle. The heat was miserable, the humidity made it worse, and everything reminded him of the Land of Giant Beasts. He'd ended up running for his life from a giant lizard on that miserable island. It wasn't an experience he was eager to repeat.

He had Colten on point so the odds of them getting ambushed were pretty low. His best tracker had only gotten better over the last few years. He was technically Axel's second-in-command now that Cobb had retired, but he was most useful in his current position.

At least he never complained about having to march in front.

Faint muttering came from directly behind him. Again. Colten might not complain, but Corina certainly had no qualms about letting her annoyance at ending up with Axel show.

Axel dropped back a couple strides to walk beside her and whispered, "You want to keep it quiet? The idea of hunting is to not let the prey know you're coming."

She had the good grace to wince. "Sorry. It seems like we just got here and he's already sending me away."

"He gave you a job," Axel said. "You and Otto are our only true wizards and both groups needed one. Have you even been checking for magic or whatever?"

"Of course I have. There's nothings magical out here, just trees, leaves, and more trees. I'm not even sure what I'm supposed to be looking for."

"What did Otto tell you to look for?"

"Anything out of the ordinary."

"I admit that's pretty vague. I guess you just need to keep looking. We're not doing much better looking for animal signs. He said we shouldn't go too far, but if we don't get further away from the village, there might not be anything to hunt."

"Sir?" one of the new scouts said. "Sergeant Colten stopped up ahead."

Then again maybe he spoke too soon. "If Colten found tracks, no more muttering, got it?"

"I know, I know. I'll be fine."

Axel gave her one last look then hurried to the front of

the group. Colten was kneeling beside a bare patch of dirt. "What did you find?"

Colten looked up. He'd been trying to grow a beard with little success. At the moment it looked like he had some mold on his face that needed to be wiped away. Despite being nearly thirty, Colten still looked almost as young as Otto.

"A track, sir. I've been following a rough game trail, but this is the first spot I've been able to find a clear track. Thing is, I've never seen one quite like this. Lord Shenk said we should expect strange beasts. Well, this certainly seems to be one."

Axel was a fair tracker himself and he examined the track. It wasn't a hoof, that much was immediately obvious. The pad suggested a cat, albeit a cat with a foot the size of his hand. A lion or tiger maybe? No, that would be too mundane.

To hell with it. He'd seen no other sign of animal life out here. Might as well hunt it down and see.

"Keep after it," Axel said. "I want half of you to put up your bows and draw your swords. Form a defensive circle around the archers. Anything comes charging at us, kill it and ask questions later. Corina, stay in the center. I'm counting on you to deal with any magical issues."

"I'll do my best." She sounded focused at least.

"Okay, Colten, let's go."

The group set out again. They were tense, Axel could tell that much just from the way they were holding themselves. Their eyes were darting all over the place. Alert was good, but this might be too much. Not that he could say anything. He felt just as anxious as they looked.

They slunk along through the silent jungle. And it was silent. All he could hear was the faint scuff of the men's boots and their breathing. He hadn't heard a bird since they left the village. It was unnatural. Though far from surprising since everything in this place was unnatural.

Sometime later, Axel wasn't sure how long since the minutes felt like hours out here, Colten signaled for them to stop.

Axel hurried up beside Colten who pointed silently through a gap in the brush. Axel's heart skipped a beat when he saw the creature. It looked like a tabby cat the size of a bear with a tail that ended in a bone club. It was standing over the carcass of some sort of bristly furred beast. Axel couldn't make out what it was, but he assumed it was a different sort of horrible monster.

When he looked away he found Colten looking at him instead of the targets. He quirked an eyebrow. Right, time to decide what to do. Not that there was much to think about. Otto sent them out to bring back meat so he could tell if it was safe to eat. If they bagged the cat, it would give them two samples. That should be plenty.

Using hand signals, Axel motioned the archers up and into position. A couple of the newer recruits started when they saw the cat, but no one made a sound.

At his signal, they drew their bows and loosed as one. The mithril arrows shot out and pierced the cat as easily as they did everything else. Too easily in fact as they kept on going into the jungle without even slowing down.

Axel cursed. They only had so many arrows. Now they'd have to retrieve them.

"Is it dead?" someone asked.

Considering it was poked full of holes and not moving, Axel was pretty sure it was.

Before he could speak Corina said, "It is. I can't sense any life force."

Axel had been somewhat fearful that it might be playing opossum, but Corina's reassurance let him relax, at least a little. "Good. Corina, take half the guys and retrieve those arrows. The rest of us will take a closer look at what we've got."

The group split up with Colten leading half the group to collect the arrows while Axel marched over to the dead monsters. The cat wasn't any prettier up close. Its fur looked less like fur than it did needles. The bone club on its tail had to weigh at least twenty pounds.

The animal it killed looked like a normal wild boar, albeit the biggest one Axel had ever seen. He didn't know about the cat, but the boar should be edible. Not that he planned to try it before Otto said it was safe.

"Why would anyone make such a thing?" asked Kirk, one of the veterans that had been with him nearly as long as Colten.

"The same reason Arcane Lords did all the mad shit they did: because they could." Despite saying it half jokingly, Axel was fairly sure that was the truth. "Get the ropes out. As soon as the others get back, we can drag the ugly things back to the village. Then they'll be my brother's problem."

Fortunately, thanks to Corina's magic, it only took the second team about fifteen minutes to collect the arrows and return. When they did, Axel had the dead animals tied up and ready to go. Dragging them would be no easy feat, but they'd manage it somehow. He put Corina, Colten, and two others on security while the rest of them started pulling.

Heaven's mercy. He knew they were going to be heavy,

but he'd pulled boulders lighter than these two beasts. Even as big as they were, they shouldn't be this heavy.

"Okay, stop," Axel said. "We won't make it back before dark like this. Let's gut them at least. That should help a little."

Mithril daggers made short work of the job and when they set out again, the carcasses pulled a little easier. It was still going to be a miserable slog back, but they should be able to manage it before nightfall at least.

By the time they reached the village it was dusk. A fire was burning in the central square and Axel could see figures reclining beside it. Since they had no fresh food, a hot meal was out of the question. Though at this point he was so worn out that even a dry alchemy biscuit would be welcome.

"What did you find?" Otto's voice came out of nowhere and Axel nearly leapt out of his skin.

"Make some noise, why don't you?"

"I made plenty of noise, you just couldn't hear me over your wheezing and grunting. You can drop them there. You're inside the safe zone."

Axel tossed the rope aside and straightened out of his hunch. His back popped and he winced. Maybe he was getting old. "We killed some kind of giant cat which had already killed a huge boar. I figured it would be best to bring both back."

"Excellent decision." Otto pointed at the animals and a moment later said, "They're both edible. Why don't you rest? I'll get Hans and the guys to cut these up. We can roast some boar meat for dinner."

"You have no idea how good that sounds," Axel said. "We'll be by the fire if you need us."

Axel trudged off, content to let Otto deal with things. Rest and then fresh meat. He could hardly wait.

CHAPTER THIRTY-THREE

L ord of the Dead walked along through the jungle, guided by Throng. His original intention had been to wait until after he'd starved out the dragonmen and claimed the orb to slaughter the Simeon villages and raise them as thralls. But when one of the dragonmen somehow slipped through the siege and then killed the thralls he'd dispatched to hunt it down, he figured increasing the number of troops at his disposal wouldn't be a bad thing.

What he couldn't figure out was what the dragonman hoped to accomplish in the jungle. According to Throng they didn't have any friends among the wild beasts. He also denied that any of the dragonmen would flee just to save themselves. Lord of the Dead didn't bother to argue, but had serious doubts that anything was so loyal that if the opportunity to escape and survive presented itself, they wouldn't take it.

Of course, what Lord of the Dead knew about dragonmen wouldn't fill a very big book. Maybe Azteca had made them that loyal. That would explain why they were still guarding the city after many hundreds of years.

Well, no matter the reason, increasing the size of his army was now of paramount importance. The dragonman could plan whatever he liked; a couple hundred thralls would be enough to stop it in its tracks, unlike the four he'd sent after it.

"How much further?" Lord of the Dead asked.

"The Chimpen Clan is the closest. We will reach their village by the end of the day."

"They're the smaller, black-haired ones, yes?"

"Yes, Master. They are also the most numerous."

"Perfect. We can use them to surround the other villages to make sure no one escapes. Make sure to stop out of sight. Since it's just the two of us, we'll need to take precautions."

"Yes, Master." A moment of silence passed before Throng asked, "Is it really necessary to do this? My people have suffered enough as it is."

Lord of the Dead stared at Throng. Now that he'd been transformed into an undead juggernaut, he should be free of such pesky things as morals and doubts.

"It certainly is necessary. Unless you can suggest another, equally convenient source of new thralls."

"No, we're the only ones smart enough to gather in villages. All the other beasts of the jungle simply prowl around and rest where they will and hope that nothing eats them in their sleep. Villages are better."

Lord of the Dead agreed. If he'd had to hunt down his new thralls one at a time, it would've taken forever.

They continued on in silence, though from the way he carried himself, it was clear that Throng was still upset. Not that he could oppose Lord of the Dead's will. As a newly made servant of Astaroth, he wasn't nearly powerful enough. That might change in a few centuries, assuming Throng survived and learned some magic. Of course, once Lord of the Dead reassembled the Rod of Terror, no lesser undead would ever be able to disobey him again. He might even be strong enough to compel Lady White back into the fold.

He smiled to himself as he imagined forcing the arrogant priestess to her knees in supplication. It would be a beautiful sight, almost as beautiful as obliterating her would be.

Daydreaming in the middle of the dangerous jungle probably wasn't the best idea, but it did help pass the time as they walked through the unchanging, silent wilderness.

"I would have thought the jungle would be louder," Lord of the Dead said.

"All the noisy animals have been eaten already. Anything that draws attention to itself doesn't last long. Even the birds learned to remain silent. This is a harsh land and only the strongest survive."

In some ways that made it very much like his old home in the Land of the Demon Binders. Though some weaklings survived by serving those who were strong. Still, the theory was the same.

Throng finally stopped about an hour before dark. "The village is fifteen minutes away. If we go any further, the lookouts will see us."

Lord of the Dead nodded. Of course there would be lookouts. "One moment and I'll deal with them."

He focused on the ether and soon sensed the presence of four life forms not that far ahead. Beyond them waited a larger cluster that had to be the village itself. He ignored it for the moment and drew corruption from the rod. Concentrating it around the lookouts, he quickly snuffed out their lives.

"It's done. Let's move a bit closer, then I can start the transformation spell."

Throng started stomping forward, louder than before. Was he trying to warn them? Of all the stupid, pointless acts of rebellion...

Lord of the Dead lashed out with his magic, raking it across Throng's undead essence. The giant monkey went rigid and snarled without a sound.

"I don't know what you think you're playing at, but keep quiet. We don't want them getting away. *I* don't want them getting away. Understand?" Throng managed a faint nod. "Good. Remember this and don't make me punish you again."

Throng staggered a step when Lord of the Dead released him then got moving again, this time silently. That was more like it.

It didn't take long to get within range of the village. When they were in position, Lord of the Dead began his spell. It was an interesting variation of the summoning spell that brought demon spirits to this world to create thralls and he couldn't have done it without the rod's power boost.

He began by infusing corruption into the ether then sent it rolling into the village. The magic paralyzed everything it touched and soon the village was filled with it. When he sensed no untouched life forms, Lord of the Dead began the second phase. He opened a micro portal and began draining the villagers' life force and using it to summon demon spirits. He loved this spell for its efficiency. It took very little out of him since the victims powered it with their lives. He didn't know which ancient priest invented the magic, but it was brilliant.

Reasonably quick as well. The process was complete in less than an hour. When he ended the magic and strode into a collection of crude huts, he found scores of short, lithe thralls covered in black hair standing with vacant expressions staring at him and Throng. A quick check confirmed that the spirits had fully bonded with their new hosts.

"That went well," Lord of the Dead said. "How far to the next village?"

Throng cocked his head. "Perhaps a week, perhaps a little more."

"Then we'd best get moving. I want to finish building my army as quickly as possible." If the other villages were populated at a level even close to this one, he'd have an impressive force indeed. Maybe enough to finish off the dragonmen rather than waiting for them to starve.

Lord Astaroth did appreciate quick results after all.

CHAPTER THIRTY-FOUR

Otto stretched and yawned. He'd gotten a decent night's sleep after their cookout last night. The roasted boar ended up tasting delicious. After nothing but alchemy biscuits, Otto and the others had thoroughly enjoyed the fresh meat. The bigger surprise had been the cat monster. They roasted a bit of its meat as well and it was quite tasty, a little tough, but otherwise fine.

And it wasn't just Otto's team that enjoyed the meat. The villagers had joined them in the feast and they seemed to enjoy it as well. They even relaxed a bit. Well, that was an exaggeration, but they didn't look like they were ready to bolt at the slightest quick move.

The fun and games were over now. As soon as everyone got ready, they were heading into the jungle. Until proven unsafe, Otto planned to stick with the paths Dhumoc mentioned. Hopefully they'd see some beasts prowling along the edges they could pick off and add to the larder.

He spotted Lady White standing a little ways off. She'd

ended up getting stuck with guard duty last night. Since she didn't sleep, she was the perfect choice.

As he approached he got a nod of acknowledgment. "Any trouble last night?"

"None. It's so peaceful in the village and I can't really understand it. The magic they're using to keep the beasts at bay must be incredibly powerful."

"If it was made by an Arcane Lord, you can be sure it is. Have you sensed anything from our enemy?"

"No, but I'd only detect an especially strong spell. I'm sure whoever it is hasn't gone anywhere. What, exactly, they're up to, I can't say."

Otto waved a hand. "We'll find out soon enough I'm sure. No doubt to our regret. But that's for later. The main thing is getting to Azteca's capital. If I can power up the portal, will you be okay?"

"It will be painful, but I can endure it. It's not like you have a way to keep it charged indefinitely."

"I certainly don't." Otto didn't add that he very much wished he did. Such a power source would be very useful.

An hour later, fed and loaded up with all the supplies they could carry, Otto and his team gathered at the edge of the village. Dhumoc was waiting. The village mayor, at least that's how Otto had come to think of him, offered a polite bow.

"You have our gratitude for the fresh meat. It has been some time since we were able to enjoy it. I would wish you a safe journey, but such a thing is impossible given where you're going. Instead, I will simply say that I hope we meet again."

"That would suit me very well," Otto said. "Where does the trail you mentioned start?"

"I'll show you. Come along." With Dhumoc in the lead, the group marched across the clearing that surrounded the village.

It was a fair hike before Dhumoc stopped in front of a very rough gap in the jungle. The way the branches and vines hung down, Otto doubted he would've spotted the entrance on his own. Checking the ether, he found a very faint, diffused energy coming off the trail. He'd never seen anything just like it. The spell looked similar, but also different from the magic that protected the village.

Well, whatever. As long as it kept them safe from wandering beasts, Otto could figure out its specific effects later. "Axel, set your marching order. Let's get this show on the road."

Axel set Colten on point. The scout had a far lighter pack than the rest of them, no doubt so he could move quickly. The rest of the group formed up with Otto, Corina, Jet, and Lady White in the center protected by Hans and his men. Axel's scouts took the front and rear. The trail's narrowness limited their options, but that was a small price to pay for protection.

With a final wave to Dhumoc, they set out.

Hours passed with no sign of monsters. The walking was relatively easy as long as you kept your eyes open for drooping vines and branches. The magic even kept the insects away, sparing them the need to apply Ulf's stinky lotion. No one uttered a word of complaint about that.

The group kept marching until well after noon before Axel called for a break. That suited Otto fine and judging by how quickly they slumped to the ground, everyone else agreed.

While the others rested, Axel motioned Otto over. Hans tagged along when he went to see what his brother wanted.

"Isn't this a little too easy?" Axel asked. "I figured we'd be fighting constantly. Other than the heat and humidity, this is nothing."

"I had similar expectations," Otto said. "But then I didn't know about these paths. From the sounds of it there's a small army of dragonmen waiting for us in the city. Likely we'll pay for our good fortune when we arrive."

Axel grunted and ran a hand through his hair. "Those are the same as the thing that attacked the capital?"

"Not exactly the same. That dragonman had been transformed into a warbeast that made it both stronger and not susceptible to Lady White's magic. They can be killed with mithril weapons. My hope is that our archers can thin their numbers before we make contact, but until we see their location and the overall strategic situation, there's no way to make a concrete plan."

"Yeah, I just don't trust it when things go smoothly."

"I'm surprised you have an opinion on it since it happens so seldom."

Axel laughed. "Fair point. I'm going to stop worrying and get some of the leftover boar meat. The giant cat monster tasted okay, but the idea of eating something that looks like an overgrown pet makes me a little sick to my stomach."

"When we run out of other food, I'm sure you'll get over it."

"I thought people were supposed to mellow with age. Though you still look like you're twenty, so maybe it doesn't count."

Otto cocked his head. "Did you never meet Father and Stephan?"

"True. It's possible the men of the Shenk line are broken."

"I think it's well beyond possible."

They stared at each other for a moment then burst out laughing. It was entirely inappropriate given where they were, but it felt good all the same to let off some pressure. Everyone else no doubt thought they were insane. Not that Otto cared. He was used to people thinking rude things about him. As long as they followed his orders they could think anything they wanted.

৩

Three days of monotonous trudging passed without incident. Otto had no idea how far they'd gone or how far they had to go, but they were moving in the right direction and nothing had tried to kill them, so he was content to keep on as they were. The jungle was exotic, exciting. You could hardly see anything beyond the path given how thick the trees were. When there was a gap, all it ever revealed was more jungle. This had to be one of the least settled, most savage places on the planet.

What he wouldn't have given for some of the mechanical horses Illsa had told him about. She promised to build some once she figured out the capacitor issues, assuming she ever did. Not that that would do him any good now.

Ahead of him the scout stopped. Otto was about to ask what the holdup was when a bow twanged.

"Axel, what's going on?" Otto asked.

"I told Colten to go ahead and take any game he saw. Looks like he saw something. Not bad timing either, the way we've been going through the meat, we'll be back on magic cookies tomorrow. Let's go see what he got. Hopefully it's another boar and not a cat."

The scouts parted to let Axel and Otto through. As always, Hans and the guys came with him, hands on their swords. At the front of the group they found Colten looking off to the side, eyes narrowed as he peered into the shadows.

"Well?" Axel asked.

"I just shot the biggest damn bird in the history of birds," Colten said. "I can see it down, but I wanted to make sure it was dead before getting closer."

"We can make sure." Hans took a step toward the edge of the path.

Otto caught him before he could leave it. "Don't be foolish. Once you're off the path, you lose its protection. If there's something watching us, you'll be a sitting duck."

"Then how will we get the meat?" Colten asked.

"I'll handle that," Otto said. "Point out once more where it is."

Colten obliged and he focused on what might be a bunch of feathers or the scrubbiest bush in history. A thirty-thread tentacle wrapped around the bird and dragged it toward them. Nothing tried to steal their prey and soon a huge bird dropped onto the path. It was an ugly thing. Its beak was tall and wide like an ax blade, only dull. Beady black eyes stared at nothing. It had a long, muscular neck, a broad body covered in black and brown feathers, and massive legs that made a turkey look like a sparrow.

"I've never seen such a thing," Hans said.

"I've never even heard of such a thing," Axel agreed.

They both looked at Otto, who shrugged. "Remember where we are. We're liable to encounter anything the mind of an Arcane Lord can dream up. This and the cat creatures are likely to be the most normal of the things we meet."

Axel shook his head. "I'm never, ever looking to you for reassurance again."

Hans patted his shoulder. "It's best not to."

Otto ignored the pair's comments and said, "Get that thing cut up. We'll have fresh meat tonight then apply the preserving powder Ulf made. I checked it for poison while I was dragging it over, there's nothing to worry about on that front. I'm going to have a look around and see if there's anything interesting."

"I thought we weren't supposed to leave the path," Axel said.

"I'm not going to leave the path, I'm going to use magic. It'll be perfectly safe, now get to work."

No one had any more objections so he moved a little ways away from the bleeding carcass and closed his eyes. His vision soared free of his body. With his increased power, Otto could easily extend his sight many miles and he did just that.

First he checked the immediate area and found nothing dangerous. Local predators had probably learned that they couldn't attack anyone on the path, which would make hunting here a waste of time.

Satisfied with that, he flew down the path. There was nothing of note within two days' march. He kept pushing, as much to test his maximum range as because he imagined he'd find anything. He was just starting to feel a tug that indicated he needed to stop when he spotted a winged drag-onman hurrying down the path.

Otto tensed at the sight of it before reminding himself that it was still many miles away and couldn't see his ethereal construct in any case. Curious in spite of himself, Otto flew in closer. The dragonman looked like he, she, whatever, had been in a fight. One wing was bent at an unnatural angle and its face had dents, for lack of a better word. Despite that, it was moving at a good clip. If Otto's group kept on the path, they would likely encounter it tomorrow evening.

On the one hand, the fact that it was injured gave him confidence that they could beat it, but on the other, he'd prefer to avoid a fight if possible. Well, leaving the path wasn't a viable option, which meant that tomorrow, they'd see how tough a living dragonman really was.

CHAPTER THIRTY-FIVE

Otto kept tensing up and he forced himself to relax. They'd been walking all day and he expected at any moment to encounter the dragonman. He'd warned Axel and Hans who in turn had spread the word to their men. They were as ready as they were going to get and yet Otto still couldn't help the feeling that he didn't fully understand what was going to happen. It was just intuition, but he'd learned to trust it.

He was debating whether or not to call it a day when Colten shouted and came running back to the group. Otto and Hans hastened to the front of the line just as the scout arrived.

"I saw it!" Colten said. "It was standing in the middle of the path just as calm as could be and looked right at me."

"And?" Otto prompted.

"Nothing. It just watched me run back here."

Otto frowned. From everything Dhumoc had said, dragonmen were fairly intelligent. It had to know Colten would come right back to warn them. Otto didn't doubt for a second that the dragonman was fully aware of the group's presence. Why would it do that if it meant them harm?

More curious now than worried, Otto reconsidered his options. Originally he'd assumed that the dragonmen were his enemies, but now that he thought more about it, the one that sent the warbeast had killed a dragonman to create it. That meant Otto's enemy was likely the dragonmen's enemy as well. While the enemy of my enemy wasn't always my friend, he might be my ally.

"Change of plans," Otto said. "Hans, grab the others. We're going to see if this thing wants to talk."

"Talk?!" Hans and Axel spoke in unison.

Otto nodded, a faint smile playing about his lips.

"You think it can talk?" Axel asked.

"I think, having seen one of them fight, that it could have caught and killed Colten had it wished to. That it just looked at him and let him go, safe and sound, suggests that it wishes to make peaceful contact. That in turn indicates that it has some means to communicate. Only one way to find out for sure."

"Is there no way I can talk you out of this, my lord?" Hans asked.

"Certainly." When Hans's jaw dropped Otto's smile broadened. "If you can provide a more likely explanation of the dragonman's behavior, I'm happy to reconsider."

Hans and Axel looked at each other and the moment stretched uncomfortably long. At last Hans said, "I can't."

"Then let's go."

Moments after that they were walking down the path. Everyone had their swords drawn, but Otto insisted on walking in front. He didn't want anyone doing anything rash. He had a thirty-thread shield around him, so only an extremely powerful strike had any hope of getting through.

They found the dragonman about a hundred yards away. It stood in the center of the path. Or maybe slumped was a better description. It looked exhausted. Wings drooped, head hung low, clawed hands resting on its knees. The guy had clearly had a rough day.

"My name is Otto Shenk. Can you speak?"

The dragonman straightened. It was taller and broader across the chest than the one that attacked the capital. "I can. My name is Skar. Are you a wizard?"

Skar was the name of the leader of the dragonmen. What was he doing so far from his people? And why was he looking for a wizard?

"I am. I've come a long ways to find the one responsible for sending a reanimated dragonman to attack my home. It did a great deal of damage and killed a number of citizens. Someone must answer for that."

"I suspect the one you seek is also the one responsible for laying siege to our home. Father said that a wizard was coming and that I should escort him back. Will you meet with my father? He seemed confident that a bargain could be reached."

"When you say your father, I assume that is the dragon that Lord Azteca used to create you, correct?"

Skar nodded. "He is bound by silver chains in a cavern beneath her palace. My people are digging out a secret tunnel that will allow us to slip past the siege."

The silver chains had to be mithril. Nothing else would be strong enough to bind a dragon.

"Very well. My companions and I will join you. How long will it take for us to reach the city?"

"Hmm. If it was just me, I would say ten days, but given the limitations of weaker races, two to three weeks is more likely."

Otto nodded. He felt no insult at being called a member of a weaker race. Compared to dragonmen, humans were undoubtedly far weaker.

"We're about to make camp for the night. Would you care to join us for the evening meal?" Hans let out a strangled sound at his invitation but didn't otherwise speak. "We have meat from an ugly, ax-faced bird."

"Meat would be most welcome. I haven't eaten since I left the palace."

Otto quirked an eyebrow at that. "You can go that long without food?"

"Father hasn't eaten since he was captured. He sustains himself with magic. We can't go indefinitely without food, but we can manage for several months, though we'll gradually grow weaker as time passes."

"Fascinating. Still, if we're to be allies, I have no desire for you to get weaker." Otto glanced at the guys and noticed they still had their swords out. "You can put those away. Oh, and someone run ahead and let the others know that Skar will be joining us. I don't want anyone panicking when we get back."

One of the younger members sprinted off. Otto followed along at a more sedate pace with Skar walking beside him.

"You're taking this much more calmly than I expected," Skar said.

"If you knew some of the things I've seen over the years, you'd know that I'm not so easily disturbed. Anyway, why did you expect me not to be calm?"

"I heard Lord Azteca speak disparagingly about ordinary

humans many times. Her words colored my expectations. You are, in truth, the first human I've ever spoken to."

Otto grinned at that. "You are certainly the first dragonman I've ever spoken to. We shall have to raise a glass to firsts, though I fear our toast will have to be made with water."

"I'm not familiar with the word toast."

Otto explained and they had an amiable chat as they covered the last hundred yards or so to where the others had set up camp. Not that there was much to set up. The one-man tents most of them slept in only took minutes for the experienced scouts to get ready. Otto's larger tent took a bit longer but not by much. Several flame-producing magical items had been lit and meat was roasting over them.

Everyone stared at Skar when they entered camp, but otherwise there was no reaction. His people had already traveled through the Dead Lands and fought an army of ghouls among other things. At this point it took a lot to rattle them.

Otto led Skar to the fire where Corina sat and gestured for Skar to join them. Otto settled into his folding camp chair and focused on the dragonman. "Perhaps we should trade stories while the meat is cooking."

As a sign of good faith Otto went first. He left out a few details but nothing significant. When he finished he said, "My fear was that we'd end up having to fight your people. I'm relieved to see that won't be necessary."

"I knew one of the lesser dragonmen had been slain while out hunting, but I didn't know his ultimate fate. To be transformed into one of those soulless monsters is worse than I feared. I am grateful to you for freeing him from that curse."

"Since he was trying to kill me at the time, I had little

choice." Otto sensed Lady White approach from behind him but he did nothing to draw attention to her. "Your turn."

Skar heaved a sigh and when he did, Otto caught a whiff of something burnt. "Before I begin you must understand, this land has been free of outsiders since Lord Azteca vanished. We hunted, tended to Father's occasional whim, and fought the odd battle with the Simeon Coalition. But otherwise all remained as it always had been. Until the day Father warned us that an evil presence had arrived."

Skar went on to tell his story, ending with the fight against the transformed monsters and his encounter with Otto's group. It was quite remarkable.

"A question if I may," Otto said. "How did your father know that both we and the priest of Astaroth had arrived?"

"Though he is trapped, Father's magic is still quite strong. He can do and see many things. His wisdom is vast beyond comprehending. He has never steered us wrong."

"I look forward to meeting him. If you're right and we can reach a mutually beneficial agreement, that would suit me very well. My only real concern is that the priest is eliminated. Anything I can gain beyond that is a bonus."

"Meat's ready," a hesitant, shaky voice said.

Otto looked over and found one of Axel's younger scouts holding a plate loaded with roast meat. He gestured and hands of ether took the plate out of the young man's grip and carried it over to the group.

"Thank you," Otto said.

He saluted fist to heart and ran away like he feared he might be the second course.

"Guess he drew the short straw," Corina muttered.

More likely Axel had simply chosen the least experienced

scout and gave him the crappy assignment. He'd noticed that was the way it usually went in the military.

"Let's eat and sleep. I hope to get an early start in the morning."

After a meal of tough but surprisingly tasty bird-monster meat, Otto headed for his tent. They didn't have a place for Skar to sleep, but he assumed someone covered in scales would be fine lying on the ground.

He reached for the tent flap, paused, and stepped through. "Did you need something?"

Lady White stepped out of the shadows. "I was curious about your thoughts on the dragonman's story. It seems a bit too good to be true. If this is a trap, we might end up surrounded by dragonmen with no way to escape."

Otto figured it was best not to point out that if worst came to worst *he* at least had a way to escape, though it would mean leaving the rest of them behind. Not a move he would make lightly.

"It sounds to me like they're the ones who are surrounded. Clearly the dragon wants something from me since Skar came specifically to find a wizard. No, I'm not overly worried about getting betrayed. Our interests are too aligned. Should that change..." Otto shrugged. "We'll deal with that when the time comes. What about you? Are you still confident that we're dealing with Lord of the Dead?"

"That might be a stretch, but in the end, I can't imagine who else it might be. Hopefully I'll be able to tell for sure when we get closer."

"Hopefully. Anyway, I'll be counting on you to keep an eye on our guest tonight while the rest of us are asleep."

"My very plan. Good night." She brushed past him and slipped outside.

Otto rubbed the bridge of his nose. He wasn't sure if his task had just gotten easier or harder.

CHAPTER THIRTY-SIX

In the end, all of Otto's fears of betrayal ended up being proved pointless. Two and a half weeks of hard marching brought them within sight of the city. From a distance it was nothing remarkable. Crude stone houses surrounded a towering, flat-topped pyramid. Only the silvery mithril portal was of any real interest.

Otto sent ether into his eyes to sharpen his vision. He could make out small figures surrounding the pyramid. They were moving around too much to count, but he had no doubt those were the enemy's troops. At least the rest of the city seemed quiet.

Lady White stepped up beside him. "We're in luck. He's not here and those are thralls rather than warbeasts. I can also sense several faint presences within the city itself, but away from the main force."

"We're wasting time," Skar said. "Father's tunnel is on the opposite side of the city. We need to go, now."

Otto turned a cold look on the dragonman. He'd been a reasonable, if impatient, traveling companion. But if he thought he was the one giving orders here, he'd best think again. "We'll move when I'm ready and not an instant before. Should you have a problem with that, you can find your father another wizard."

Skar bared his fangs, an intimidating sight no doubt, but Otto understood full well that there was no other wizard even close to his skill anywhere on the continent. So he just stared back and waited. As expected, Skar backed down. If he wanted to be in charge, he shouldn't have let Otto know how important he was.

"Good. Now, you were saying, Lady White?"

"The weaker presences I sense are almost certainly slave spirits. If I can find them, I can compel them to tell me what Lord of the Dead is up to."

"That would certainly be good to know. Once we're finished interrogating these creatures, we can move on to the tunnel."

Lady White shook her head. "It would be best if I went alone. Our group is too large to sneak through the city. Should we draw attention to ourselves, it would mean trouble. I'll see what I can do and join you later. Finding the tunnel shouldn't be difficult."

"You're certain? If there's a fight we won't be able to come to your rescue."

Lady White smiled. "Are you worried about me?"

"Somewhat. You *are* our expert on all things Astaroth related. Losing you would put us in a weaker position."

"Well, don't worry, I won't do anything crazy. If it looks too dangerous, I'll come join you sooner."

"As you wish. Good luck."

"May I join you, Mistress?" Jet asked.

"No. Stick with Otto." So saying, Lady White hurried

toward the city.

Judging by her sour expression, Jet wasn't thrilled with her answer. Not that it could've come as a surprise. Jet was little more than an ordinary woman. She had no magic or combat skills to defend herself from supernatural threats. Of course, Otto didn't believe for a moment that Lady White had rejected her offer out of concern. More likely she figured Jet would be in the way.

"Look at it this way," Otto said. "If anything happens to Lady White, you're our next most knowledgeable expert on the cult of Astaroth. We can't afford to risk both of you."

Jet gave a distant, "Yes, Lord Shenk." But her gaze remained on Lady White's rapidly retreating back.

"Can we go now?" Skar asked. "The longer we linger here, the better the chances we'll be noticed."

"By all means, lead the way."

"Finally." Skar stalked off to the left and the rest of the group fell in behind him.

Corina moved up beside Otto. "Why are you being so nice to Jet? She's barely even part of the team."

Corina sounded jealous, which struck him as odd. He dismissed the idea as soon as it appeared. It was a ludicrous notion. "I'm being nice to her because a little kindness costs me nothing. However minimal her role, she is still a part of this group and as such can cause us problems should she become too disgruntled. Her knowledge of Astaroth's cult is valuable, so eliminating her out of hand would be a waste. In any case, why do you care?"

"I don't. I was just curious."

He let the obvious lie pass and fell silent. Otto was starting to think that bringing two non-undead women on this mission hadn't been the best idea. Corina especially seemed off. She'd never been this irritating when she was his apprentice. Though he still trusted her, if her behavior didn't improve, he'd have to think about getting her transferred out of the capital when they got back.

Skar led them back into the jungle as they continued to circle the city. All random thoughts were long gone from Otto's mind. Off the path, they could run into just about any sort of mutated beast. That they went stride after stride without encountering such a thing came as a surprise, though a pleasant one.

Otto took a quick glance at the ether, but couldn't see Skar doing anything magical. How did he even know where the tunnel was? Much as Otto wanted to ask, this was hardly the place for random questions. As long as he got them to the right place, the "how" didn't make any difference.

And get them to the right place he did. The tunnel entrance was a hole about six feet in diameter and sloped down into the earth. When they got close a pair of wingless, tailless dragonmen emerged to welcome them. Not that it was much of a welcome since they didn't say a word.

"Come," Skar said. "Father is eager to meet you."

"The feeling is mutual. Can you let them know that Lady White will be along in a little while and they shouldn't attack her?"

"I can, but how will she find us?" Skar asked.

"I'll mark the location in the ether. She'll have no trouble tracking it down, and since our enemy is out of the city, no one else will be able to."

"That's fine, only hurry. There have been enough delays."

Otto only needed seconds to put the marker in place. "Done. What's the hurry anyways? Your father has been trapped here for hundreds of years, an hour or even a day more or less isn't going to make any difference."

"All I know is that I can feel Father's urgency like a pressure in the back of my mind driving me to hasten the meeting along. Until you stand before him, the pressure will not go away."

It seemed strange that Lord Azteca would allow the dragon to have that much influence over her creations. Otto gave a mental shake of his head. Trying to figure out the mind of an Arcane Lord was beyond him, especially this one.

"By all means, let's get this meeting underway."

Skar didn't need to be told twice. He focused on the guards and said, "The final member of our party will be along eventually. Do not harm her."

Order given, he led the way into the dark tunnel. As soon as they were beyond the entrance, Otto conjured a light so everyone could see. This was ostensibly friendly territory so there was no need for stealth. Which was a good thing since casting darkvision on everyone would strain even him.

The tunnel went down for about thirty yards before leveling out. Otto tried and failed to detect the dragon's presence. That was odd. Something as powerful as a dragon should shine like a beacon in the ether. Likely it had some way to shield itself from magical sight. That would be a useful trick to learn.

At last the tunnel widened out into the largest cavern Otto had ever seen. Near the center of it, a massive, scaled creature lay pinned to the floor by mithril chains. The dragon easily measured fifty yards from its nose to the base of its tail. The tail itself had to be at least another thirty yards long. Its green scales were a perfect match for Skar's. It certainly wasn't hard to believe this creature was his father.

"Lord Shenk?" Hans's voice trembled.

"Calm yourself. We're all allies here. There's nothing to fear." Otto thought he sounded pretty convincing. And he wasn't all that frightened. No doubt his truncated emotions had a lot to do with that.

"I've brought the wizard, Father," Skar said.

"Well done, my son." The dragon's voice was a deep base rumble that vibrated in Otto's chest. "I can sense his power. He may be capable of doing what needs to be done."

Otto moved a little bit ahead of the others. "Perhaps it would be wise for us to exchange stories."

"I already know yours. I plucked the information out of Skar's mind. And you already know our current situation. The thralls outside are numerous enough to keep my children trapped. Even now, their creator is off collecting more of the cursed creatures. Only Azteca's barrier keeps them from attacking at once."

"Will that be a problem for my companion? She's undead as well."

"The barrier doesn't extend into the earth. She can pass through the tunnel without issue."

"Do you know why they're so interested in this place?" Otto asked. "As a wizard, my own interest is obvious. I'm sure Lord Azteca's library holds a wealth of magical knowledge. But what's here to interest a priest of Astaroth?"

"Why does it matter?" the dragon asked.

"This priest sent a dragonman that he'd transformed into a warbeast to attack my home. If you want my help, then I will know everything."

"You have more courage than most humans. I respect that. Very well, I shall tell you a story, a brief one, from long ago. Long before I was captured by Azteca and reduced to a

SHADOW OF THE DRAGONS

prisoner, a dear friend of mine and I spent much of our youth scouring the world looking for artifacts, evil ones, that we might keep them out of the hands of men that would use them. We were successful to some extent, finding many vile objects, the worst of which was called the Rod of Terror. It was forged by the greatest priest of Astaroth this world has ever seen under his master's direct guidance."

Otto nodded. That certainly sounded like something that would motivate a priest of Astaroth. "So you're the caretaker of this rod?"

"No, only half of it. We decided that it was so powerful it would be best to break it into two pieces. Melcor kept the rod itself and I kept a crimson orb that focused and magnified its power. The priest already has the rod, I can sense its corruption even from here. The only way that's possible is that Melcor is dead."

Otto frowned. "You're saying this priest is strong enough to kill a dragon?"

"I don't know. Someone or something else may have killed Melcor and the priest simply got lucky and found his lair. Whatever the case, he has the rod and if he gets his hands on the crimson orb, stopping him will become next to impossible even for me."

Otto looked around at the empty cavern. "You're clearly not in possession of the orb now. Where is it?"

"When I was captured, Azteca claimed all the artifacts I had collected. They're above somewhere."

That made sense. No doubt an Arcane Lord would have a ball studying a bunch of evil artifacts.

"Okay. What, exactly, do you want me to do?" Otto asked.

"I want you to free me. Your magic should be strong enough to melt the mithril chains."

Otto eyed the chains. The links were about as big around as his thigh and each end was driven into the stone floor. The anchor points fairly crackled with magical energy. As expected of such a critical juncture, Lord Azteca had reinforced the stone, probably enough to make it even tougher than the mithril. Heating that much mithril wouldn't be easy even for him. If you tried to focus on a narrow spot, the heat would dissipate into the rest of the link. But it might be doable, emphasis on might.

"Why would I want to free such a powerful potential threat?" Otto asked.

Skar growled and bared his fangs.

Otto ignored the dragonman. The threat was an empty one. They needed him, but Otto wasn't entirely certain that he needed them.

"I will swear an oath, both to never trouble your homeland and to police this nation to prevent any trouble from rising. I will also grant you unrestricted access to the library."

Otto considered the dragon's— "It just occurred to me that we haven't been properly introduced. My name is Otto Shenk."

"I am Brazon the Green. Do you know that in all the years she kept me here, Azteca never even asked my name?"

"That doesn't surprise me in the least. I'm a student of the Arcane Lords, and their arrogance was one of the most remarkable things about them aside from their power. You were a resource to her, nothing more."

"And do you consider yourself superior to them?" Brazon asked.

"Not especially. I am ever and always a practical man. I view the world through a simple lens, will this decision make my life better or worse. I have yet to decide where freeing you falls on that spectrum. You would certainly make a powerful ally, but I have no way of knowing when you might betray me. Leaving you here removes that risk and also the potential gains. It's by no means a simple decision."

"You are a rational man. I can appreciate that. We are currently in a standoff with the creatures outside, so there's no immediate danger. Go look at the library. Perhaps that will make the decision easier. Skar, show them the way."

"Yes, Father." Skar's tone indicated tightly controlled anger. "This way."

Skar guided them to a staircase that led up into the palace. He stomped his feet as he climbed and the muscles in his back were clenched so tight they were rippling visibly under his scales. Seeing the massive dragonman acting like Abby used to when she was a toddler throwing a tantrum nearly made Otto laugh. It was pathetic, but pointing that out would accomplish nothing.

At the top they turned down a hall and soon started climbing another set of steps.

"Which floor is the library on?" Otto asked.

"The second." Skar stomped up a few more steps then said, "You should do as Father says. He is very wise and following his orders has always gone well for us."

"Your father is trapped and desperate. He'd say anything if it got him free of his chains. I suspect that I'm the first person with the potential to free him that has reached this land since Lord Azteca was banished to the netherworld. Under such circumstances, you must acknowledge that I have a right to be suspicious."

"Dragons are not humans," Skar said. "We value our honor and our word above all things."

"You say this based on your numerous interactions with humans and dragons other than your father?"

Skar growled. "Are you questioning my honor?"

"No, I'm questioning your lack of experience. Before you met us, how many humans did you meet?"

"Only the Arcane Lords."

"Exactly, and they hardly counted as human anymore. What about dragons, other than your father?"

"None." Spitting out that one word seemed to cause him physical pain.

"You see where I'm going with this? Based on your ignorant opinion, I should act in a way that might put my homeland in danger one day. I can't make such a decision so lightly. In the end, I may agree to your father's terms. Or I may not. Either way, neither your advice nor your threats will make any difference."

They reached the top of the steps and a few yards down was a closed wooden door. Otto checked it for magic and found nothing.

"That's the library," Skar said. "I'll leave you to your reading. Think hard and fast about what you're going to do. Father says the priest is gathering more thralls as we dither. If they return with a real army, we may not be able to hold them back on our own, barrier or not."

"I have every intention of doing so. Lady White should be along soon. Would you escort her here when she arrives?"

"Very well."

Skar stalked off down the steps.

Think fast and hard, hmm? Fast thinking rarely led to good outcomes, but in this case, Otto feared time was not on his side.

CHAPTER THIRTY-SEVEN

Lady White was used to silence and being alone, but as she made her way through the empty city, even she found it a bit creepy. She'd been following the faint scent of corruption that belonged to only one of Astaroth's servants, a slave spirit. Lord of the Dead must have left his servants behind when he went to gather more forces. That made sense. Slave spirits were useless in combat situations, being not especially fast, or especially smart. They were absolutely obedient and tireless, which made them ideal for menial tasks.

She paid little attention to her surroundings. The squat stone buildings were as empty as they were tedious. Neither life nor corruption filled them. Even a graveyard had more life than this city. It was strange. Why would Azteca bother building such a huge city given her limited number of servants? It seemed impossible that she had more beastfolk in the past than were living now, though it wasn't impossible.

Whatever, it didn't matter for the current situation. She needed to wrap up her investigation as quickly as possible and rejoin Otto. It was sweet of him to worry about her safety, his explanation notwithstanding. No one had ever done that before. It was one more reason she'd come to highly value their friendship.

A dozen yards ahead she spotted a house with its door smashed down. The slave spirit was inside. She looked deeper into the city. There was something else there, another creature of corruption. It felt like a proper demon instead of a thrall, but not a strong one.

She dismissed it for now and stepped into the building. Three vulture-headed slave beasts stood on the far side of the room staring at nothing. He'd given them no orders, so they were in standby. Convenient for her.

Drawing on her magic, Lady White thrust tentacles of corruption into the skull of the nearest slave. Its gaunt, nearly skeletal body thrashed as it fought her control, but in the end she won. Had Lord of the Dead been close enough to reinforce its will, things would have gone differently, but without its master's backing, the slave beast had no hope of victory.

Black eyes with faintly glowing red centers stared at her. It offered nothing beyond its attention.

"Do you serve Lord of the Dead?" she asked.

"Yes, Mistress." It spoke in a dull monotone. Her magic held it in total bondage. Even showing what little personality it had was impossible.

She nodded, not surprised, but still happy to have her guess confirmed. "What is his goal here?"

"To acquire an artifact. Astaroth himself commanded that he do so."

No doubt something the dragon was protecting. "What does this artifact look like?"

"A crimson orb."

"And what does it do?"

"It combines with the Rod of Terror, making it stronger."

That wasn't an artifact Lady White was familiar with. Perhaps Lord of the Dead had kept it hidden from her. Astaroth knew they all kept plenty of secrets.

"Tell me everything about the rod."

The slave spirit started speaking. Apparently, after she left the Land of the Demon Binders, the other cults had turned on Lord of the Dead and driven him into hiding. His suffering pleased her in an offhand way. In truth, if he hadn't decided to cause trouble, she wouldn't have given him a second thought.

They wandered the wilderness until it became clear that the other lords had no intention of trying to hunt them down. Eventually they settled in a cave and Lord of the Dead set about rebuilding his force of warbeasts. After some years had passed two strangers arrived. They wanted information and were willing to trade the rod for it. Lord of the Dead threatened them, offering to let them live if they just handed it over. One of the strangers transformed into a huge red dragon and made it clear that they wouldn't be destroyed so easily.

Lady White frowned at that. A second dragon couldn't be a coincidence. She couldn't imagine any information that would be so important that someone would hand over an artifact of such power to a maniac like Lord of the Dead.

In the end it seemed Lord of the Dead bargained successfully with Astaroth to get the information they wanted. The strangers set the rod down and left. At their master's command, Lord of the Dead came here to find the second piece of the rod only to discover that it was guarded by a force of dragonmen as well as another actual dragon. Lord of the Dead was now building up his forces for an all-out assault.

Lady White considered her options, but only for a moment. She needed to let Otto know what she'd learned. Then they could come up with a proper plan. Getting her hands on the artifact would be nice, but keeping Lord of the Dead from claiming the orb was paramount.

Who knew what chaos he could cause should he succeed in claiming it.

ↄ

Lord of the Dead was well and truly sick of the jungle. He hated the way his vision was obscured. It teemed with so much life that he couldn't really sense anything clearly. And worst of all, every stride he took toward Throng's village brought him further away from the city and his ultimate goal. He took some solace in the fact that he'd been successful in both of the previous villages, adding the residents to his collection of thralls. When they were combined with the ones he left surrounding Azteca's palace, he would have over three hundred. And that didn't include however many they got in the final village.

He let out a mental sigh. An undead shouldn't be so impatient, but he couldn't help himself. He felt both extremely close to and far away from achieving his goal. Fantasies of the power he'd wield when he finally got his hands on the crimson orb flitted through his head.

But only for a moment. He savagely stomped them to death. Focus! His daydreams were what got him into trouble back in the Land of the Demon Binders. He couldn't make the same mistake this time. Thoughts of Astaroth's wrath made him shudder.

Turning to Throng he asked, "How much further?"

"Not far. We will arrive around midafternoon."

At last. Considering how far they'd come, it would likely take at least two weeks walking nonstop to get back to the city. Once they arrived with reinforcements, he'd order a full-scale assault on the palace. Even dragonmen couldn't stand against the force he'd built. Only the undead barrier stood between him and total victory and Lord of the Dead had an idea about how to deal with that. He'd been thinking about it off and on and the answer was as simple as it was difficult. If he channeled enough corruption into it, eventually it would have to break.

Once the obstacles had been removed, it was simply a matter of finding the orb and restoring the rod to its full might. He nearly grinned at the thought before reminding himself once more to focus. One step at a time. He couldn't get too far ahead lest he make some fatal mistake.

A quick glance back over his shoulder confirmed the thralls were still following along. There was no way they could disobey him, but he'd never commanded so many at once and that dented his confidence a bit. Those doubts needed to be buried in the same grave as his eagerness.

"The village is about three hundred paces ahead," Throng said.

Lord of the Dead almost thanked him for driving the whirling thoughts out of his head. It was time to get down to business.

Drawing on the power of the rod, he began the same ritual he'd used to transform the first two villages. When he sent the corruption forward, he frowned. There were no life forces for it to act upon. Where were all the villagers?

He released the spell and turned on Throng. "The village is empty. Where have my new thralls gone?"

"I don't know."

Lord of the Dead grabbed Throng by the face and dragged him to the ground. "You must know. You're the leader of this village. You must have a place where you gather in times of danger. You wouldn't let the young and females go into the jungle by themselves. And how did the village even know we were coming? Did you warn them somehow?"

"No, Master. Likely one of the scout patrols spotted us and fled to warn the village. And we have no gathering place. The warriors will protect the others as they travel through the jungle. In time a scout will see if it's safe to return. If the scout is slain, the others will know to stay away. That's how I set up the system."

Lord of the Dead sensed no lie. In fact, Throng couldn't have lied to him if he wanted to. It seemed his new confidence had been misplaced. Disappointing as it was, he still had a sufficient force to complete the job.

They'd wasted enough time out here. They needed to return and wipe the dragonmen out once and for all.

CHAPTER THIRTY-EIGHT

The library was everything Otto expected from an Arcane Lord. Shelves upon shelves of books stretched from wall to wall. There was also an open area in the center with chairs and a table where you could read and relax. If anything, it was a bit more low key than he'd expected from the eccentric Lord Azteca.

But that was fine. He'd take a look around until Lady White rejoined them.

"Axel, Hans, you and the guys can rest. Have a bite to eat if you want. I'm not planning on doing anything right away. I'll be wandering the stacks."

With everyone released from duty, Otto strode off to see what he could find. He had neither the time nor the inclination to make an exhaustive search. For now he would just grab a few random books and see what sort of theories interested her. He suspected most of them would be about flesh shaping. It was Lord Azteca's specialty after all.

Two rows from the front he reached in and grabbed the first book that caught his eye. The cover was plain brown leather with no title or other information. The spine was equally blank. Weird, did she have such a perfect memory that she could remember everything without labeling them? He would put nothing past an Arcane Lord at this point.

Flipping to the first page he started reading.

Otto nearly dropped the book. It wasn't a book of magic or even history. It seemed to be a romance novel, and a racy one at that. He shook his head. It had to be some kind of code.

By the time he reached the end of the first chapter, he was convinced that there was no code, only poorly written smut. Maybe he should bring a couple back for Sin. This seemed like the sort of thing she might enjoy.

"Is something wrong, Master?"

He'd been so deep in thought he hadn't even sensed Corina approaching. "Yes, something is definitely wrong. How wrong, I won't know until I look at a few more books."

"What is it?" she asked.

Otto handed her the book. "See for yourself."

While Corina read, Otto scanned the rest of the shelf. All the spines were the same unmarked brown leather. That they looked exactly like the one he'd just pulled down couldn't be a good sign.

He turned back to Corina and found her cheeks flushed as she eagerly turned the page. Hmm, perhaps Sin wasn't the only one that might like a few copies as a gift.

"What do you think?" he asked.

She flinched and looked up. "It's, um, interesting. Would it be okay if I kept this one? I want to see what happens."

Otto chuckled. "Sure. Be my guest."

She beamed. "Thank you!"

Taking her prize, she hurried back to the sitting area.

Looked like she didn't plan to offer to help him search. That was fine. The trip had been long and stressful. She deserved a bit of relaxation as much as anyone did.

Otto got back to work, pulling and checking more books at random and finding nothing but more smut. How many novels did Lord Azteca have? Assuming, heaven forbid, that all of the books in the library were like this, there had to be tens of thousands. Then again, if she were a dedicated reader and lived for hundreds of years, that wasn't impossible.

Somehow freeing the dragon to get access to all this struck him as a poor deal.

"Lord Shenk!" Hans called. "Lady White has returned."

Thank heaven. Hopefully she had good news. He'd gotten all the bad news he could stand for today.

He returned to the sitting area and found Lady White standing just inside the door. She looked no worse for her side trip which was a good sign.

"Did you learn anything interesting?"

"A few things. First and foremost I confirmed that it is, indeed, Lord of the Dead that we're dealing with." She went on to tell him everything the slave spirit had relayed. "So he wants the dragon's orb to complete the artifact. Should he get it, well, we don't want that."

"We certainly don't. As you may have noticed, the dragon's cavern is basically empty and distinctly orb free. That means it's somewhere up here. I propose we find it and take it for safekeeping. Perhaps I could even transport it to Colt's Workshop. There isn't a safer place that I can think of."

"If you do that," Lady White said. "Lord of the Dead is liable to sense it and go in pursuit."

Otto snorted at that. "If he's stupid enough to try, he'll find the workshop far more difficult to deal with than a few dragonmen, impressive though they are. But first we need to find and claim it. Axel, I need one of your scouts, preferably one that's young and not terribly bright looking."

Axel stood. "None of them are terribly bright looking, but one of the new recruits should fit the bill."

He pointed at a young man Otto guessed was about twenty-five. "Mitt, you're up. What's the mission?"

"I want him to check the rest of the palace and make sure there are no dragonmen hanging around. Assuming we're in the clear, we'll begin the search for the orb."

"What if there are?" Mitt asked with a decidedly nervous hitch in his voice.

"Tell them you're looking for the garderobe but got lost. I'd do it with magic, but I'm not certain how sensitive the dragonmen are to it and I'm sure Brazon would notice even from downstairs. No, I fear this is a job for a scout not a wizard."

"Yes, Lord Shenk," Mitt said. "I'll do my best."

"Be sure not to touch anything," Otto cautioned. "Any door you approach might be warded and you don't want to trigger it. Just make sure there are no dragonmen around. Understand?"

"Yes, my lord. I'll be careful."

Axel went to the door and pulled it open. He looked left then right before saying, "All clear. Off you go."

Mitt darted out and was soon lost from sight. Axel closed the door behind him and said, "Tell them you're looking for the garderobe? That's the best excuse you could come up with?"

"It's perfectly reasonable. What would you have had him say?"

Axel opened his mouth then snapped it shut. "Fair

enough. I can't actually think of anything off the top of my head. Think he'll find anything?"

"I don't think he'll find any dragonmen. I'm pretty sure they're all on the first floor watching the thralls." Otto snapped his fingers. "Speaking of which, how hard are thralls to kill?"

That last was directed at Lady White who said, "Fairly hard, though they are on the bottom rung of demonic entities. Why?"

"Well, we've got hundreds of mithril arrows. I was thinking it might not be a bad idea to wipe out the thralls here before Lord of the Dead shows up with more. If the archers can handle it from a safe position inside the palace, it would be worth the effort."

"Mithril-tipped arrows would certainly be an effective way to destroy them. A hit to the head or torso would purify the demon spirit and destroy the thrall."

"Perfect. What do you think, Axel? Would your men be up to a little target practice tomorrow?"

"Sure. Other than a couple of those weird beasts, they haven't had much to do. Wouldn't want them getting rusty."

Otto grinned. Tomorrow they would finally get a bit of payback for Lord of the Dead sending that monster to attack the capital. Otto could hardly wait.

○

In the two hours Mitt was gone, Otto had done a spot check of multiple books throughout the library and so far had found nothing beyond novels. He didn't want to just assume they were all fiction, but so far he was having a hard time coming to any other conclusion. If Lord Azteca could somehow see him from the netherworld, she was doubtless laughing her incorporeal head off. Had he the ability to kill her a second time, he would've happily done so.

So it came as a great relief when Mitt pounded on the door and Axel let him in. The scout looked a bit pale and sweat soaked his uniform, but otherwise he didn't have a mark on him.

"What did you find?" Otto asked.

"Nothing much, my lord. No dragonmen, lots of doors I didn't dare open, and lots of hallways lacking in decorations. Arcane Lords were rich, were they not? Rich folks usually like having fancy things around, right?"

"They were certainly rich," Otto said. "But they weren't really human, so you can't very well hold them to human standards of aesthetics. Anyway, good job. Since the coast is clear, let's have a look around. Corina."

She still had her nose buried in the book and didn't even look up when he spoke.

"Corina!"

She started and looked up at him, her face bright red. "Yes, Master?"

"We're leaving. Can I count on you to put that foolish book out of your mind long enough to help me search for wards and other magic?"

She bent the page to mark her place and as a book lover Otto winced. Then he remembered the book's contents and felt less bad about it. "I'm with you, Master. It's a very interesting book. You might enjoy it if you gave it a chance."

Otto seriously doubted that.

"May I be of some use, Mistress?" Jet asked.

"You can't see the ether," Lady White said. "So you can help the most by staying out of everyone's way."

Jet flinched as though she'd been slapped.

It was hardly Otto's place to interfere, but he thought it wouldn't hurt if Lady White treated her servant with at least basic politeness. It was remarkable how much better service you got when you did so.

"Come on." Otto went first and Hans and the others immediately took a defensive formation.

They went corridor by corridor, checking every door, and finding nothing of interest on the library floor. Mitt guided them to the stairs and they climbed up without issue to resume the fruitless search. None of the doors even had defensive wards.

When they reached the next set of steps Otto asked, "How many floors are there?"

"Two more, my lord," Mitt said.

They were also getting smaller as they went up, which meant they were rapidly running out of places to search.

"Master, where did she do her magic?" Corina asked. "We haven't seen any labs."

"Flesh shaping would happen in pits, so I assume there are more underground chambers like the one holding the dragon. I hope that's not where she put the orb. It would be a pain trying to find them."

They climbed to the next level and tried again. Still no wards, but they did find the treasury. It was filled to the ceiling with gold, jewels, and every sort of mundane wealth you could imagine. But nothing magical. Otto already had access to all the wealth he could ever want, so it didn't overly interest him. Everyone else stared at the mass of coins like a starving monkey shown a pile of bananas.

"We're not here for gold," Otto said. "Let's move on."

The others tore their gazes away from the gold and

followed him to the final set of stairs. As soon as they reached the top landing, Otto immediately sensed powerful magic.

"This is it."

The landing was about ten feet square and a single wooden door exactly like every other door they'd passed blocked their way. He checked it in the ether and found no wards. The potent source of magic he sensed was beyond it. Assuming this was the magical treasury, he couldn't imagine there were no defenses. Lord Colt's Workshop still had fully functional wards despite the centuries.

Was it because he'd left a simulacrum behind to maintain them? No. Lord Azteca surrounded herself with living servants that she created. None of them would be able to betray her. You could even argue that her force of dragonmen served as a sort of living ward.

Just to be safe, Otto conjured an ethereal hand and used that to push the door open. Nothing happened and no physical traps were triggered.

An orb of white light appeared at his metal command and he sent it into the room. A number of benches filled the space and all of them were covered with artifacts, all of which glowed in the ether.

"It's here," Lady White said. "I can feel Astaroth's presence in the artifact. It's like he imbued it with a fragment of his essence."

She walked past Otto and into the treasury. He was about to ask for a volunteer to go first, but this worked too. Nothing happened as she crossed the room, so the rest of them followed her inside.

Otto started to join Lady White then turned back. "Don't touch anything."

"Do any of us look suicidal?" Axel asked.

"No, but in cases like this, it's best to make sure. You never know when someone might see something shiny and lose their mind."

Warning given, he hurried to catch up. Lady White was standing in front of one of the benches set up near the right-hand wall. In the center of the bench sat a red sphere about the size of Otto's clenched fist. It was smooth and shined in the light. In the ether it looked like a black blot. As far as he could tell it wasn't actually doing anything. That was certainly a good thing for all of them.

She reached out to touch it then hesitated. "Do you know what this is?"

"Other than a surprisingly pretty ball of corruption, no. Do you?"

"It's a solidified sphere of Astaroth's blood. No wonder Lord of the Dead wants it so badly. Even if it did nothing, this would be considered the most holy relic of our faith on this world." Otto had never heard Lady White speak in such reverent tones. He'd always assumed her faith to Astaroth was just a way to gain greater power. Perhaps it was genuine.

"Does it do anything? As far as I can tell, the orb isn't leaking energy."

"The only way to know for sure is to pick it up."

She just stood there not picking it up.

"Are you planning to do so?"

"I was trying to savor the moment. You really don't have a romantic bone in your body, do you?"

"No. What I do have is an ever-growing heap of problems that need solving. It would be helpful if you could tell me just how big a problem this thing is going to be."

"Fine." She snatched up the orb and frowned. Corruption

oozed out of her hand and hit the orb's surface without penetrating. "It does nothing and I can't interact with it. It seems that, disconnected from its partner piece, it's harmless."

"Finally, some good news. I'll take it to Colt's Workshop and be right back." Otto held out his hand and Lady White reluctantly dropped the orb into it.

The surface felt slimy and his first instinct was to drop it. He resisted the impulse and tried to become one with the ether. Nothing happened. He'd never failed at this technique since he first learned it. Only magical exhaustion or protective wards could stop him and neither of those applied here.

He looked down at the orb. Was this thing the problem?

"Hold it for a second." He passed the orb back to Lady White and tried again. Otto shifted to the ether with no issue then reappeared in the same spot. "I can't take the orb with me when I teleport. So much for transporting it somewhere safe."

"Do you have an alternate plan?" she asked.

"I guess we kill Lord of the Dead and all of his thralls. A bit riskier of a plan than I'd like, but I don't see an alternative."

"And the dragon?"

Otto grimaced. "I'm not even sure I can free him. Melting those mithril chains will take a tremendous amount of energy. Just getting through one will probably put me into backlash and I'd just as soon not be helpless should Lord of the Dead show up unexpectedly. I'll decide for sure after we see how hard killing the thralls outside turns out to be."

"And the orb?" She caressed the thing like it was her lover.

"Let's leave it here. I can put a spell on the door. It won't be a proper ward, but at least it will let me know if anyone enters."

"Perhaps it would be best if I remain behind to guard it and you enchant the library door."

"What is it about this thing that so obsesses you? It feels disgusting when I touch it and it interferes with my magic. I can hardly imagine a worse thing."

"I couldn't begin to explain it to a nonbeliever."

Otto shrugged. He didn't consider Lady White insane, exactly, but she was definitely a little bit off. "I guess that's fine. We're going back. Maybe I'll make a fire with some of the awful books and fix some hot soup."

"Mistress?" Otto frowned when Jet spoke from right behind him. "May I touch it?"

Jet reached toward the orb and Lady White jerked it back. "You may not. This is a holy relic and only a true priestess may handle it."

Jet's worn face twisted in a grimace of bitter hate before smoothing once more. "Yes, Mistress."

She meekly returned to the doorway where the others were waiting.

"If there's trouble, contact me," Otto said. "Otherwise, I'll check in tomorrow."

Lady White nodded, her expression rapt as she stared at the orb. It almost looked like she was hypnotized.

Otto swallowed a sigh and went to the exit. Had he gained or lost by finding the orb? He couldn't decide and that worried him.

CHAPTER THIRTY-NINE

The night passed without issue and without any dragonmen showing up. After a rather uninspired breakfast of dried meat and tepid water, Otto left the team to get ready while he climbed up to the top floor. Inside the treasury he found Lady White sitting on the floor with the orb in her lap, petting it like the dogs some of the noble ladies favored. Otto had seen many things over the last few years, but this sight troubled him more than most. Any thoughts he'd harbored of counting on Lady White should things get tough were rapidly draining away.

He cleared his throat and she finally looked up. "Is there a problem?"

"That's what I came to ask you. We had a peaceful night. I assume you did as well."

"Indeed, no one troubled me. I have my doubts that the dragonmen even come up here."

That certainly made sense if none of them were wizards. "I'm going to speak with Skar and his father then do my best to wipe out the thralls. Is that something you can help with?"

She cocked her head. "What do you mean?"

"I mean I'm not sure how your particular sort of magic interacts with demons summoned from your master's hell. Will it affect them?"

"It won't destroy them, but I can hold them in place or even force them back if they're weak enough. Your mithril arrows will be much more effective. Once the demon spirits are destroyed, you need to burn the bodies to ash so Lord of the Dead can't reuse them."

"Can I assume that you prefer to remain here then?"

She nodded. "I feel that as I meditate on the sphere, my connection to Astaroth grows. My power hasn't increased yet, but it's only a matter of time. Having me stronger when it's time for the final confrontation can only be to your benefit."

Otto had serious doubts about her explanation, but he nodded. Maybe she really was accomplishing something. He was no priest and so had no idea one way or the other. It sounded like their mithril weapons would be sufficient and that was all that mattered.

"In that case I'll wish you luck and be on my way. Should I send Jet to join you?"

"No! No, keep her away. Her needy gaze is a distraction I don't want while I'm trying to focus."

"As you wish. When the slaughter is finished, I'll be back to discuss our next move. Until then." He stepped back and reached for the door. A quick glance confirmed that she was already fully engrossed with the orb.

Otto closed the door and retraced his steps. As he descended to the library he couldn't help wondering if some tiny amount of Astaroth's will remained in the orb. Lady White seemed almost hypnotized by it. Though far from devout himself, this seemed like far more than a priest finding a holy artifact.

As long as it didn't interfere with her actions when the final battle arrived, Otto would keep his thoughts to himself.

He rounded the corner to the library and found Skar standing in the doorway, blocked by Hans and Axel. What did the dragonman want now? Probably to pester them about freeing his father.

"Skar," Otto said. "I assume you're looking for me. Did you need something?"

Skar turned to face him. "Have you made up your mind?"

"No." The dragonman bared his fangs. Otto was beginning to think this was an expression of frustration as much as one of anger. "But I have decided on our next move. We're going to eliminate the thralls out front. That way we won't have so many to deal with when Lord of the Dead returns."

Skar snorted. "Those things killed several lesser dragonmen and drove us into the palace. What hope do you humans have of killing them?"

"According to our resident expert on thralls, they're vulnerable to mithril. It just so happens that my soldiers are armed with mithril weapons, including hundreds of arrows. We're going to shoot them from a safe distance. If they react the way we expect, killing the whole bunch shouldn't be an issue."

"I doubt it will be so simple," Skar said. "But if you can do it, we would be free to hunt and replenish our meat supply. That would be most welcome as we're getting low. That said, freeing Father will assure our victory. That should be your priority."

Otto smiled and shook his head. "Has anyone ever told you that you have a one-track mind?"

"No. I've never heard that expression before now. I will relay your plan to Father. Good luck."

Skar stomped back toward the stairs and was soon out of sight. Though Otto knew he was intelligent, sometimes Skar reminded him of those birds that repeated the same thing over and over again. He hated those birds.

"Excellent timing, Lord Shenk," Hans said. "I don't think that fellow believed me when I said you were out. I doubt we could have stopped him from forcing his way in."

"You shouldn't even try," Otto said. "We're not doing anything secret in the library. He can come in and look around all he wants. It makes no difference to me beyond the minor annoyance. Axel, are your archers ready?"

"Whenever you are. Thing is, I didn't notice any arrow slits when we were exploring the upper levels. I never saw a castle without them."

Otto cocked an eyebrow. "Why would an Arcane Lord need arrow slits? Anyone stupid enough to attack her city would be obliterated in an instant. Anyways, there's a door on this level that leads to the second-floor ledge. It's about three feet wide and runs all the way around the palace. That should be wide enough, right?"

Axel nodded. "Three feet is plenty. When did you find that? I didn't notice it when we did our walk-around."

"This morning. It's a hidden door, built into the wall. You wouldn't notice it without magic. It also only opens from the inside. Hans, you and your team are in charge of making sure it doesn't close while we're out there."

"Yes, my lord," Hans said.

"The morning's wasting," Otto said. "Let's get this done."

Everyone lined up and followed him through the empty halls. The secret door was down a dead-end side passage that stopped at a blank wall. An ethereal hand flicked the latch hidden in the wall and pulled the door open enough for Hans to grab it and open it the rest of the way.

The archers strung their bows and followed Otto out. Below them, the thralls were milling around aimlessly. If they were aware of their impending death, they gave no sign. He wasn't sure if they were stupid or if Lord of the Dead had given them specific instructions. Didn't matter anyway. Unless they could fly, they weren't getting up here.

"Pick your targets and fire when ready," Otto said.

Bows creaked as the archers pulled them back. A moment later they twanged and arrows leapt out. Each one struck a thrall square in the chest, passing through undead flesh as easily as they did everything else.

Otto watched through the ether as the corruption at their cores was burned away and the once-more-dead bodies collapsed. Mithril really was perfect for this sort of thing. Especially in arrows since it didn't risk any of his people getting within striking distance.

It ended up taking thirty-five shots to drop the thralls on this side of the palace. Pretty good accuracy. But Otto had an idea that would be more efficient. Sending ether through the mithril in his hand, he created a resonance bond with the mithril arrowheads and plucked them out of the ground.

"What are you doing?" Axel asked.

"Just watch. If this works, we can save your arrows for round two."

He led the way around to the next side of the palace. The thralls were moving around, agitated, but seeming uncertain what they should do. Clearly they realized something had happened to their fellows but had no idea what to do about it. They were even too stupid to try and find cover.

Otto shrugged. That made his job easier.

Focusing on the arrowheads, he sent them streaking into the mass of thralls. They zipped back and forth, mowing the creatures down one after the next. If they tried to dodge, he simply adjusted the arrow's path. After a few seconds it became clear that managing all thirty-five was inefficient.

He pulled all but ten back and focused on those. That was way easier and his greater control made it simple to nail each thrall right through the chest. In less than a minute, all the thralls on this side were dead.

"That's a hell of a trick," Axel said. "How is it you keep getting scarier and scarier?"

"Too much free time. You don't need to be scared of me, only my enemies do. Now, let's clear the rest of them."

And so they did. Well, so Otto did. Not wanting to waste arrows, he tore the thralls apart on his own until none remained around the palace. Task complete, he pulled the arrowheads back and returned all but ten of them to Axel. They had all the material they'd need to make new ones and that would give the scouts something to do while they waited for the next attack. And Otto had no doubt there'd be one. Given how obsessed Lady White was with the orb, there was no way a fellow priest would give up trying to claim it.

"We still need to burn the bodies," Otto said. "We can get the dragonmen to help with that. Let's find Skar."

"I found him." Axel pointed down into the courtyard where Skar and a dozen dragonmen had emerged from the palace.

"That's convenient." Otto headed for the secret door.

Just inside, Hans and the guys were waiting, swords drawn and ready for trouble. Corina stood a little ways away, a faint frown twisting her lips. Of Jet there was no sign.

Probably stayed in the library. That was fine. She had no combat skills to speak of and couldn't wield magic. Otto wasn't sure exactly why they'd brought her along other than as some sort of test of her loyalty.

Whatever, she was Lady White's problem, not his.

"I didn't get to help," Corina said when Otto walked past her.

"There was nothing for you to do. I will be counting on you to help with burning the bodies. Given the environment, I doubt there's much in the way of dry wood around, so it will come down to magic. Between the two of us, there shouldn't be much trouble."

She smiled, clearly pleased to have a job, even a nasty one. When they left the empire, he'd assumed that there would be a lot more for her to do, but so far things hadn't gone at all the way he'd expected. They were, in fact, going far better. Which worried him. Whenever something went his way, he fully expected to be slapped in the head by reality sooner rather than later.

The group descended to the first floor and Otto strode right past the dragonmen still on guard duty and out the front door. None of them tried to stop him which suggested that Skar had ordered them not to.

In the courtyard he found the leader of the dragonmen poking a fallen thrall with his toe as if he expected it to get up and attack.

"They're all quite dead I can assure you," Otto said.

Skar looked up. "How did you do this when my finest warriors were driven back by them?"

"Mithril-tipped arrows. Every shot destroyed the demonic spirit animating the thrall. Since you had neither bows nor mithril, you were in a poor fighting position. If we'd had to fight them without our weapons, it would have been a different story. Can I get you and your people to help gather the bodies into a couple of large piles? They need to be burned."

"Why?" Skar asked. "They're dead."

"For now, but when Lord of the Dead returns, he could summon new spirits and reanimate them. I don't care for the thought of having to kill these things a second time, do you?"

"No. We will assist you. And thank you for destroying them. While I still think you should free Father, this was a big help. I already dispatched hunters to restock our meat supply. Should another siege befall us, we will be well supplied."

Otto nodded. Always a good idea to be prepared. And he knew another fight was coming. It was just a question of when.

CHAPTER FORTY

The march back from the empty village was no more interesting than the march to it. Lord of the Dead strode forward nonstop, his undead body tireless. He wished he could've opened a portal through Astaroth's hell, but the two times he tried it, he'd ended up so tired he could barely cast a spell for most of a day. Not exactly the kind of shape you wanted to be in when you arrived in enemy territory.

So he walked. The heat didn't bother him; neither did the dark of night or the bugs that occasionally landed on him only to die an instant later. Throng and his other slaves followed along silently. It was a procession of the dead and no one was around to appreciate it. Not that they would have. Had anyone been around, Lord of the Dead would have happily killed them and added their body to his forces.

Two days in, the tedium was broken by a faint and unwelcome twinge in the back of his mind. It was the very specific feeling triggered by the destruction of one of his thralls. It was enough to stop him in his tracks. The dragonmen wouldn't dare attack such a large force. But if not them, then who?

Another twinge hit him, then another and another. His servants were dying one after the other. Grimacing, he focused on the imp he summoned. A moment later the courtyard appeared in his vision. Archers, human archers, were standing on the second-floor ledge peppering his thralls with arrows. What were humans doing here and how did they get past the siege in the first place without fighting his thralls or getting spotted by his imp?

He shook off the question. For now, it was sufficient to know that they had. He debated sending his imp in for a closer look but immediately rejected the idea. Those arrows were terrifyingly effective at killing his thralls. He doubted the imp would do any better.

Speaking of those arrows, how were they killing the thralls so easily? You should be able to turn a thrall into a pincushion without killing it.

He ordered the imp to show him the ether, but there was nothing visible. If not magic, then what? The answer came a moment later and made him feel sick. It had to be mithril. Weapons made of that cursed metal were banned from the Land of the Demon Binders for a reason. One hit was enough to destroy a weak demonic spirit and the various cults used them almost exclusively to make servants and low-level troops.

Lord of the Dead looked up at the sky. Had Astaroth's enemies in Heaven sent these warriors to stand in his way? No, that was ridiculous. Heaven interfered directly in the mortal realm even less than Hell did. An archangel might have sent a message to some of their followers, but even that seemed doubtful.

While he stood there thinking, the last of the thralls visible to his imp were destroyed and the archers moved around to the other side of the palace out of sight. The twinges immediately started again.

He ordered the thralls to take cover, but there was nowhere to hide in the courtyard and they kept falling. By the time he told them to escape, it was too late and soon all the thralls he left behind were destroyed. A third of his force, gone, just like that and there wasn't a damn thing he could do about it. And now he had mithril-armed soldiers to worry about along with dragonmen. If the soldiers had brought mithril weapons for the dragonmen, he had no hope of victory.

♂

It took most of a day and a fair bit of magic, but finally the bodies of the thralls were no more. Otto hadn't paid much attention to what they looked like while he was killing them, but as the dragonmen were tossing them into piles he couldn't help noticing that they were basically giant monkeys. Why had Lord Azteca chosen them as test subjects? Otto had seen a couple monkeys brought in by traders from the City of Coins and they were cute, small things with big eyes and puffy tails. He distinctly remembered telling Annamaria that under no circumstances could Abby have one as a pet.

These things wouldn't make anyone a good pet. Not that the dragonmen were especially cute either.

He rubbed the bridge of his nose and left the stink and smoke of the courtyard behind. Corina had done her best, but she ran out of power hours before the job was done and had gone in to sleep. Or more likely read another of the useless books that filled the library. Well, that was fine. There were no pressing tasks for her at the moment.

For his part, Otto wanted an alchemy cookie, and ten hours' sleep. Then it would be time to fix the portal.

He froze halfway across the courtyard. Lady White said Lord of the Dead had left behind some of his servants. Didn't sound like they were a threat, but he might as well clean them up. There was no way their enemy didn't know all his thralls had been destroyed, so leaving them intact was pointless.

That would be a good job for the scouts.

Otto yawned and walked through the palace door. The dragonmen on guard duty ignored him and he returned the favor. It had become clear that the lesser dragonmen weren't the sharpest swords in the armory. Of course, that made them no less lethal.

The slog up to the top floor seemed especially long today but he made it and in the magic treasury found Lady White in the exact same spot, sitting on the floor with the orb in her lap like it was her new favorite pet.

She looked up when he entered and quirked an eyebrow.

"The thralls are all dead, but I figure this would be a good time to deal with those things Lord of the Dead left behind. What did you call them?"

"Slave spirits. They're basically harmless, but I suppose it couldn't hurt to destroy them. Do you want directions to where they were hiding?"

Otto shook his head. "I want you to take Axel and his scouts there and make sure they get them all."

She looked down at the orb. "I'm—"

"No. I didn't bring you on this mission to sit around day

after day mooning over that thing like it was your long-lost lover. Corina and I are both used up." That was actually an exaggeration. Should it be necessary, Otto had plenty of reserve strength. Unless it was life or death, he never used up all his power. "Time for you to step up. And take Jet with you. Her moping is starting to get on my nerves. You two need some quality servant-and-mistress time."

"She's useless."

"I don't care. She's yours, deal with her. One way or the other, it makes no difference to me. Her gloomy presence is dragging everyone down, myself included."

Lady White stood and grimaced. If all that time sitting cross-legged on the floor left her stiff she gave no sign. "I can't just kill her outright, much as I'd like to. She's still a loyal servant of Astaroth."

"I wasn't under the impression that your cult cared all that much about such niceties."

"It's complicated. And it's not like there's a rule book we can follow. There's just a sort of rule of thumb that says you don't kill those who are loyal without a good reason. Since we may end up having to explain our reason to Astaroth should he be displeased, we tend to not take such things lightly."

"Details of your religion, interesting as they are, don't concern me at the moment. Go make my life easier. I'll stay and guard the treasury until you return."

She clutched the orb to her chest. "I can take it with me."

"And risk running into something nasty that we missed? I think not." Otto pointed at the bench where he'd found the thing. "Just set it there. I promise it will still be here when you get back."

She looked torn, but he didn't care. And he was too tired

to soothe her feelings. If all Lady White did was sit here, she was as useless to him as Jet.

"Fine. I suppose a couple hours won't make that much difference." She set the orb where he said.

"Have you learned anything useful from it?"

"I'm afraid not. I'm beginning to wonder if there's anything to learn, but even if there isn't, I find holding it soothes my spirit and, I like to think, strengthens my connection to Astaroth."

"I suppose that can only be a good thing. Good hunting."

She took the hint and strode out of the room.

Otto rubbed his eyes. Why, in heaven's name, did everyone seem intent on making his life difficult?

ᴑ

Jet leaned against one of the bookcases in the library and scowled at the wall. Since they'd arrived, she'd been pretty much ignored by everyone, most pointedly her mistress. Lady White's disdain couldn't have been clearer. The truth became painfully obvious when Jet wasn't even allowed to touch the crimson orb. If it truly was a crystallized drop of Astaroth's blood, then as a faithful follower of the demon lord, Jet had every right to touch it. At least that was the way she felt. It wasn't like she had the power to force the issue.

For years Jet had believed it was her fault that Astaroth ignored her prayers, but lately she'd come to a different conclusion. Lady White was doing something or keeping some secret that was preventing her making that final, important connection to their master. The reason why was as obvious as a war hammer blow to the head. She didn't want Jet to become competition. There could be no other explanation.

The problem for Jet was, what could she do about it? There was no one else to teach her the secret, whatever it might be. Lord Shenk had been kind to her, in his rather cold way, but he was a wizard, not a priest. Even if he were inclined to tell her something useful, he didn't have the correct knowledge.

The library door opened and Lady White strode in. "Otto wishes for us to hunt down Lord of the Dead's slave spirits. He asked me to guide the scouts to where I last saw them."

Axel and his men stood. "He said something about that. We're ready when you are."

"Where is Lord Shenk?" Hans asked. It was rare for him to be separated from his charge and he looked uncomfortable.

"He's taking over guard duty on the treasury," Lady White said. "This shouldn't take more than a couple hours. If you wish to speak with him, that's where he is."

Hans nodded but showed no sign of leaving. Perhaps he'd decided that inside the palace was safe enough that a guard wasn't necessary.

That worked out perfectly for Jet. Surely Lord Shenk would let her touch the orb.

Lady White pointed at her. "You come too."

Jet's eyes widened. "Me, Mistress? I'm of no use in a fight."

"A fact of which I am painfully aware. However, you've never seen a slave spirit from the Land of the Demon Binders. This is a rare opportunity for you."

Jet panicked. She didn't want to go out into the city. She wanted to go upstairs and try and convince Lord Shenk to let her touch the orb. But she couldn't just disobey. Lady White wouldn't stand for it.

"Interesting as seeing a slave spirit would be, I'd prefer to stay behind. If there are hidden dangers out there, I fear I might slow you down or get in the way. My strengths and weaknesses are very clear to me, Mistress."

"Useless and a coward," Lady White muttered. "I should never have made you my disciple. Fine, stay here. This won't take long in any case."

Lady White spun and stalked out with Axel and half the scouts on her tail.

Jet blew out a breath of relief. That had been too close. She'd wait ten minutes then try her luck upstairs.

"You should probably try and help out with the dangerous stuff even though it's not your forte." Jet nearly jumped when Corina spoke from behind her. The young wizard had a book in her hand. "Our masters tend to be impressed by that sort of thing."

"I thought you were sleeping."

"I was. Voices woke me up so I decided to grab a new story. They're quite good. I've never read anything just like them."

By Astaroth she seemed young sometimes. "There's nothing impressive about showing off and getting in the way. Far better for everyone if we understand our strengths and weaknesses and do our best within those limitations. I can't use magic like you. I am literally just an ordinary woman who happens to be knowledgeable about demonic matters."

"I still think Lady White would've liked it if you went with her." Corina shrugged. "I don't know her as well as you do, so I'm sure I'm wrong."

She wasn't wrong, unfortunately, but Jet had other priorities at the moment. "Excuse me. I think I'll stretch my legs a bit."

Jet hurried away before Corina could say anything else and slipped out into the hall. She let out a long sigh and headed for the stairs up. Not a soul crossed her path as she climbed and soon she stood in front of the treasury door. After a moment of hesitation, she pushed it open.

Lord Shenk was seated on the floor with one of the artifacts, a black metal rod of some sort, resting in his lap. He looked up when she entered, his expression neutral. "Did you not wish to accompany Lady White?"

"I told her I'd only be in the way." Jet hesitated, uncertain how she wanted to approach this. In the end, directly was all she could think of. "Can I hold the orb? Please, just for a minute or two."

His expression twisted into something unreadable before he answered, "If you wish to touch the disgusting thing, be my guest. But don't pick it up."

She frowned. "Why not?"

"Because I said so. Please get your touching over with so I can get back to work."

"You can keep working. No need to worry about me."

"You think I can concentrate with you feeling up that ball of congealed blood? I know you and Lady White worship Astaroth and this is some sort of holy artifact to you. That's grand, but the way you obsess over it is unnerving. It doesn't even do anything without its companion piece."

"I suppose a nonbeliever would never understand. I accept your terms." She walked over to the bench and placed her hand on the sphere.

And nothing. No bolt of power or inspiration struck her.

Astaroth's presence didn't speak to her. The orb did feel pleasant under her fingers. Like a fresh coat of the master's blood covered it. She rolled it this way and that, running her hand over every inch as if there was something hidden that she would miraculously discover.

But of course there wasn't. The orb was exactly what it appeared to be.

Much as she would've liked to spend an hour or two enjoying the feel of it, Lord Shenk's glare was getting sharper by the second. It seemed she was getting close to the end of his patience.

Reluctantly, she took her hand away and sighed. "I appreciate your indulgence. If I may ask one more favor, please don't tell Lady White I came up here. She wouldn't approve."

"If she doesn't ask, I won't mention it. If she does, I won't lie for you. We're allies and that's no way to treat someone you trust. Now, please go away. I'd very much like to finish analyzing this artifact."

She bowed and hurried away. Cold though he was, Lord Shenk at least treated her with a modicum of respect. Clearly Jet had chosen the wrong person as her master.

CHAPTER FORTY-ONE

After a good night's sleep, Otto headed straight for the city portal with the entire team, minus Lady White, who had resumed petting the orb, and Jet, who seemed terrified to leave the palace. He couldn't really blame her. Things appeared safe and quiet at the moment, but Aztecaland had to be one of the most hostile environments he'd visited. Only the Dead Lands surpassed it.

He didn't know exactly how long it would take Lord of the Dead to get here, but he wanted to get this done while he had time. Otto had no intention of fleeing before all threats to the empire had been dealt with, but having the option wouldn't be a bad thing, especially since undead and other creatures of corruption couldn't pass through the mithril gate.

"Did you decide what you're going to do about the dragon?" Axel asked.

"I'm not going to do anything about him. It's far safer for us to leave him chained where he is. If the fight with Lord of the Dead goes badly, I may change my mind, but for now, I'm content to leave things as they are."

"And do you imagine Skar is just going to let us finish our business and leave unmolested?"

"That's one of the reasons I'm getting the portal ready. I vastly prefer using it to running through the jungle with a bunch of angry dragonmen on our tail."

"I second that," Hans said. "Of course, we could always launch a preemptive strike, take 'em out before they turn on us."

"No, we are not going to pick a fight with our allies until Lord of the Dead is dealt with. Once that matter is sorted, we can see. I would much prefer to simply leave as soon as our business is concluded."

"And leave all those magical goodies behind?" Axel asked. "I'm shocked."

Otto grimaced. "I studied several of them yesterday. They all require you to use corrupted ether. As a still-living man, that's a problem. Lady White could probably make use of some of them, assuming she can drag herself away from her new obsession, but for me, they're basically trash."

They reached the edge of the courtyard where the portal waited. It was strange seeing a portal with so few runes on it. Clearly Lord Karonin hadn't been exaggerating when she said Lord Azteca seldom visited her fellow lords.

Otto studied the runes. There were none from the empire. He recognized one that matched the portal outside Amet Sur's black pyramid. Ah, here we are. The rune for Markane's portal. That was perfect. No one would want to visit the dead island anyway.

"I'm going to begin. Under no circumstances can I be disturbed. Is that clear?"

"Yes, Lord Shenk," Hans said.

"What happens if someone interrupts?" Axel asked.

"Then our easy way home is lost. It's not like I have a spare mithril patch on me or time to go home and make one."

Axel swallowed audibly. "That's certainly good motivation. We'll keep the area secure. You do what you have to."

Otto nodded and dug the patch out of his satchel. Now that he'd done this once, he hoped the second time would go more smoothly. Not that hoping was an especially good strategy. But in this case, it was the only one he had.

Skar made his way to the cavern where his father remained a prisoner. Once the wizard arrived, he'd assumed his first act would be to set Father free. That was the only sensible thing as far as Skar was concerned. It wasn't right to keep someone as powerful and wise as Father chained up like a stupid animal. Skar's anger flared up just thinking about it.

He suppressed the emotion as quickly as it appeared. Anger just got in the way of thinking clearly. He would be of no use if he let his emotions control him. Shame it was so much easier said than done.

At the bottom of the steps he nodded to the lesser dragonman on duty. Skar didn't think Father would be in danger from anyone and thought of the posted dragonman as an honor guard more than anything. A few more strides brought him to Father's side. Even chained to the ground, the dragon's massive body was taller than Skar.

"The human wizard still refuses to free you. Even now

he's wasting his time and energy doing something to the portal."

"I can sense the magic from here," Father said. "He's modifying the portal in some way that I don't fully understand. What little I know about humans suggests such a thing would be impossible for anyone other than an Arcane Lord. If this wizard is capable of such a feat, I may have underestimated him."

"Is the human truly so impressive?"

"For a human, he certainly is. Compared to Azteca or myself, he's nothing. Not that comparing a human to an Arcane Lord or a dragon is especially fair. We're simply too different."

"Do you have a plan to compel him to do what you want?"

"No. There is no way to compel someone to use magic against their will. It would take all his focus and determination to free me. Even if we tried to force the issue, the results would only be failure. No, my son, Otto must act of his own accord or not at all."

Skar growled a little. He'd been optimistic that Father would have a better plan. "He's been to the treasury, perhaps if you offered it all to him, he'd do what you wanted."

"Unlikely. All the magical artifacts are unusable by a normal human. They're cursed things I collected over the centuries before my capture. Even Azteca couldn't use them, though she did recognize their danger and brought them here at the same time that she brought me. I think little of that witch, but that was one decision I fully appreciate. Those things have no place in the wider world."

"Then are we truly reduced to depending on the human's benevolence?"

"We truly are, my son. Help him however you can. Do everything in your power to prove that we aren't a threat to him or his empire. Or better yet that we can be reliable and trustworthy allies. He already has an undead priestess at his side, so clearly he has no bias toward nonhumans."

Skar bowed his head. "I will do my best, Father, but he never asks for anything, so it's difficult."

"We can only do our best. I have been here for many centuries. If I must wait for another wizard to show up, I can do that."

Father's durability couldn't be questioned, nevertheless, Skar wanted him free. And he would do everything in his power to make it happen.

CHAPTER FORTY-TWO

Otto had taken a full day to rest after fixing the portal. The process had gone perfectly and he was confident that they now had a way to escape should the worst happen. It wouldn't be easy given the time it took the portable capacitor to charge the portal, but it was better than nothing by a fair distance.

That had been nearly a week ago and he was now back to full strength. The scouts had used their time well. All the broken arrows had been replaced and they were back to having a complete complement plus backups. Given how effective the mithril arrows were, Otto was glad he told Axel to bring as many as they could manage. Avoiding a direct physical confrontation with Lord of the Dead and his thralls would be ideal. Not that Otto had any confidence they'd get that lucky. The team had been extraordinarily fortunate so far and there was no doubt that wouldn't last forever.

Now it was simply a matter of waiting. He spoke to Lady White every day and she assured him that Lord of the Dead was getting closer all the time. In fact, she expected him to be at their doorstep either tomorrow or the next day. The fight was going to be awful, but Otto, and, he felt certain, everyone else, was eager to have it over with so they could go home.

Speaking of home. One thing Otto hadn't done was teleport back to check on the empire. He was confident that everything would run smoothly in his absence and he wanted to give everyone the chance to prove they could handle the day-to-day operations on their own, especially to themselves.

He groaned and stood. Every eye in the library focused on him. Well, all save Corina's, she was oblivious to everything save her latest book. She'd become obsessed with them, nearly as badly as Lady White was with the orb.

"I'm going to check in and see if anything's changed. If the enemy is close enough, I may take a peek myself."

Since this was what he'd been doing around this time every day, no one felt the need to comment. They all just went back to their various card games. At least no one was complaining.

He slipped out the library door and made the now-familiar trek up to the top floor. When he pushed the treasury door open, he found Lady White in her usual spot cuddling the orb. No matter how many times he saw it, he couldn't wrap his mind around what she got out of such behavior.

Oh well, it wasn't like he had anything else for her to do. She looked up after a moment. "Has it been a day already? I lose track of time when I'm contemplating the orb."

Contemplating the orb, that was an interesting way to describe it. "Where is Lord of the Dead now?"

She closed her eyes and her pale brow furrowed. "About twenty miles out and making good time. He'll reach the city by nightfall."

Fighting at night was not ideal for human warriors. He could always conjure lights if it came to it, but using even a fraction of his power for something like that was a waste. Actually, that would be a perfect job for Corina.

"Will you be ready to fight when the time comes?"

"I will. Lord of the Dead knows I'm here. When the battle begins, only one of us will survive. He claims leadership of the cult, but I will not serve him. Our positions can be rectified in only one way. Astaroth will decide which of us he wants as his champion."

"Thanks for the update. When he's a mile out, let me know and we'll get the archers in position on the ledge. It'll be up to us to hold off Lord of the Dead's magic while the archers do their work."

"That will be difficult for you."

Otto's first reaction was to bristle at the insult, but he immediately caught himself. Lady White wasn't the sort to throw out insults. At him, anyways. "Why is that?"

"Lord of the Dead wields corrupt ether, the same as I do. While I have no doubt that you could defeat me should it come to battle, Lord of the Dead is getting a massive power boost from the rod. His strength will be easily three times my own. Whereas your attacks will be muted simply due to the miasma of corruption that surrounds him."

"You can sense all this from so far away?"

She nodded. "This might seem like an odd way to describe it, but the flavor of this corruption is perfectly aligned with Astaroth's hell. Now that I can get a better feel for it, I believe the rod acts as a permanent portal to the

Endless Graveyard. That's why he can summon and control so many demon spirits without using sacrifices."

"And the orb? What purpose does it serve?"

"This is just a guess, but I believe that this drop of Astaroth's blood creates a resonant link between the rod and his hell thus allowing the portal to open even wider and sustain ever greater numbers of thralls, possibly even true demons."

"Right, that sounds every bit as bad as I feared. Of course, if we kill him, that solves all our problems. For the moment at least. Make sure you don't lose track of time." Otto gave the orb a pointed look.

"Though I may not look it, I am fully aware of everything going on around me as well as the approaching danger. Have no fear on that account."

He had his doubts, but chose not to comment. "Well enough. I'll see you when it's time."

Otto turned on his heel and marched out. Twenty miles. Assuming they weren't sprinting, and the jungle would make that nearly impossible, Lord of the Dead should arrive in about five hours, give or take. That seemed like both very little and a great deal of time. Well, they were ready, it was just a matter of putting everyone in place and spearing fish in a barrel.

Smiling to himself, he returned to the library. He could only wish the fight would go that well.

When he entered, everyone looked up.

"How long?" Axel asked.

"They're about twenty miles out. Five hours, at most."

"Then they'll arrive after sunset. Not ideal for us."

Otto shook his head. "No, far from ideal. When the fight begins, providing light will be Corina's task."

She was still reading and hadn't heard a word he said. He sent a thread of ether into the book and a moment later a line of fire followed.

Corina yelped when the dry pages burst into flame.

Otto snuffed them out a moment later. "When I'm speaking, I expect you to be paying attention."

She couldn't meet his gaze. "Yes, Master."

"If I see a book in your hand before things are settled, so help me I'll burn every trash novel in here to ash. Do I make myself clear?"

"Yes, Master."

"Good. I'm going to talk to Skar. As far as I'm aware we should be set, but if any of you have last-minute preparations to make, you'd best do so now."

With that Otto turned and left the library. Annoyed as he was by Corina's recent behavior, he felt certain she'd come through when there was actual danger. At least she'd better, for all their sakes.

He reached the bottom floor and paused. He didn't actually know where Skar was. It would probably be easiest to talk to Brazon and have him summon Skar, or better yet just fill him in. Otto wasn't especially eager to talk to the dragon, not that their brief conversations to date had been unpleasant. Otto just found the huge creature intimidating and he didn't like the feeling.

At the bottom of the stairs he found a single lesser dragonman on guard duty. He didn't so much as blink in Otto's direction. As far as Otto knew they were incapable of speech. Not the most effective of guards, but maybe they counted on their father to give them orders about who to attack.

Otto turned deeper into Brazon's prison, conjuring a light as he did so. He could have used darkvision, but the yellow orb's warm light felt comforting in the darkness. Foolish sentimentality, but the truth all the same.

When he reached the dragon he found its huge eye focused on him. The yellow orb was half as big as Otto was tall and had a vertical slit. Even the veins were visible this close up.

"Have you reconsidered?" Brazon asked. "I sense the great darkness that's approaching. My help may be necessary."

"It may be," Otto said. "However, I couldn't free you now if I wanted to. Melting just one of those chains would leave me too weak to fight, assuming I could do it at all. I've come to ask you to let Skar know the enemy is close. We expect him to arrive sometime after sunset."

"I have already alerted all my children and recalled the hunters. They will all be here when the time comes. But they will not be going out to fight. Not against this enemy. They will defend the palace."

"My plan exactly. Their numbers are too great to fight in the open courtyard. Can you use your magic even as you are?"

"To a limited degree. Azteca's magic has worn down over the centuries, slowly allowing me ever greater freedom. In another millennia I'll be able to melt the chains myself."

Otto smiled. "It's good that you have another option. Is there any chance you'll be using that limited magic to help out during the fight?"

"To the extent that I can, I will. I have no more desire to see my children die than you do to see your comrades die. Plus, with no one between me and the enemy, it's possible they'll find some way to kill me. I'm powerful, not invincible."

"I suspect we'll be glad to have all the help we can get. If you'll excuse me, I need to get ready."

"One moment," Brazon said. "I have to know. Is there anything I can do or say that would convince you to free me?"

Otto thought for a moment. The dragon didn't seem like an evil or particularly destructive being. The odds were good that if Otto freed him, he would do exactly what he claimed; keep the jungle safe and cause the empire no problems. Unfortunately, there was a big difference between what the odds said and no chance at all. If there was even a tiny chance that a dragon might attack them, then the risk was too great. After all, it took at least three Arcane Lords to subdue Brazon. What chance would Otto have if the dragon betrayed him?

"I can only think of one thing. If I had some guaranteed way to kill you should you betray me, that would do it. Otherwise, I just don't think I can take the risk."

"So you still don't trust my word?"

"If our positions were reversed, I'd say anything to get free. I might even convince myself that I meant it. But once the chains were gone, would I think differently? I don't know." He shrugged. "Skar assured me that dragons were more honorable than humans. Given some of the humans I've met over the years, that's probably true. But it's not a guarantee, and that's what I need."

Brazon made a couple of low grumbling sounds and it took Otto a moment to figure out that he was laughing. "So you won't trust me, but you want me to trust you with something that would instantly kill me?"

Otto shrugged. "I'm not the one in chains. Assuming we

both survive what's coming, we can chat some more. Until then."

He turned and walked back the way he'd come. Everything he'd said was the truth. If an artifact capable of killing the dragon instantly existed, he would do his best to set it free. Either that or he'd immediately use it to eliminate a potential future threat.

CHAPTER FORTY-THREE

Lady White tried to quiet her mind and focus once more on the wonder that was the crimson orb. The longer she spent holding it, the more she could feel her master's presence. When they first found it, she'd had her doubts about it really being Astaroth's blood. But those had faded after the first day. Whenever she held it and cleared her mind of all distractions, it felt like her body was vibrating in tune with the orb. She'd never experienced anything similar, not even when she traded her true name and her soul to become a hellpriest.

And now Lord of the Dead was here. His presence was like a thorn in her brain preventing her from concentrating. Had she the power, Lady White would have happily killed him for that offense alone. To add insult to offense, every step he took in her direction drove the thorn a little deeper.

Finally she shook her head and stood. There was no chance of proper meditation now. Until matters were settled, she would have to accept that she was finished with her contemplations.

She set the orb on its bench, but her hand lingered. Leaving it alone seemed wrong. Ludicrous of course; the orb might be Astaroth's blood, but it didn't actually contain any of his personality and will. At least not that she'd noticed.

If she couldn't meditate, what should she do to pass the time until the final battle began? None of the other artifacts overly interested her. They were all corrupt, demonic things, which meant that their abilities would be largely useless against thralls and undead. Had their opponents been alive, that would've been another matter.

She was still thinking when the door burst open and Jet rushed in. "Hurry, Mistress. Lord Shenk needs you at once. The dragonmen have betrayed us."

"What!?" Her jaw dropped but only for a second. It was possible that his continued refusal to free the dragon had turned the dragonmen against them. That they should attack now, with Lord of the Dead on their doorstep seemed stupid beyond reason.

"Mistress, please."

Right, the timing didn't matter. Dealing with it did.

Lady White hurried out of the treasury, brushing Jet aside like the useless bug she was. She made it to the second floor without encountering any enemies. In fact, everything seemed far too quiet. When she reached the library door she found it partway open. Inside, the soldiers were playing cards while Otto and Corina chatted together off to one side.

What, in Astaroth's name, was going on here?

Otto looked up at her and raised an eyebrow. "I thought we still had a few hours."

"We do. Jet came to the treasury and said the dragonmen had betrayed us and that you needed help."

"As you can see, all is well. I spoke with Brazon not long

ago and we both agreed that continuing to work together was for the best. And I certainly didn't send Jet to get you."

Lady White ground her teeth. "When I get ahold of her, I'm going to wring her neck."

Otto stood, a frown creasing his face. "Did you bring the orb with you?"

Her eyes widened. "No."

Lady White spun and sprinted for the door. Otto was right on her heels.

Jet wouldn't dare betray her. The spineless worm didn't have the guts. Unless it had all been an act. Making Lady White underestimate her while she waited for the right time to make her move.

She growled. If that was the truth, then Lady White had been played like a junior initiate. Astaroth was no doubt laughing at her right now.

They reached the treasury without running into Jet. The bench that had held the orb was empty.

◝

Otto studied the treasury, but no matter how hard he looked, the orb was nowhere to be found.

"It seemed she was a bit less loyal to the cause than you led me to believe," Otto said. "Well, let's see if we can find her."

He closed his eyes and sent his sight flying out. Quick as thought, he searched the first two levels, finding nothing. Hall by hall, floor by floor, he looked everywhere.

"She's not in the palace," Lady White said. "I can sense the orb moving further away. She's either in the courtyard or she just entered the city."

Otto sent his ethereal eyes outside. From a bird's-eye view, it didn't take long to spot Jet sprinting for all she was worth toward the jungle.

He flew down, adding thread after thread to keep extending his vision. He was at thirty-five before he caught up. She dodged down a side street. Otto couldn't hear, but from the way her chest was heaving, she had to be reaching her limit.

Unfortunately, so was he. At forty threads he had to stop. This was the edge of his attack range. Bitter as it was, he had to accept that she'd escaped.

He blinked once and found himself back in the treasury. "She's gone. Straight into Lord of the Dead's waiting arms I'll wager."

Otto could almost hear Lady White's teeth grinding. "What is she thinking? I gave her a safe place to live, made her my disciple. And this is how she shows her loyalty?"

"Perhaps she's thinking that Lord of the Dead will give her what she wants in exchange for the orb."

"He can't give her what she wants any more than I can. There are no secrets or shortcuts. To become a hellpriest like me, you have to kill everyone that knows your name then offer it in sacrifice to Astaroth along with your soul. Only Astaroth himself can change the rules, certainly Lord of the Dead can't."

"Sometimes people believe what they want to believe rather than facing reality. It's an unfortunate habit we humans have. Still, what's done is done. We have to prepare for the worst-case scenario. Come on, we need to brief everyone."

The pair left the treasury and returned to the library.

Everyone was standing, faces tense and hands on the hilts of their swords.

"How bad?" Axel asked.

"Bad enough," Otto said. "Jet stole the orb and we assume is taking it to Lord of the Dead. When he combines it with the rod he already possesses... Lady White, you take over."

"Right. With the orb in place, the rod's power will at least triple. He will have the power to summon demons directly from Astaroth's hell and to make his thralls even more powerful. As far as his offensive magic is concerned, I'm not completely certain, given that I've never seen Lord of the Dead in a fight. I assume he's stronger than me but my specialty lies outside of direct combat."

"Great," Axel said. "Will our mithril weapons still work?"

"Absolutely," Lady White said. "In fact, they will be your best hope for survival. Not only will they kill any thrall or demon you face, but having mithril close to your body will purify the corruption, thus weakening any spells Lord of the Dead might cast. Arrows, unfortunately, might be less effective, assuming he takes precautions."

"So we have to fight those things toe to toe?" one of the scouts, Otto didn't know the young man's name, asked.

"Probably," Otto said. "We won't know how effective arrows are until the battle begins. If they work, fantastic. If not, then we do it the hard way. We've had it easy up until now. Pretty soon it will be time to earn your pay."

Corina hesitantly raised her hand. "I don't have a mithril weapon."

"You don't need one." Otto walked over and tapped the apprentice ring on her left ring finger. "This is mithril and will protect you just as well as a weapon. Don't forget to channel your spells through it. The purifying and strengthening effects will make your magic much stronger. That might be the difference between taking an enemy down or not."

"I'll remember, Master." Corina drew herself up to her rather unimpressive full height. "I'll make you proud, I promise."

Otto did his best to smile his reassuring smile rather than his predatory one. "I'm already proud of you, so don't take a foolish risk and get yourself killed. We only win if we all survive."

She beamed at the compliment. "Yes, Master."

He gave her shoulder a final squeeze and turned to face the rest of the group. "I need to update Brazon. The loss of the orb changes all my calculations. I have a backup plan, but I can't do it without the dragon's help."

"What backup plan?" Axel asked. "You never said anything about a backup plan."

"We didn't need one before. Remember in the Dead Lands when I activated the portal and it weakened the ghouls? I figure I can do something similar here. The problem is, with Valtan dead, there's no one to power the portal."

"Which is why you need the dragon's help," Hans said.

"Precisely. I'll likely have to promise to free him after the battle, which is a risk, but at least we'll all be alive to worry about it. I'll be back shortly."

Otto left the others behind and made his way once more down to the dragon's cavern. He hated to go bargaining in such a weak position, but then again at least he wasn't chained to the floor, so he had that going for him.

He reached Brazon's side and the dragon said, "I didn't expect to see you until after the battle."

"I didn't expect to visit you until after the battle. Unfortunately, our situation has deteriorated." Otto explained about the stolen orb. "That changes our strategic situation a great deal. Can you use your magic to power the portal?"

"I can, but you'd have to guide the ethereal flow into the correct rune. After that, maintaining it would be simple. My endurance is another matter. I could manage an hour at most, then I'd be drained."

An hour was less than Otto would have liked, but better than nothing.

"Assuming I do, what's in it for me?" Brazon asked.

"Not getting killed by Lord of the Dead?"

"And?"

"And, assuming we live, I'll free you. Under the same terms you mentioned. You agree not to trouble the empire and you keep Aztecaland peaceful."

"Agreed. When do you wish to begin?"

"I don't know." Otto rubbed the bridge of his nose. "It will depend on the flow of the battle. I'll contact you when it's time."

"Very well. You made the right decision. I truly have no interest in you or your empire. Dragons are very territorial. Once we settle in a place, we never leave it unless driven out by a stronger dragon."

Otto offered a polite bow. "That's very reassuring. If you'll excuse me."

He retraced his steps to the exit. Had he made a good deal or a bad deal? Time would tell, but his lack of certainty did nothing to calm his already jangled nerves. Of course, if he could get out of this mess with nothing worse than jangled nerves, he'd consider himself lucky indeed.

◯

Jet sprinted through the jungle, her heart racing and not just from the exertion. She couldn't decide what surprised her more, that her plan worked, or that she'd escaped the city safely. In her arms, she cradled the wondrous crimson orb. Surely Lord of the Dead would share the secret of becoming a hellpriest with her in exchange for this. Jet cursed her stupidity for choosing to follow Lady White instead of the leader of the cult. She'd been so full of hope, but all she got for her efforts were lies and disappointment.

Well, no more. Jet would get what she was due, one way or another.

She stumbled over a hidden root and staggered into a tree, jamming her shoulder. She paused to catch her breath and wipe the sweat from her brow. Since no magic had struck her down, she assumed she'd gotten a safe distance from the city. Part of her actually felt bad about betraying Lord Shenk. He'd shown her kindness of a sort. He was one of the few people that ever had. But if she had to sacrifice him to attain her destiny, then she would do so.

With her breathing back to normal, she pushed away from the tree and got moving again. This time she kept her gaze on the jungle floor. There were plenty of roots and vines to trip up the unwary. In that way it was much like life.

According to Lady White, Lord of the Dead was approaching from the northeast. Jet was hardly a scout, but even she knew enough to get her bearings. The only question was whether or not she would find him before some of the jungle's nastier inhabitants found her.

Jet kept moving, only occasionally looking up to check the shadows and confirm that she was moving in the right general direction. Time didn't mean much as only the growing burning in her tired legs let her know she was making progress. The jungle looked the same despite the miles she'd covered.

Eventually a chill ran down her spine and she stopped. A faint rustling reached her. Wisps of darkness curled around her feet and when she looked up, she found the nearby trees appeared to be dying. The darkness had to be visible corruption. That meant she was close.

Jet hurried toward the noise. Thirty or so strides later she rounded a tree and found herself face to chest with the largest monkey she'd ever encountered. It had charred gray fur and stood at least eight feet tall. It stared at her with burning red eyes.

"Take—" The word came out as a terrified squeak. She cleared her throat and tried again. "Take me to Lord of the Dead. I have something he wants."

The giant monkey snorted through its nose, turned, and trudged away. Jet fell in behind it, confident that it would take her where she wanted to go.

She glanced left and right and caught movement in the shadows. Figures nearly as big as her guide were moving around out there. More thralls no doubt. Deeper darkness curled around her ankles, numbing her feet. This was clearly no place for the living.

Hopefully, once her transformation was complete, it would feel more inviting.

Not long after they set out, her guide stepped aside, revealing a pale, harsh-looking man with a pointed, dark beard, black robes, and glowing red eyes. He held a black rod in his hand that ended with an open, skeletal hand just the right size to grasp the orb. Darkness oozed out of the rod. The corruption was so thick here she had trouble breathing.

"It seems you've brought me a gift," Lord of the Dead said. "A most welcome if unexpected one."

Jet shook her head and did her best not to tremble. "Not a gift. I want something in exchange."

Lord of the Dead's lips quirked up in the faintest hint of a smile. "And what would that be?"

"I want to be a hellpriest, like you and Lady White. I know she's keeping something secret from me. She doesn't want me to become her equal. Give me the secret and the orb is yours."

"There is no particular secret. You have to sacrifice your soul and your true name to Astaroth. In exchange, you become like us, assuming he considers you worthy. Is that not what Lady White told you?"

"It is, but too many people know my name for it to work. I refuse to believe there's no other way."

Lord of the Dead laughed. A colder, more humorless sound she'd never heard. "We don't make the rules, Astaroth does. When the first demon binder contacted him, this was what he told us. No one that I know of has ever become a hellpriest any other way. I suppose if you could convince Astaroth to grant you the power you seek directly, that might also work, but the Lord of the Undead isn't known for his flexibility or his generosity. However, I can arrange for you to ask him."

Jet's brow furrowed in confusion. "What—"

There was a sharp pain and she knew nothing more.

Lord of the Dead looked down at the woman's corpse and shook his head. He'd met plenty of stupid people over his long life. It was unavoidable, really. But this woman took the top prize for absolute foolishness. Imagine walking up to him carrying the thing he wanted and trying to bargain. If she'd hidden it, then maybe. Of course he still could have killed her and compelled her corpse to show him where the orb was hidden. What would Astaroth do with her soul? Considering her uselessness, he'd probably just let it get absorbed into the essence of his hell and make it a bit stronger.

Her ultimate fate didn't interest Lord of the Dead. He had what he needed now. Once the Rod of Terror was complete, the pitiful defenders would have no hope of defeating him. The corruption would overwhelm Azteca's wards and the palace would fall soon after.

He smiled and touched the skeletal hand to the orb. The fingers wrapped around it without his having to do anything. As soon as they closed tightly, darkness exploded out in all directions. Ecstasy filled him. Power unlike anything he'd ever dreamed of danced at his fingertips. With this he could conquer this continent then return to the Land of the Demon Binders and crush the arrogant fools that dared cast him out.

His revenge would be sweet indeed.

Pain lanced through his brain, a none-too-subtle reminder that he needed to finish one thing at a time.

"Yes, Master. The city and its defenders will fall."

"Why did you have me kill this one?" Throng toed the dead woman's body. "I could've just taken the orb. Is killing others of your kind not a taboo among humans?"

"I haven't been human in a long time and no, it isn't.

Humans kill each other all the time and think little of it. It's one of their more positive traits. As for this one, she had no value alive and only moderately more dead." Lord of the Dead waved the rod over her body and it rose, transformed into a thrall as easy as that. "There, now she'll be of some use."

"Do we continue our march on the city, Master?" Throng asked.

"Indeed we do. By the time the sun rises it will be a city of the dead and I will be its king."

CHAPTER FORTY-FOUR

Otto stood on the second-floor ledge and stared out over the jungle. The sun was turning the sky a stunning orange and purple, but Otto had eyes only for the dark blot on the ground about five miles out. The trees were rotting and falling to the ground. Lord of the Dead had carved a black scar through the jungle that a blind man could follow. Just seeing it gave Otto a pretty good idea of the sort of power they were dealing with. Their chances had seemed lousy before, but now he was pretty sure he'd been overly generous.

On either side of him, Axel's scouts were spread out, bows strung and arrows nocked. Otto wasn't sure how effective they would be, but it was a good place to start. Hans and the guys had gone down to the first floor to reinforce Skar's dragonmen. Having their mithril weapons close should help mitigate some of the effects of the corruption. His loyal bodyguard hadn't been best pleased with the order, but that was where he could do the most good for now.

Lady White stood a step behind him to his left and

Corina was beside her to the right. Corina's job was to produce light once the sun fully set and Lady White would use her knowledge and abilities as she thought best. Otto didn't really understand them well enough to give her orders.

As the darkness grew ever closer Axel asked, "What do you think of our chances?"

Otto turned a jaundiced eye on his brother. "Your sense of humor is dreadful. What's wrong, are you regretting not taking Stephan up on his job offer?"

Axel barked a laugh. "Hell no. I'd rather fight an army of demons than spend a week in the same castle as Stephan and his pig of a wife. Frankly, I don't know how Mother stands it."

"Mother has the patience of a saint. After all, how long was she married to Father?"

"Good point. Whatever happens, it hasn't been terrible, spending more time together these past dozen years."

"Some of it was pretty terrible, but…" Otto fell silent as a hideous black dog half again the size of Father's hounds strode into the courtyard. It was a rotten thing with glowing red eyes. Patches of bone and flesh poked out from under its hide.

"A hellhound," Lady White said. "No doubt summoned to serve as a scout. There will be more."

"Well, let's deal with this one." Otto connected a thread to one of his mithril arrows and sent it racing toward the hellhound.

It pierced the monster's side and blasted out again in a shower of gore. The beast let out something between a howl and a whimper. Otto silenced it a second later when the arrowhead zipped back through its skull. The hellhound collapsed and melted into a puddle of black goo.

With an effort of will, Otto recalled the arrowhead and found the mithril pure and free of blood and flesh. At least he didn't have to clean it, that was something.

"I thought a demon would be tougher," Axel said.

"Careful what you wish for," Otto replied.

"Hellhounds are among the lowest-ranked demons," Lady White said. "And are highly vulnerable to mithril. Of course that applies to all demons, but higher-ranked demons can endure longer before their essence is purified."

"How high of a tier do you think he can summon?" Otto asked.

"Impossible to say. Mid-tier at a minimum. Understand that the tier rankings aren't terribly precise, just a general guide to help new demon binders figure out what sort of demons they can handle."

"Caveat noted."

"Here they come!" one of the scouts shouted.

Sure enough, pouring out of the woods were hellhounds, some sort of weird skeletons with black flames in their torsos, and scores of giant monkeys. All of them charged across the courtyard as fast as they could.

"Let 'em have it!" Axel shouted.

Bows twanged and arrows arced in. Many demons were pierced and even the skeletons went down when an arrow passed through the flames in their ribcage. One four-armed thrall took an arrow through its arm. It ripped the arm off and tossed it aside, arrow and all, without breaking stride.

It was terribly difficult to fight things that didn't feel pain. Or if they did feel pain, didn't react to it.

At the edge of the courtyard but out of sight, a concentration of corrupt ether gathered.

"Bows down! Swords out! Now!" Otto shouted.

The archers didn't hesitate. They dropped their bows behind them and drew their swords in only seconds. As soon as they did, Otto ran pure ether through them and raised a shield. He barely got it formed when a wave of corruption rolled out, blanketing the courtyard and continuing on toward the palace.

The darkness struck his barrier.

Otto winced as the corruption followed his thread back to him but didn't break his focus. The energy hit his mithril-enhanced hands and was negated, leaving only the tips of his fingers singed. He breathed a sigh of relief. As soon as he got home, he was focusing exclusively on infusing the rest of his bones with mithril. It was entirely too useful not to.

Though no one had been harmed, the attack had allowed the thralls and demons to reach the base of the palace wall. As soon as they did, the giant monkeys started climbing. They'd reach the edge in seconds.

"Archers, fall back and collect your bows!" Axel said. "Everyone else, step forward and prepare to repel the assault."

He had barely given the order when a black-furred head poked over the lip of the ledge. Axel split it in half with a single blow. The blow was well struck, but there were plenty more monsters to take its place. From the pounding, it sounded like some of their enemies had decided to attack the front door.

If they got through and attacked from both directions, that was the end. Otto had hoped to wait to use the portal, but that was no longer possible.

He turned to Corina. "Go tell Brazon it's time for the portal. I'll send a thread with you and he can use it as a guide. And stay with him."

"But I want to help."

"You're not helping by arguing with me. Go now and go quickly. It would be nice if we were still alive when you delivered the message."

She frowned and for a moment he thought she might argue some more. But finally she ran for the secret door. Thank heaven for small favors.

He turned to Lady White. "Will you be okay once the portal opens?"

"Does it matter?"

Otto increased the length of his thread without thinking about it. Corina was hurrying, so that was good.

"No, I suppose it doesn't. I was thinking you could go inside if it would help. We're going to be fighting room to room before long."

"What are you going to do?"

Otto reached a dozen threads. Up and down the ledge the scouts were hard pressed, but so far none of the thralls had gotten a foothold.

"Assuming the portal clears the ether enough, I'm going to hunt down Lord of the Dead. There's so much corruption in the ether, I can barely use magic even with the mithril purifying it."

"If you're going after him, I'm coming with you. This is my score to settle."

Otto nodded. He wouldn't object to some backup.

He felt a surge of power come roaring along the thread. He immediately extended it to the portal, specifically the rune that connected to the Dead Lands. No way was he opening a portal to Garenland. The risk was too great.

The runes lit up and light flooded the city. The thralls howled in pain.

This was his chance.

"Axel, I'm going hunting. Use your best judgement and try to keep everyone alive. I'll see you when it's over or in hell." Otto gathered ether in his legs and leapt out over the mass of thralls and across the courtyard before landing in the street.

His knees and ankles swore at him, but he took no real damage. Lady White landed beside him a second later, her face twisted in a pained grimace that he felt certain had nothing to do with the long jump.

"Can you sense him?"

She pointed up the street. "That way. He's the darkest bit of corruption out here."

Otto nodded and drew his mithril sword and anti-mithril dagger. As soon as he did, the discomfort vanished. He swallowed a breath of relief. He'd been counting on the dagger to work as well against corrupt ether as it did against the pure variety. Looked like his gamble paid off.

Given that Otto couldn't sense anything while he held the dagger, he said, "Lead the way."

CHAPTER FORTY-FIVE

Axel took a moment away from killing monsters to watch his brother land on the far side of the courtyard and vanish into the city with the creepy pale lady right behind him. Despite the effectiveness of their mithril weapons, he still would have preferred to have Otto with them. Of course, if he could deal with the mastermind, that would certainly be a good thing. Pity *if* was the most important word of that sentence.

A low moan drew his attention to one of the skeleton demons or whatever the hell they were. It had crested the top of the ledge and was reaching for the leg of a rookie that was busy hacking away at some other weird-looking thing that Axel figured would haunt his nightmares for the rest of his life.

Three quick strides closed the gap and he sliced the reaching hand off six inches from the young man's ankle. A thrust through the chest snuffed out the black flame. The skeleton disintegrated before it hit the ground.

The youthful scout kept fighting, seeming completely unaware of how close he had come to dying.

Since the portal activated, the monsters had definitely gotten slower, but their numbers showed no sign of diminishing. For every one they killed it seemed two more emerged from the city and ran into the courtyard. There had to be an end to them, at least Axel hoped there was.

One of the scouts screamed as an orange, four-armed thing hurled him off the ledge to the ground. The fall didn't kill him, but the hellhound that breathed a blast of blue flames at him did. A few seconds later, his charred body rose and turned toward the palace, clearly ready to join in the assault on his former allies.

In the column of small favors, at least he couldn't wield his mithril sword anymore.

The other scouts finished off the orange monster, but there were more coming all the time. It was time for a strategic withdrawal.

"Fall back! We'll hold them at the door. Move!"

Axel got there first and waved his men through. They streamed past him, monsters of all sorts nipping at their heels like herding dogs.

When the last man was in, he leapt through. The men slammed the door shut just ahead of the first monster. The magic did its thing, locking the door tight.

Axel lay on the floor and panted for breath as he stared at the ceiling. All around him the men were doing the same. He offered no criticism. From the pounding outside, it wouldn't be long before they were fighting again.

Far too soon Colten appeared and looked down at him. "What's the plan, sir?"

He found it equally pleasing and amusing that Colten imagined he had a plan. "We fight and hold them off as long as we can in the hopes that my brother can deal with the source before our strength runs out. If we can't, we die."

"Not your best plan ever, sir. Though when we're working with Lord Shenk, it does seem to be our fallback. Assuming we make it home, Cobb will be sad he missed this one."

"When we make it home and tell him the story, Cobb is going to laugh at us and tell us how glad he is to be retired. Then we'll all drink ourselves unconscious."

"Definitely a better plan than our current one."

There was a loud crunch. Axel sat up and found a hairy orange fist the size of a ham had punched through the stone door.

"I was hoping it would be sturdier," Axel muttered.

Colten held out a hand. "Time to get back into the fight."

Axel let Colten pull him to his feet. "Up, you lot! There're demons in need of killing and we're just the ones for the job."

Hans drove his mithril sword through the chest of a black-furred monster that one of the dragonmen had knocked down. For all their strength and toughness, the dragonmen's claws and fangs couldn't kill the demons. And while they could rip the thralls to pieces, the amount of time and damage it took to destroy one meant a dragonman could be tied up for minutes leaving it vulnerable to attacks from the side and behind. Ultimately, they'd found it easier to use the dragonmen's strength to knock the monsters down, making it easier for Hans and his men to finish them off with the mithril weapons.

Much as he hated it when Lord Shenk left him behind, Hans had to admit this was the correct place, strategically, for him to be right now.

The front door of the palace had been smashed to pieces, but a wall of dragonmen made for just as effective of a barrier. The light from the portal made it easy to see what they were facing. Whether knowing what was coming helped or hindered the defense he had yet to make up his mind.

There was a lull in the fighting and the front rank of dragonmen swapped places with the row behind them. Skar rotated out and ended up behind Hans. His green scales didn't have a mark on them, which put him well ahead of some of his fellows, one of whom had been forced to withdraw to the side with bloody, blackened wounds on his arms and chest. Hans had pressed the flat of his blade into them until they stopped steaming. That should at least prevent any more corruption from seeping into the wounds.

"How are you holding up?" Hans didn't look away from the battle as he spoke.

"Dragonmen are far more durable than you humans. We could fight for days without rest if necessary."

"I'm pretty sure this is going to be over way before that. Lord Shenk said we had an hour from the moment the portal became active. If we're still fighting when it goes dark, we lose the modest advantage it grants us."

Hans lunged into a gap and ran a hellhound through the skull. It collapsed into black goo.

When he recovered Skar asked, "Do you have faith that your master can defeat this enemy in that length of time?"

Hans wished he could give an absolute yes, but the truth was, when they spoke, Lord Shenk hadn't seemed sure himself. "I don't know, but if anyone can, he can. You wouldn't believe some of the things I've seen him do. Hell, I was there and I hardly believe some of them. I have faith that he'll do all he can and if he fails, we won't be around long enough to complain."

Skar made a little chuffing noise that Hans interpreted as amusement. "That is one way to look at it."

The conversation was interrupted by what sounded like a thunderous pounding of hooves. Hans hadn't heard anything like it since the time they were nearly trampled by a herd of cattle. Only this time he wasn't inside his magical armor.

He peered around the melee and spotted what looked like a battering ram with legs. Lots of legs. At a glance he counted over a dozen pairs of very human-looking legs attached to a huge, pointed log made of bone and rotten flesh that dripped on the ground with every pounding stride. It reminded him vaguely of a giant centipede.

If that thing hit the line, there was no way even the dragonmen could hold.

"Incoming!" Hans shouted. "Everyone break to either side on my order."

He watched intently. The timing would have to be perfect.

"We can't let it in," Skar said.

"We can't stop it," Hans countered. "I suggest you order your dragonmen to dodge as well, but it's your call."

The battering ram got closer by the second. Vibrations ran through the floor and up Hans's spine.

Not long now.

"Dodge!" Hans shouted.

Like a well-oiled machine, the men of his squad moved as far to the side as the entryway allowed. The dragonmen held their place, continuing to fight and bracing themselves at the same time.

The battering ram made no distinction between friend and foe, smashing demons and thralls with the same enthusiasm it would have crushed Hans's men.

When it hit the dragonmen their claws scraped the stone floor, leaving grooves under their feet as they fought to stop it. The battle was a losing one. For all their strength, they couldn't stand up to its momentum.

Scaled bodies went flying. One ended up under the ram's many legs and was torn to bloody bits.

It was an impressive show of bravery if not intellect.

"From the flanks! Now!" Hans shouted.

The guys lunged in unison, driving their blades up to the hilts into the slowed ram. Its remaining momentum cut deep gashes in its side even as the mithril purified the corruption that kept it alive.

It took ten seconds to finally collapse and start rotting away.

Hans leapt onto it and ran down its length toward the still-staggered demons. "Kill as many as you can before they recover!"

His men joined him and they set to slaughtering demons as fast as they could swing their swords. Unfortunately, unlike human soldiers, the demons recovered their wits far faster.

As soon as they started counterattacking Hans shouted, "Back inside!"

They made it to the doorway, but the dragonmen were still recovering and in no shape to help hold the opening.

The guys formed up with Hans in the center. They hacked down any demon that came close. They were holding for now. How long that would last was an entirely different question.

CHAPTER FORTY-SIX

Otto followed Lady White down the street. They didn't run—too much danger of stumbling into a trap—but they did hurry. At least the light from the portal made it easy to see. It also made Lady White wince with every stride, but there was no helping that.

He glanced down a side street and found it empty. How much further away was he? Every second gave Lord of the Dead's minions more time to breach the palace and kill everyone. While Otto had great faith in Axel and Hans, defeating a small army of demons was a big ask.

"Are we getting close?" Otto didn't bother to pitch his voice low. Lord of the Dead would have no trouble sensing them approaching.

"Yes, we should be nearly on him."

Otto tightened his grip on his weapons. He wasn't looking forward to a fight without his magic, but given what they were dealing with, he doubted there was much chance of him winning a wizards' duel. Twenty strides later they stepped out into a little square. In the center of it was a black disk as tall as Otto. As he watched, a hellhound emerged and sprinted off toward the palace. What he didn't see was any sign of Lord of the Dead.

Lady White let out a gasp. "It's a portal connected directly to Astaroth's hell. I never imagined such a thing was possible. As long as it's open and he doesn't run out of power, Lord of the Dead can summon as many demons as he wants."

"That's a problem. How do we close it?"

"You don't." A pale man in a black robe stepped out from behind the portal. He clutched a spike-covered black rod in his right hand. The rod ended in a skeletal hand that clutched the crimson orb. "You've come a long way to die, my former subordinate."

"You tried to kill me once already," Lady White snarled. "Figured I'd see how you did when we were face to face."

Lord of the Dead barked a laugh. "You couldn't have beaten me before I got the Rod of Terror. What makes you think you could beat me now?"

"You might hold the rod, but I can wield the corruption it emits as well as you. Plus, I didn't come alone."

"Neither did I." Lord of the Dead snapped his fingers and a huge gray-furred monkey stepped out from behind the portal. It made the four-armed orange ones look like children. "Your bodyguard can play with Throng while we commence the real battle. I hope he's more loyal than the last one I met. She couldn't turn against you fast enough. Not very impressive."

Lady White said nothing to dispel his misunderstanding of their relationship. That suited Otto fine as he preferred to keep his magic a secret until it could do some good. A surprise spell might just be enough to turn the tide.

"Jet was a useless weakling, too pathetic to accept the

rules our master laid down. She was no great loss. Let's see if you can do more than talk."

Throng roared and charged toward Otto who leapt to the side to give himself room to fight. All thoughts of Lady White vanished when his opponent closed the distance between them.

A fist the size of his head swept past Otto, missing by inches.

His mithril sword lashed out, cutting a deep gash in the offending arm, but not severing it as he'd hoped. This opponent was clearly on another level from the ones he'd fought earlier.

"I'm going to crush you to pulp!" Throng roared.

Otto jumped back just before a double hammer fist came down with enough force to crack the stone.

As soon as his feet touched the ground he darted back in and sliced a shallow gash in Throng's chest. Neither of the wounds amounted to much, but it was reassuring to know he could hurt the monster. Whether he could kill it without magic was another question altogether. At least it wasn't as fast as it was strong.

"I'm surprised you can talk," Otto said as he waited for Throng's next move. He wasn't a skilled enough duelist to risk going on the offensive.

"Why?" Throng's deep voice was nearly a growl. "Just because I look like a beast doesn't mean I'm stupid."

"Clearly not. Still, you're the first of your kind I've heard speak, so I was surprised. Can the others?"

"There was one other, but he is dead, killed by Skar. The dragonman will pay for that death along with his many other crimes."

Throng darted forward, fists leading.

Otto slipped left and slashed again, opening yet another shallow cut in Throng's torso. It seemed the conversation was over. Just as well. Otto had no time to waste talking. Unfortunately, his sword wasn't proving much more useful than his words. Getting a kill shot would force him to close in and that would be an excellent way to end up crushed.

They danced around a bit more, Otto putting a few more nicks in Throng's hide while doing no real damage. The giant meanwhile kept making huge, sweeping attacks that were easy to read and dodge even for a poor swordsman like Otto. Odd, but he wasn't about to complain.

After their most recent exchange, Otto managed to get a little space and risked a glance at Lady White. She was on her knees, face twisted in pain, and Lord of the Dead stood over her, the rod leveled in her direction.

That was definitely not good. If she lost, Otto would be forced to fight both enemies at once and he hadn't the least confidence he could win.

He only had one choice. If Lord of the Dead's magic was too strong, he'd just have to negate it.

A flick of Otto's wrist sent the anti-mithril dagger flying across the square. It hit point first in Lady White's shoulder, but not square.

He looked back to find Throng closing in, a huge fist headed his way.

A hastily conjured shield saved him from the worst of the blow, but even then he ended up flying across the clearing. Wrapped in a bubble of barely purified ether, he couldn't decide what hurt more, the impact or having to wield such corrupt energy.

Otto skidded to a stop and groaned. Despite his pain, he began cycling ether through the mithril of his sword until he had enough pure energy to work with. Next, threads connected to the arrowheads in his pocket. They flew out and circled him like a flock of birds. He ended up having to continuously loop through them to keep his threads from breaking due to the ambient corruption.

Snarling through the pain as he forced himself to his feet, Otto said, "Let's try that again you big ugly bastard."

Throng growled back then charged.

Otto's arrowheads shot out, punching through the huge creature and making new holes with each pass.

Despite the damage, Throng didn't slow.

Otto dove out of the way of a punch that would've crushed his skull had he been a moment slower. His sword lashed out in passing, making a deep cut in Throng's leg.

Rolling to his feet, Otto raced to put some distance between them. Throng hobbled after him, but far slower now. That last blow must have cut deeper than he first thought.

This was his chance to end it.

The arrowheads flew in, burying themselves in Throng's chest, but not coming back out. He would let the mithril do its work. Chopping the thing apart a piece at a time clearly wasn't working.

Throng kept coming, but slower every second. At last he collapsed at Otto's feet and stared up at him.

"You have to stop Lord of the Dead," Throng said. "If he wins, we will hunt down my people and turn them into things like me."

Otto frowned. "Isn't he your master?"

"The metal you struck me with has loosened his control. I only joined him because my desire for revenge overwhelmed my good sense. I regret many things, but none more than that." Throng's mouth worked but no sound came out. Just when Otto thought he'd reached his limit Throng continued. "He is evil. Evil beyond anything I ever imagined. Stop him. I beg you."

Those were the brute's last words. Otto saw no more corruption in his carcass. When time permitted, they would have to burn the body, but time certainly didn't permit right now.

"Don't worry," Otto said. "I have every intention of killing Lord of the Dead. Should your people be saved as well, so much the better."

A bit of mental effort yanked the arrowheads back out of Throng's body. The gore and flesh sizzled off of them until they were as perfect and silver as the day they were forged.

Now to deal with Lord of the Dead.

○

Lady White had no idea how Otto would fare in a fight with the massive, overpowered undead and she didn't have the focus to spare to worry about it. Lord of the Dead stood facing her, an arrogant grin twisting his lips and making him even uglier. His whole body practically vibrated with corrupt energy.

Could she really beat him?

Yes, Astaroth curse him! Any doubts would weaken her magic. She had to believe it or she had no chance at all.

"I'm so pleased you traveled all this way to see me," Lord of the Dead said. "When my thrall was destroyed, I feared I'd have to wait decades if not centuries for another chance to punish you for your disobedience. So thank you for your thoughtfulness."

"I didn't come here to be thoughtful, I came here to kill you."

He laughed. Arrogant son of a bitch.

"Kill me? As I am now, I doubt all the cult leaders together could defeat me, much less an underling whose talents lie outside of combat. Still, I will take pleasure in your pointless flailing before I end your worthless existence. Perhaps, should Astaroth be in a cruel mood, you'll find your former minion waiting to enjoy whatever punishment awaits failures like the two of you."

Lady White had heard enough. She gathered energy, formed it into a black spear, and hurled it at his heart.

Lord of the Dead didn't even flinch. The spear just veered away from him without any visible effort on his part. And that had been one of her more powerful spells. The tiny amount of confidence she'd had withered to nothing. If that spell failed, nothing else she could do would have a chance.

"Do you understand now? You're as helpless against me as a newborn thrown into the middle of a lake. Soon, Throng will turn your bodyguard into pulp and then you will join him in the eternal torment awaiting you. But for now, I think I'll punish you personally."

As an undead, Lady White seldom felt pain. In fact, she hadn't felt so much as a twinge since her battle with Jackal. But when Lord of the Dead's magic hit her, it felt like her very essence was being sucked away. Her whole body locked up and she couldn't even open her mouth to scream.

"Painful, isn't it?" Lord of the Dead asked in an offhand tone. "This technique is a more powerful variation of the one Jackal used. I taught it to him after all. I can even control how fast your corrupt essence is drained away, thus drawing out the pain forever should I wish it. And rest assured, I do."

Lady White could barely understand the words he was using, so disordered had her mind become. Seconds passed like hours as she drifted in a world of pain.

And then, like someone had dropped a shield in front of her, the pain vanished. She also noticed a cut on her back. How had that happened?

The answer was beside her. Otto's anti-mithril dagger lay on the ground. He must have seen her predicament and thrown it. She couldn't believe he'd give up his most powerful weapon for her, but she also wasn't about to complain.

"What—" Lord of the Dead only got one word out before she snatched up the dagger and lunged at him.

He barely evaded the first slash. Her second cut took off the fingers of his right hand and sent the Rod of Terror clattering to the ground.

"No!" He hurled darkness at her, but Lady White felt nothing.

She couldn't even sense the magic. It was the oddest feeling. How long had it been since the ether was denied to her? Centuries, certainly.

"Throng! Kill her!"

Lord of the Dead lunged toward the rod with his intact hand, but she warded him off with a few slashes, forcing him back until she stood between Lord of the Dead and his prize. That a giant monster wasn't trying to crush her meant Otto was winning his fight as well. That didn't surprise her in the least. Lady White had seldom met a more formidable human.

More darkness rushed toward her only to vanish a few inches short of her body.

Lord of the Dead screamed in frustration.

A moment later his scream took on a different tone when

a mithril arrowhead blasted through his abdomen before exploding out his back in a shower of gore.

Otto strode toward them, sword drawn and six more arrowheads in the air around him. He scowled, eyes narrowed and looking grim.

A wall of darkness appeared between them and Lord of the Dead. Arrowheads zipped through it, but no shout of pain followed.

"Dispel it with the dagger," Otto said.

Lady White slashed through the wall and it promptly vanished. There was no sign of Lord of the Dead.

"He no longer has the artifact. Why hasn't the portal closed?" Otto asked.

In fact, demons still emerged from it regularly, all of them ignoring her and Otto and running straight for the palace.

"I don't know why it hasn't closed." Lady White looked down at the rod and licked her lips. This was her chance to claim it. But would he let her?

"Axel and the others are still in danger," Otto said. "If you need to pick that cursed thing up to close the portal, then do so. I'll take my dagger back."

She flipped the blade around and offered it to him hilt first. "You saved me. I never imagined you'd give up your greatest weapon for my sake."

He shrugged and slipped the dagger back into its sheath. "What are friends for? The portal."

Right, focus on the problem at hand.

Lady White reached the rod. The instant her fingers grazed the black metal, she was hurled across the square. A gentle force caught her and set her on her feet.

Otto raised an eyebrow as she walked back. "Can't say I was expecting that. What happened?"

"As best I can tell, the rod is still bonded to Lord of the Dead. I can't use it until he's slain."

"That's not ideal. Okay, you stay here and get ready to close the hell portal as soon as he's dead. I'll hunt him down."

Lady White shook her head. "We should stick together."

"Ordinarily I'd agree with you, but leaving the rod unattended isn't an option. If Lord of the Dead gets past me, you'll have to stop him from claiming the rod until I get back." Otto dug a thin glass rod out of his satchel. "You remember how to use the message sticks?"

How dumb did he think she was? No, she dismissed the thought. It was the stress of the moment; Lady White knew Otto respected her.

"I remember. If Lord of the Dead comes back, I'll let you know. And good hunting."

"Thanks."

With that final word of parting, Otto stalked off into the city. She didn't ask how he'd find Lord of the Dead without her. At the end of the day, he was right, they couldn't leave the rod unprotected and they certainly couldn't move it. That meant one of them had to stay here. Even injured, Lord of the Dead was more than a match for her. He'd proven that easily enough, galling though it was to admit.

She just had to trust Otto to finish what she started.

CHAPTER FORTY-SEVEN

Axel cut a skeleton demon in half and blew out a breath. He'd lost track of how long they'd been fighting, but it felt like forever. The only thing that had saved them was the narrowness of the hidden door and the hall beyond. No more than one or two demons could force their way through at a time. And even so, every time a hellhound showed up it would breathe blue flames at them and force them back a stride. Soon they would reach the main corridor and all bets would be off.

Speaking of the rotten, dog-looking things, another of them stepped through the ruined doorway. A moment later an arrow took it in the forehead, killing it instantly. That was the strategy he'd settled on to delay the inevitable retreat.

And that was all it was, a delay. He had no doubt that in the next minute or two they'd have to make a break for it.

Apparently he wasn't the only one that thought so. Colten moved closer and asked, "When the time comes, are we going up or down, sir?"

Axel cut the head off some weird-looking zombie thing then answered. "Down. We'll meet up with Hans and the dragonmen for a final stand. Maybe the dragon can be of some help. Hell, even Corina's magic might buy us a minute or two."

"I like Corina," Colten said. "But if we're depending on her to save us, we're doomed."

Axel couldn't argue with that.

A surge of brutal fighting ended any conversation and cost him two more scouts.

That's when the floor shook and a massive, four-armed skeleton forced its way through the gap. Unlike the littler ones, this one had black flames in its eyes rather than its chest. He appreciated them; the ugly things at least showed them where to aim.

And aim the archers did. A pair of arrows streaked out, only to get slapped aside before they could hit home. Not only was this one big, it was fast too.

Axel knew a sign when he saw it. "Back to the first-floor landing! Go!"

No one needed to be told twice. The scouts broke and ran with Axel bringing up the rear and Colten on point. That wasn't an accident. With his uncanny sense of direction, Colten was sure to get them to their destination. The others were good, but Axel planned to take no chances on running into a dead end.

He risked a glance over his shoulder. The giant skeleton had dropped to all six limbs and was rapidly closing the gap. Its claws clattering on the stone floor gave Axel a chill. Behind it came a snarling mob of ugly that Axel didn't even want to think about. It was going to be damn close whether they reached the stairs first or the demons reached them.

Axel offered a little prayer to any watching archangel that they won the race.

And they did, by the narrowest of margins. As soon as Axel cleared the doorway he spun and sliced a skeletal arm off as it groped through the entrance. That didn't slow the monster down any, and he soon found himself hacking and dodging for all he was worth as the remaining arms darted in and out.

One hand got through and shredded his tunic. Luckily for him, the mithril mail underneath turned the blow aside with nothing to show for it save some new bruises.

When the last arm had been severed, Axel strode in and cut its skull off, ending its thrashing.

"What now, sir?" Colten asked.

Axel was starting to understand why Otto got annoyed when everyone asked him that. "We'll hold up here for as long as we can, then we head for the basement and our last stand. Hopefully it won't come to that."

Colten looked skeptical and Axel didn't blame him. He felt just as skeptical, but he had to at least sound confident.

The truth was, Axel figured the odds were they were all going to die here.

※

Hans couldn't begin to say how glad he was when the dragonmen regained their feet and fought their way to the front of the line. The two minutes his squad had been forced to hold the entrance on their own were among the longest of his life. Though it still didn't feel as comfortable in his hand as his trusty steel blade, Hans swore he would never complain about having to wield a mithril sword again.

He stood panting as his team worked with the drag-onmen to slay demon after demon. It was an impressive display and he was proud of them. There wasn't a more disciplined group in the imperial army he felt certain.

Despite the danger in front of him, Hans couldn't stop thinking about Lord Shenk. Worrying about someone that could kill them all in the blink of an eye seemed foolish, but he couldn't help himself. His job was to keep his lord safe and he couldn't do that if he didn't even know where he was. Hans imagined having to tell Abby that her father was dead and the image tied him in knots.

"Your men fight well." Skar had disengaged from the melee to take a breather. It made Hans feel better that the incredibly powerful dragonman still got tired.

"They're the best we have. Your people are impressive as well."

"We were created to be so. Created to serve as the guards of a master that vanished centuries ago. It seems pathetic to say it out loud."

"You serve your father now, isn't that better?"

"Yes, better, but less satisfying. My soul wants to serve Lord Azteca. I can't explain it any better than that."

Hans was saved from having to reply by a roar that shook the air. By the archangels, what now?

The answer came a moment later when the largest demon yet, an eight-foot-tall bloated corpse with two heads and three arms, one of which was growing out of its back, came lumbering toward the entrance. Each of its arms carried a crude ax made out of bone. That seemed a poor choice of weapon material, but somehow Hans doubted it was regular bone.

"Do you think it can fit through the door?" Hans asked.

"Barely," Skar said. "But I'd prefer that not happen."

Hans wholeheartedly agreed. Stopping it, on the other hand, would be no easy feat. Unlike the battering ram from earlier, this monster gave its smaller brethren time to get out of the way as it approached. That suggested some level of intelligence. Hans preferred his opponents stupid, but you had to deal with what was in front of you.

"Take a step back!" Hans shouted. "Don't attack until it starts to enter. The door frame will hinder its movement."

The guys hastened to obey and to his surprise, so did the dragonmen.

Hans's plan didn't amount to much. Instead of trying to squeeze through, the monster drew back and struck the entry with stone-shattering force. Literally. Stone went flying and three blows later it easily stepped through the now far larger opening.

"So much for plan A," Hans muttered. "Do we fight or fall back? We can't hold the entrance now anyway."

"That thing might attack Father. We have to kill it."

Hans didn't give a damn about the dragon, but if they lost their allies, they'd be in trouble.

"You take the lead, I'll back you up. The rest of you deal with anything that comes in behind it."

His order wasn't met with much enthusiasm, but everyone formed up again.

Skar roared and charged, his flame breath leading the way. Hans didn't know why he bothered. None of the demons they'd fought seemed flammable.

A bone ax came swooping in at Skar's head.

He ducked then pounced, leaping forward and raking his claws across the monster's bloated stomach. The sickly yellow flesh parted easily, spilling stinking guts out and releasing a cloud of gas that looked exceedingly toxic.

Skar fell back coughing and gagging.

The arm in its back came down, ready to slice Skar in half.

Hans lunged forward and swung his sword. Ax and hand went flying. Even better, the mithril negated the toxic cloud, dispersing it and sparing Hans any ill effects.

The monster roared, whether angry, in pain, or something else, Hans didn't know.

A responding howl from the monsters outside sent a shiver down Hans's spine. It was calling for backup.

He needed to end this quickly.

Giving no thought to defense, Hans waded in, sword swinging. The first slash cut a huge lump out of the monster's massive gut and sent more innards spilling to the ground. The poison might be gone, but he was going to have to watch his footing.

As soon as he thought it, his foot slipped.

Out of the corner of his eye he caught a glimpse of the right-side ax coming down. No way could he block it in time. Despite Lord Shenk's best efforts, it seemed it was his time to die after all.

A second passed and nothing cleaved him in half.

"Hurry and kill it!" Skar was wrestling with the monster's right arm.

Hans didn't need to be told twice. He sprang straight up, sword leading, and ran the monster through. Wrenching the sword side to side for good measure, he rode it to the ground and didn't pull his blade free until it stopped moving.

The clash of weapons and roar of combat made it clear that his victory hadn't settled the issue. The combined force of dragonmen and humans was getting pushed back and would soon be in danger of getting surrounded.

"We need to fall back," Hans said.

"Not to Father's cavern. The staircase up will do. We can hold them there and fight level to level if we have to."

Hans hated that plan, but they couldn't divide their forces. "Fall back! To the stairs!"

He and Skar rejoined the group and made a fighting retreat toward the staircase door. At least it wasn't an awfully long ways from the entry hall. Swinging even a mithril sword for so long left Hans's arm on the verge of falling off.

Tired or not, he kept fighting, cutting down every variety of savage monster a madman's nightmare could conjure up.

"We're almost there," Skar said. "I'll take the center. Get the door open."

Hans dropped back a step and Skar shifted to fill the gap in their line.

The door was just behind them and Hans rushed to open it. He almost got a mithril sword through the gut for his trouble.

"What the hell are you doing here?" Axel asked. On the stairs above him, the scouts were holding off a demonic force of their own.

"Regrouping. We got pushed out of the entry hall."

"Shit! We were planning to join you and fight to the basement."

Hans shook his head. "Skar won't allow it. We're making our stand here, for better or worse."

Axel's laugh was bitter. "I doubt it could get much worse."

Hans dearly hoped he was right.

CHAPTER FORTY-EIGHT

Otto stalked through the shadowy streets with one eye closed. He'd conjured an ethereal construct and connected it to one of his mithril arrowheads and now it was flying overhead. It was a beautiful setup. The mithril made it easy to maintain and use pure ether, so he felt no pain as he searched. A minute ago he spotted a hint of movement and as far as he knew, Lord of the Dead was the only one out here. The oh-so-mighty leader of the Cult of Astaroth was running like his life depended on it.

Which it very much did.

The problem was, Otto didn't dare run after him for fear of stumbling into a trap. Another hint of movement, this time ducking into one of the huts. Why would he do that? There was only one way in or out of those stone buildings.

Something was fishy, but Otto didn't have time to worry about it. Lady White couldn't close the portal until Lord of the Dead was destroyed. And every second he delayed, more demons emerged.

Picking up the pace and ignoring his many aches and pains, Otto hurried to the hut. Nothing troubled him during his jog there and when he checked the door frame he found nothing in the ether to indicate a trap. Everything in him screamed that this was a mistake, but he gripped the hilt of his sheathed anti-mithril dagger and stepped through anyway, leaving the ethereal construct outside so he could watch his back.

Inside, Lord of the Dead stood facing him. His black robe was rumpled and gobs of what Otto assumed served as his blood dotted the front. The man couldn't get any paler, but somehow he managed to look even more corpselike.

"Stop, please," Lord of the Dead said. "Surely we can make a deal. I have vastly more to offer you than Lady White. The most powerful priest of Astaroth must be of more value than a cast-off failure."

"We might have been able to do business once, but only before you sent a monster to attack my home. For that offense alone I would kill you a dozen times. Unfortunately, I can only do it once."

There was a flash of movement outside.

Otto spun and thrust.

His sword slid through something and a moment later the rotting carcass of some sort of little demon wavered into view.

Magic gathered behind him.

Otto drew the black dagger and slashed an incoming spell apart.

A flick of his wrist sent the demon's body flying across the room to splatter against Lord of the Dead's chest. Before he could react, Otto closed the distance between them and ran him through. Just to be sure, he drove the anti-mithril dagger into Lord of the Dead's shoulder, thus cutting him off from his magic.

They stood a foot apart staring at each other. The hellish crimson light began to dim in Lord of the Dead's eyes.

"It wasn't supposed to go this way. I was going to build an empire for Astaroth's glory. This continent, no, this world, was to be mine."

"Life is full of disappointments," Otto said.

Lord of the Dead coughed and some black ooze flecked his lips and chin. "Isn't that the truth. Lady White was one of my greatest servants. She betrayed me and she'll betray you too."

"She didn't betray you. You used her as a scapegoat for your own failures. Had you remained loyal to her, she would still be serving you in the Land of the Demon Binders. But your loss is very much my gain, so I'm not about to complain."

"If she had been a properly loyal servant, she would have died quietly rather than live to make her master's life difficult."

Otto was about to offer a rejoinder to that bit of stupidity, but before he could speak he noticed the light had fully gone out of Lord of the Dead's eyes. He sheathed the anti-mithril dagger and checked the ether. Sure enough, Lord of the Dead's body was just a body.

It was over, at least this part was. He jerked his blade free, went outside, and collected the arrowhead that had clattered to the ground when he drew the dagger.

Now to get back and help Lady White shut that hell portal.

⟳

Lady White paced, tapped her toe, paced some more, all the while never taking her eyes off the rod. It lay there, corruption streaming out of it, mocking her. A few yards away, demons continued to emerge from Astaroth's hell every few minutes. She felt confident that the flow was slowing, but it was impossible to say for sure.

Otto thought she could close the portal and she hadn't said anything to contradict him, but the truth was, she had no idea how the rod worked, and if Astaroth's will had any control over what happened, he might not allow her to close it. Of course, she wouldn't know for sure until she tried.

She finally dragged her gaze away from the rod and looked in the direction Otto had gone. Even injured and on the run, Lord of the Dead was a formidable enemy. She shook her head at her own foolishness. Otto wasn't the sort to get taken by surprise. Despite his youth, she had never met anyone more dangerous.

A chill ran up her spine and she immediately focused on the rod. It looked exactly the same, but somehow she knew that she could safely pick it up. If you'd asked her how she knew, Lady White wouldn't have been able to answer, she just did.

Steeling herself, she bent down and grasped the black metal in the clear space between the spikes. A bolt of power ran through her and she found herself floating in the Eternal Graveyard. Directly ahead of her stood the giant skeletal form of Astaroth himself. Even though she knew it was a vision, his power still nearly overwhelmed her.

"I knew it was a mistake to trust that useless fool,"

Astaroth said. "But no matter. You will take up the rod, slaughter the living, and raise an empire of the dead in my honor. Your new name shall be Lady of the Dead."

Lady White's heart hadn't beat in a long time, but if it had, it would've been racing right now. Doing as Astaroth commanded would put her in direct conflict with Otto. A conflict she didn't want and doubted she'd survive.

"The human worm is nothing. Overwhelm him with demons then finish off the survivors and the dragon. With that done, nothing will be able to oppose you."

"I swore an oath on my true name not to betray him. Will the magic not prevent me taking such an action, Master?" She tried not to sound hopeful lest she give offense.

"Breaking such an oath will be quite painful for you, but with the rod enhancing your power, it won't prove fatal. I sense your reluctance. Does this speck of a human frighten you so?"

"He is an impressive wizard, likely the most powerful living." She hesitated then added. "He has also shown me loyalty and kindness even when he had to go out of his way to do so. I would've been destroyed long ago if it were not for his intervention."

Pain racked her body as Astaroth turned his ill regard upon her. "It sounds to me like you have misplaced your loyalty. Whatever this human may or may not have done for you, first and foremost, you serve my will. Perhaps you need a further reminder of who your proper master is."

Pain unlike anything she'd ever dreamed of in her entire life or undeath assailed Lady White. It felt like her very essence was being torn apart. It lasted for what could've been moments or days for all she knew. And then it was gone.

"I trust you have no more doubts about where your true loyalty lies," Astaroth said.

"None, Master. All shall be as you say."

"Indeed it shall."

She blinked and found herself back in the square. Otto stood on the far side, his mithril sword drawn.

Her throat worked as she tried to swallow the lump choking her. Just thinking about betraying him triggered the ritual that bound her not to work against Otto. But this minor pain was nothing compared to what Astaroth would do to her should she fail.

"Lady White," Otto said. "Were you unable to seal the portal?"

She tried to speak, to lie, anything. But her bond with Otto wouldn't allow it. With a scream she closed her eyes and pushed against the binding with all her will. It felt like something broke inside her when the binding shattered, but after, she was free to speak and act as she wished.

Lady White opened her eyes and stared in horror as Otto slashed the black dagger through the portal, making it collapse. He nodded once and put the dagger back in its sheath.

"I doubt that would have worked while Lord of the Dead was still alive. His will would have just reformed it, don't you think?"

"Probably. Now that task falls to me."

"Excuse me?" Otto cocked his head, seeming uncertain he'd heard her correctly.

"Astaroth commands that I take up Lord of the Dead's mission."

"Is that right? How unfortunate." Otto reached under his tunic and pulled out a silver disk. "I assume your master allowed you to break the oath you swore to me. It's a pity really. I'd hoped to never have to use this."

Lady White wasn't sure what he was talking about, but she didn't dare let him do whatever he was planning to do. She gathered corrupt ether and formed it into a black spear.

"Stop, Alice Young."

Her body froze, every muscle tense. The black spear dissipated, dissolving back into the ether. Tendrils of pure ether connected her body to the disk.

"Set the rod on the ground, Alice Young."

She tried to resist with all her will, but like any other puppet, she was under the control of the one pulling the strings. The Rod of Terror clanked to the ground and the moment it did, her mind cleared of Astaroth's powerful presence. He was still there of course, but just barely, in the background like usual.

"Back away, Alice Young."

With jerky steps Lady White moved away from the rod. Otto moved with her until he stood between her and the rod.

"Don't move, Alice Young."

She froze, her body as rigid as steel.

"Lord of the Dead told me you'd betray me. I didn't believe him. I didn't want to believe him. I've enjoyed our many conversations over the past few years." Lady White thought he actually looked a bit sad. That pleased her for some reason. "I shall miss them."

White-hot pain shot through her when Otto slid his mithril sword through her breast. The pure fire slowly consumed her corrupt essence. Much like a demon, being slain with mithril meant she wouldn't be reborn in Astaroth's hell. Her essence would dissipate into oblivion.

She found she welcomed it.

⌒

Otto looked down at Lady White's black robe and sighed. Her body had already transformed into fine ash. The mithril amulet Lord Karonin had helped him make worked perfectly. It really was a shame that he'd been forced to destroy someone so interesting.

Even better, the rod was no longer pumping out corruption. Without that, the demons wouldn't be able to sustain themselves for long in this reality. Axel, Hans and the others should be fine now. Otto didn't doubt for a moment that they'd found some way to survive. Hans and his brother were too clever and talented not to. Still, best not to dawdle. Some of the demons might linger longer than the others.

He had no desire to touch the rod with his bare hands, so he wrapped it multiple times with Lady White's robe. A ginger tap with his right forefinger confirmed that it was safe.

Otto snatched it up and ran back toward the palace. He passed several puddles of black goo that had doubtless been demons not too long ago. If the newest arrivals were already in this state, the rest should be equally out of commission. Good. He'd had enough fighting to last another decade or maybe century.

He strode through the front door, ignoring the demonic remains littering the area. His magical senses guided him through the wreckage deeper into the palace, past several dead humans and dragonmen. He didn't recognize any of them at a glance and wasn't eager for a closer look.

The survivors were sitting, lying or leaning just outside the first-floor landing. Every one of them looked as exhausted as he felt. Hans started to stand, but Otto waved him back. He had no interest in formality right now.

"Is it over?" Axel asked.

"More or less. There are a few odds and ends to sort out and I have to keep my promise to free Brazon. That'll take a few days at a minimum. After that, it's back to the empire and some well-deserved rest."

It showed how tired they were that no one cheered.

"Where's Corina?" he asked.

"Still with the dragon I guess," Axel said. "The last demon dropped less than a minute ago and no one had ambition enough to go get her."

"I'll go," Otto said. "I need to update Brazon anyway. You all can rest for as long as you need to. How bad were our losses?"

"Five scouts," Axel said. "Considering what we were facing, it could've been a lot worse."

"I lost two of my squad." Hans forced himself to his feet. "It was a hard fight and they acquitted themselves honorably."

"That's good to hear. Much as I'd like to bring them back for a hero's sendoff, the bodies will need to be burned as a precaution. I didn't notice any corruption in them when I walked by, but better safe than sorry."

Hans nodded, looking more dour than usual.

Skar pushed away from the wall. "If you're going to speak with Father, I'll join you."

"As will I," Hans added.

Otto didn't need an escort or a bodyguard right now but he was too tired to argue. Instead, he simply turned on his heel and set out for the steps to the basement. Hans asked no questions as the trio marched through the silent halls. Otto was most grateful for his consideration.

At the bottom of the steps Corina was waiting, a huge smile on her face. "I knew you'd be back safe. Where's Lady White?"

"She didn't make it." Otto walked past her without another word.

Behind him he vaguely heard Hans say, "Leave it alone for now, lass."

That man was due a raise when they got home.

He stopped in front of Brazon. The dragon looked exactly the same, but maintaining the energy flow to the portal had to have taken a toll on him. "It's done. Once I've recovered, I'll see about severing those chains. I've got a couple ideas about how to do it."

"That is well." Brazon's reply came out as a long sigh. "The city and the jungle feel nearly free of corruption already. In a day, all will be as it should."

Otto nodded. Everything back to the way it should be. That result suited him very well. "What about the rod? Is there some way to separate it into its constituent pieces once more? Leaving it intact strikes me as a poor idea."

"You're quite right about that. Working together, we should be able to manage it. Will you leave half with me and take the other?"

"That was my plan. I'd prefer to take the orb if that's acceptable to you."

"Perfectly acceptable. I assume you have a secure place to store it."

Otto considered the many vaults filled with magical items scattered around the empire and nodded. "I believe I can manage. For now, I'd like to leave it here."

"That's fine. Will you begin tomorrow?"

"Assuming I'm recovered enough, yes."

"That is also acceptable. I shall sleep as well."

The dragon closed his huge eyes, signaling the end of the conversation. That suited Otto fine. The sooner he could lie down, the happier he'd be.

CHAPTER FORTY-NINE

Otto ended up sleeping not just through the night but half the day as well. When he climbed out of his bedroll, he found most of the soldiers still sleeping. Even Hans was snoring away. Only Axel and Corina were awake and she had her nose stuck in a new novel.

He ambled over to Axel, who offered him a wordless nod, a flask of water, and an alchemy cookie. Otto gratefully ate and drank. As soon as the magical food hit his stomach, energy filled him. He let out a sigh. That was so much better.

"What's the plan for today?" Axel asked.

"I need to melt some chains. You guys need to collect any corpses that haven't melted away and burn them. I don't know what the rotting body of a thrall dedicated to the Lord of the Undead may do, and I prefer not to find out."

"Skar's way ahead of you. He had his people out and collecting bodies before I woke up this morning."

"That's convenient. If the dragonmen are handling body

collection, you can let everyone sleep for as long as they need to. I'm headed to the basement."

"Want some company?"

Otto shrugged. "Up to you. The process isn't going to be very exciting, but if you wish to observe, it won't bother me any."

"Mostly I'm sick of watching them sleep. I had horrible nightmares last night."

"Shocking. You'd think you'd spent several days fighting demons. Corina."

She flinched and looked up. "Master? You said it was okay if I read another one after the battle."

"I'm not going to chastise you, but I do need you to tell the others that we've gone to see about freeing Brazon."

Corina slumped with relief. "I will, Master. Count on me."

Otto forced himself not to roll his eyes and headed for the door. Axel fell in beside him. "Want to talk about what happened yesterday?"

"Meaning?"

"Meaning you and your pale girlfriend went out together and only one of you came back. Doesn't take a genius to figure out what happened."

"Lady White and I didn't have the sort of relationship you're suggesting. She was my friend and a useful ally. When I finished off Lord of the Dead, their master commanded her to pick up where he left off. A demon-worshipping priestess can't exactly refuse her master's commands. An empire of the dead, even one an ocean away from home, doesn't appeal to me. Destroying her was unfortunate, but necessary."

"You seem to be taking it well. It's not like you have so many friends that the loss of one shouldn't sting a bit."

"This is as much emotion as I can muster, Axel. Ever. It

will be the same when you die. It will even be the same when Mother dies. It's one of the prices of the power I've gained."

"And is it worth that price?"

"If I lacked it, we'd all be dead many times over."

Axel stopped in the middle of the empty hall and Otto turned to face him. "That's not what I asked."

"I know perfectly well what you asked, but the question is irrelevant. I did what I did with my eyes open. For better or worse this is who I am and who I will be for the rest of my very long life. It's not something that can simply be undone like a bad hairstyle."

Otto resumed his march and Axel did him the kindness of asking no more questions. In the cavern there were three lesser dragonmen on guard duty along with Skar. The idea that they imagined they needed to guard the massive green dragon struck Otto as absurd, but given what Lord Azteca created them for, protecting the one they perceived as their master was no doubt instinctive.

"Are you finally prepared to do the right thing?" Skar asked.

Otto swallowed a biting reply. "When I give my word, I keep it. But I will be needing your help to make it work."

"We can't do magic," Skar said.

"I'm perfectly well aware. What I need is for you to pull the links apart once I heat them to melting. Be sure to grip them well back from the molten end. Mithril melts at about three times the temperature of steel. Durable as you are, I suspect a burn from something like that would hurt."

"We'll be ready. Just say when."

Otto went to the nearest chain. This one ran from one side of Brazon's body across his shoulder, pinning him to the floor. The links were easily a foot in diameter, smooth as glass and still polished after all this time. Otto wouldn't have been surprised if Lord Colt had been responsible for their creation.

Hopefully he'd been having a bad day when he made them.

Otto conjured a thread and wrapped it around the link to serve as a guide. He made the route as narrow as possible to minimize heat loss. Speaking of heat, he rubbed his fingers together and began amplifying it.

He needed fifteen threads' worth just to get the mithril to glow orange. Not nearly hot enough to melt. Otto added more threads, slowly building up the heat until at thirty the metal started to glow white.

Almost there.

At thirty-five it started to drip.

"Now!"

Skar and his brothers snarled and pulled as they struggled to separate the molten metal.

Otto pushed harder, going all the way to forty threads.

With a final heave of effort, the dragonmen pulled the link in half. Otto immediately ended the spell and pulled the heat back out, hardening the metal and making sure no one would get burnt.

He wobbled but didn't pass out or fall to his knees. That was a nice change of pace.

Wiping the sweat from his brow he said, "One of those a day will be enough for me. If my count is right, there are six more, though if I do them in the right order, I think Brazon will be able to slip out from under the one holding his tail."

"That was more difficult than I expected," Skar said. "We will be ready when you arrive tomorrow."

"Good enough. When your people finish gathering the

bodies let me know. I should be sufficiently recovered in a few hours to oversee burning them."

Skar lowered his head, the first overt gesture of respect he'd shown so far. As for Brazon, the dragon slept through the whole procedure.

Must be nice.

O

It had taken a week, but Brazon was now free of his chains. Otto didn't know exactly what he'd expected the dragon to do, but just continuing to lie there, unmoving, wasn't it. At least he was awake now. The giant yellow eye staring at him was somewhat disconcerting, especially since there were no longer any bindings preventing the dragon from moving.

They had also succeeded in separating the Crimson Orb from the Rod of Terror. The orb was now sitting in his satchel like an especially ugly tumor.

"I had my doubts that you would keep your word," Brazon said. "Plenty of the humans I met before my capture would have thought nothing of betraying me once they had what they wanted."

"Betrayal is a tricky thing," Otto said. "It's an easy choice, but once you begin betraying, it can become a habit. I prefer to keep my word if it's at all possible."

"You are wise beyond your years. Is it still your intention to leave today? It would please me to have a chance for further discussion."

Otto shook his head. "I've been gone for long enough. However, I did leave a rune circle in the library upstairs. That will make it easy for me to come and go."

"Why not use the portal?" Brazon asked.

Never one to mince words, Otto replied, "I plan to disable the link between here and Garen. It's not that I don't trust you, it's just that I prefer not to take chances."

Brazon's chuckle sounded more like the rumble of thunder. "Real trust takes time to establish and what has been broken can't always be repaired."

Otto offered a polite bow. "Your understanding is much appreciated. May I ask a potentially impolite question?"

"Go ahead. Whatever you may think you know about dragons, rest assured that I, at least, am not so easily offended."

That was good information to have. "Why have you not left the cavern? I would've thought that after so long imprisoned you'd be eager for fresh air and sunlight."

"I am every bit as eager as you imagine, but, though magic has sustained my life, my body has atrophied. My dragonmen will bring meat and that will restore me, but it won't be a quick process. I estimate at least a century for a full recovery."

"That long? Well, given how long you've been trapped, I suppose it's not unreasonable. In any case, I wish you speedy healing. Until we speak again." Otto bowed.

"Farewell, Otto Shenk. May the winds of fate blow gently for you."

Otto turned on his heel and strode out of the cavern and up the stairs. Everyone should be gathered by the portal by now and he was eager to get going. Despite what he said, Otto was in no hurry to return for another chat. Brazon seemed pleasant enough, but he was still a dragon and that made Otto nervous.

Just outside the shattered entry he found Skar waiting.

The leader of the dragonmen offered a little bow of respect. "Thank you for freeing Father."

"I kept my word, no more and no less. I wish you and your people all the best. Hopefully we can all enjoy a nice long quiet spell."

Skar chuffed a laugh. "That would suit me very well, but I doubt the jungle will be so generous. That said, I would be very happy to never see another demon."

"That makes two of us. Farewell."

Otto left Skar behind, crossed the courtyard and made the short walk to the portal where the rest of his team was waiting. They were all loaded down with supplies. Corina stood beside the portal, the portable capacitor already connected and ready to activate.

"Are you sure you don't wish me to come with you, Lord Shenk?" Hans asked.

"Totally sure. I'm traveling through the ether, so you couldn't join me anyway. Now that the rod's deactivated, teleporting with the orb isn't a problem. As soon as you're gone, I'm going to deactivate the Garen rune, let Captain Coleman know he can leave anytime, then I'm headed for the palace." Otto frowned and did some mental calculations. "Scratch that last one. If I'm right, it'll be night when we arrive. I'll just go straight home and report to Wolfric in the morning. All of you can consider yourselves on leave for the next two weeks barring a major emergency. I'll arrange a bonus as well."

"Maybe something extra for the families of those who didn't make it back?" Axel said.

"Good idea. I'll arrange the money, you can handle delivering it. But that's for later. Corina, power it up."

The capacitor sparked when she connected it to the

portal and soon the runes began to glow. A few minutes later the portal opened and everyone marched through. As soon as it powered down, Otto used a forty-thread burst of heat to cut a scar across the Garen rune. That would keep it from properly activating until someone repaired it. Not a perfect solution, but the best he had at the moment.

Satisfied that his work here was done, Otto became one with the ether.

An instant later he appeared in a small clearing a hundred yards from the beastfolk village. He picked up the rune coin he'd left behind and pocketed it. A breeze off the ocean made the heat bearable as he walked toward the village.

When he arrived, he found sailors lounging in the sun, barefoot, and generally looking totally relaxed. Given everything that had happened over the last few weeks, Otto found the sight annoying. He forced the emotion aside as quickly as it appeared.

Walking up to the nearest sailor he asked, "Where's Captain Coleman?"

The sailor opened his eyes, saw Otto, and scrambled to his feet. "Lord Shenk, welcome back. The captain is, I believe, having a meal with Dhumoc. The two seem to have become friends. Though a less likely duo I can hardly imagine."

Otto couldn't possibly have cared less who the captain decided to spend his free time with. "Thank you. I remember the way to his hut."

Leaving the nervous sailor behind, Otto walked across the village to Dhumoc's hut. There was no door to knock on, so Otto just brushed the blanket that covered the entrance aside and stuck his head in.

Captain Coleman sat on the floor facing Dhumoc. Both men held bowls of something that smelled vaguely of stew.

"Captain," Otto said.

Coleman started, looked his way, and began to get up.

"Relax. I have no intention of ruining your meal. Our business is complete and everyone else has returned via the portal. You can return to port as soon as you're ready."

"Understood, Lord Shenk. We'll need a couple days to collect water, then we'll set sail."

"That's fine, Captain. There's no need to rush. I'll be returning via magic as well, it's just going to be you and your crew."

"What has become of the city?" Dhumoc asked.

"It's safe and the dragon is now freed from his prison. I have no idea about Skar and Brazon's long-term plans, but perhaps they'll make contact with you one day."

Dhumoc offered a faint nod. "It would be good to go home again."

That sounded like a fine idea to Otto as well. "Safe journey, Captain."

Otto pulled his head back out of the hut, became one with the ether, and went home.

CHAPTER FIFTY

Otto had been home for three days, spoken to everyone that needed speaking to, and now it was time to check in with Lord Karonin. He briefly considered going last night, and he knew the time of day didn't matter to her, but somehow it still felt rude to just show up that late. His mother's lessons in manners must still be rattling around in his head.

But it was morning now, the sun was up, and the house was still quiet. He'd get a quick bite to eat and be on his way. He smiled and reached for the bedroom door. The best thing about being back was the food. The alchemy cookies kept him alive, but that was about all he could say for them. Certainly they didn't begin to compare to the chef at Franken Manor.

He opened the door and froze. Abby was standing directly across from his door, staring at him. Why was she even up much less dressed and standing at his door?

"Did you need something?" he asked.

"I have a question that's been gnawing at me for a while and I want a real answer."

"Depending on the question, you may not like the answer. But if you ask, I'll tell you the truth. You'll be an adult soon enough, it's time to start treating you like one."

"Do you hate me?" She asked her question with a little quaver in her voice.

Otto thought for a moment. How harsh did he want his answer to be? He promised not to lie to her and he meant it, but there were shades of the truth.

At last he said, "No, I don't hate you."

He decided not to add that he thought no more of her than he did the servants or the furniture. She was just... here, another thing to be tolerated.

"Do you hate Mom?"

Otto's face twisted into a bitter scowl. "I used to. Now I don't care what happens to her one way or the other. On the day she dies I won't shed a tear, nor will I celebrate. I won't even make a mental note of her passing. Her continued existence is entirely irrelevant to me."

Abby looked like she wanted to cry, but Otto was incapable of offering comfort.

"Is that all?" he asked.

Abby nodded, seeming unable to speak further. Appetite gone, Otto became one with the ether.

A moment later he appeared in the hidden tower. As always, the unchanging top floor soothed him. It was the one place he could count on being the same. That was a rare and delightful gift.

"So you made it back alive." Lord Karonin's cold, ghostly face appeared backlit by the greenish aura of the netherworld. "How did you find Aztecaland?"

"Harsh. Still, I never imagined getting a chance to speak with a dragon, so that was interesting."

"I'm sure you have questions. Why don't you tell me everything, then I'll see if I can answer them."

Otto did so, leaving nothing out. If there was one person he felt completely safe sharing his secrets with, it was someone long dead and trapped in the netherworld.

When he finished, Lord Karonin said, "I warned you that a priestess of Astaroth could only serve one master and it was never going to be you."

Otto shrugged. "It was a good decade. That it wasn't longer is unfortunate, but that's life. The amulet you helped me create worked perfectly at least."

"Of course it did. Amet designed the original one after all." A little smile curled around her lips. "What did you think of Azteca's library?"

"It was... interesting. I never imagined an Arcane Lord would have an interest in collecting trashy romance novels."

Lord Karonin laughed. "She didn't collect them, she wrote them. It was her hobby. Heaven knows why. Out of all of my peers, she was the one I understood the least. She would spend days creating the nastiest, most bloodthirsty monster she could think of, then spend two weeks penning the sloppiest drivel you could imagine. The worst part was, she never wrote down any of her spells or techniques. It was all in her head. With her apprentices long dead, her secrets are likely lost forever."

That was certainly a shame, but out of all the various magical disciplines, flesh shaping interested Otto the least. There were more than enough naturally occurring monsters in the world; he felt no need to add more.

"What do you think I should do with the Crimson Orb?

Lady White claimed it was a drop of Astaroth's solidified blood. My plan was to just stick it in one of the storehouses. Unless you know of a way to destroy it."

"The answer is so obvious I can't believe neither you nor the dragons thought of it. Set it on a mithril plate. Over time, it will dissolve. And when I say over time, I mean centuries, not decades."

Otto nodded. That was simple enough. "In any case, Brazon has invited me back to visit whenever I like. I think it would be interesting to see what a dragon likes to talk about."

"As long as you're confident that you won't be eaten or incinerated, there's no harm in it. Dragons wield magic in unique ways. A friendly one might teach you something even I can't."

Otto was shocked to hear her admit that. "I do have one more question before I leave, Master. Do you think Lord Azteca left some way for her spirit to interact with the world? I encountered no simulacrum and there was no anchor like yours."

"Looking for a new mentor? Colt and I not enough for you?"

Otto smiled at that. "When it comes to magical knowledge, Master, there's no such thing as enough, only more."

"It really is a shame you decided not to follow through and become an Arcane Lord. To answer your question, I doubt she made such preparations. Azteca lived very much in the here and now. Long-term planning was not her specialty."

"I guess no one's perfect." Otto bowed. "I'll be on my way. Until next time, Master."

He became one with the ether. An instant later Otto

appeared in the nearest of Lord Karonin's armories. They really were his at this point, but in his mind, he would always think of them as hers. He chose the first one he found out of simple convenience. He'd taken enough odds and ends out of it over the years that there was room on the workbenches for the orb.

An effort of will agitated the ether and produced a light. Books and magical items filled the space. Even after all this time he'd barely made a dent in exploring them all. A glaring gap against the back wall marked where the suits of magical armor had once stood. Illsa hadn't been at all impressed with them when he showed them off.

He took a deep breath of musty air and blew it out again. Enough navel gazing. He walked over to the nearest workbench and took off the amulet he'd been wearing as an insurance policy against Lady White. Using it to destroy the artifact she'd been so obsessed with seemed a delightful irony. He set the amulet on the bench then put the slimy-feeling orb on top of it.

The horrid thing could rot there for eternity, he didn't care in the least. That final task complete, Otto became one with the ether.

It was time to get back to running the empire.

AUTHOR NOTE

Hello everyone,

I hope you enjoyed reading about Otto's latest adventure. I had a ton of fun writing it. It felt like visiting an old friend who I hadn't seen in a few years. If you'd like to know more about my writing and be the first to hear about new releases, you can join my newsletter on my website. www.jamesewish er.com

Until next time, thanks for reading,

James

Malice

Hearts of Corrupt Fire

Aegis of Merlin Omnibus Vol 1.

Aegis of Merlin Omnibus Vol 2.

The Complete Aegis of Merlin Omnibus

The 72 Demons

The Blood of Solomon

A Friend in Need

The Immortal Apprentice Trilogy

The War With Audin (Prequel Novella)

The Hunt For Revenge

The Army of Darkness

The Apprentice Reborn

The Soul Bound Saga

An Unwelcome Journey

Darkness in Tiber

Depths of Betrayal

The Black Iron Empire

Overmage

The Divine Key Trilogy

Shadow Magic

For The Greater Good

The Divine Key Awakens

The Dragonspire Chronicles

The Black Egg

The Mysterious Coin

The Dragons' Graveyard

The Slave War

The Sunken Tower

The Dragon Empress

The Dragonspire Chronicles Omnibus Vol. 1

The Dragonspire Chronicles Omnibus Vol. 2

The Complete Dragonspire Chronicles Omnibus

Soul Force Saga

Disciples of the Horned One Trilogy:

Darkness Rising

Raging Sea and Trembling Earth

Harvest of Souls

Disciples of the Horned One Omnibus

Chains of the Fallen Arc:

Dreaming in the Dark

On Blackened Wings

Chains of the Fallen Omnibus

The Complete Soul Force Saga Omnibus

Other Fantasy Novels:

The Squire

Death and Honor Omnibus

The Rogue Star Series:

Children of Darkness

Children of the Void

Children of Junk

Rogue Star Omnibus Vol. 1

Children of the Black Ship

Children of The End

ABOUT THE AUTHOR

James E. Wisher is a writer of science fiction and Fantasy novels. He's been writing since high school and reading everything he could get his hands on for as long as he can remember.